Mountain Lake, Minnesota Trilogy

A Seeking Heart

A Heart Surrenders

When a Heart Cries

MOUNTAIN LAKE, MINNESOTA TRILOGY

· Book One ·

A Heart Surrenders

KIM VOGEL SAWYER

HENDRICKSON PUBLISHERS

A Heart Surrenders

Hendrickson Publishers Marketing, LLC
P. O. Box 3473
Peabody, Massachusetts 01961-3473

ISBN 978-1-59856-926-1

First Hendrickson Edition Printing — June 2012

Dedicated to Sabra Henson and Philip Zielke—
two lifelong friends who encouraged me
to never lose sight of my dreams.

Contents

Klaassen Family Tree

Simon James Klaassen (1873) m. Laura Doerksen (1877), 1893
   Daniel Simon (1894) m. Rose Willems (1892), 1913
      Christina Rose (1915)
      Katrina Marie (1916)
   Hannah Joy (1895–1895)
   Franklin Thomas (1896) m. Anna Harms (1900), 1918
   Elizabeth Laurene (1898) m. Jacob Aaron Stoesz (1897), 1915
      Andrew Jacob and Adam James (A.J.), 1917
   Adam Earnest (1899) m. Samantha Olivia O'Brien (1900), 1918
   Josephine Ellen (1900)
   Arnold Hiram (1903)
   Rebecca Arlene (1906)
   Theodore Henry (1909)
   Sarah Louise (1911)
Hiram Klaassen (1872) m. Hulda Schmidt (1872), 1898

O'Brien Family Tree

Burton O'Brien (1870) m. Olivia Ruth Stanton (1873–1900), 1891
   David Burton (1894)
   Samantha Olivia (1900) m. Adam Earnest Klaassen (1899), 1918

Chapter One

*D*avid O'Brien stood stiffly at the back of the Mountain Lake Congregational Church, his chin angled upward and his blue eyes holding a telltale sheen. His beloved sister, Samantha, stood beside him, hand resting in the crook of his arm. He wasn't sure if the quivering he felt was caused by his nervousness or her excitement.

He sneaked a glance at the young woman at his side. She was so beautiful. He felt his chest expand with pride. The gown, a shade of cream, was a soft material and perfect with her russet hair, similar in color to his own. David thought her hair usually fell free in unruly curls around her face or was pulled back in a bow, but today it was twisted up in the back. He'd describe it as resembling an egg in a nest. A few tendrils had pulled away into curls on her slender neck. She turned her face up to his, and the joyous expression in her eyes, the same blue as his own—cornflower blue, he'd heard it said—brought a lump to his throat.

At the front of the church, the organist ended the hymn with a mighty thrust of the pedals, and the final note echoed through the small sanctuary. A pause, and then the woman reached up to open the cover of a small enameled music box resting on the top of the organ. The tinkling notes of the traditional wedding march, *Lohengrin*, sounded through the church. David pressed her arm against his rib cage and squeezed Samantha's hand reassuringly. He paused long enough to whisper, "Are you ready?"

She nodded, her lips curving into a smile of readiness and her eyes shining with anticipation. Those eyes were aimed straight ahead toward the black-suited young man waiting at the head of the center aisle.

They began their slow walk in time to the music. David's gaze ranged from side to side as they moved up the aisle, watching as the people seated on the backless benches turned their heads to follow their passage. Happy expressions all, with the exception of one. A young woman with dark hair seemed to glare at Samantha as they moved slowly by. David's eyebrows drew together in a frown. A quick glance at Samantha confirmed that she hadn't noticed the other woman's sour expression. He wanted nothing to spoil this day for his sister. She deserved this happiness after all she had been through.

They reached the front of the church just as the final notes of *Lohengrin* rang out. The organist gently closed the lid on the music box before moving to one of the front benches.

The black-suited minister smiled at the pair from behind the pulpit. "Who gives this woman?"

David cleared his throat and answered, "I, her brother, do." He started to turn toward his place, but Samantha tightened her grip on his arm, holding him.

She lifted her face to him, and he stooped downward for the fleeting yet heartfelt kiss she planted on his cheek. When he straightened, he returned her loving smile with one of his own and made his way to his seat.

He sat straight on the bench, pressing his knees together and holding his hands in his lap, his gaze resting on Samantha. As happy as he was for his sister and as much as he admired and respected her Adam, this day was proving more difficult for him than he had imagined it would.

David and Samantha had been separated for seven years— seven lonely, difficult years for both of them. Four months ago they'd been reunited, thanks to Adam and the Klaassen family, and for David they had been the happiest four months of his life. He knew Samantha was marrying a fine man with a fine family—there were no regrets concerning her choice—but it was hard to see her become a wife and belong to another so soon after they had rediscovered each other.

The young woman seated at his right quietly reached over to give his hand a brief squeeze. He glanced at her, and her reassuring smile brought a lift to his heart. David was glad for the presence of Adam's sister beside him. Josie was Samantha's age and had become a dear friend to Samantha. Although David didn't know her well, Samantha often talked of Josie's sensitive, caring spirit. He managed to give her a grateful look before both of them turned their attention back to the front of the church.

The minister challenged Adam and Samantha on the seriousness of the commitment they were making to one another, read some Scripture passages of instruction on holy matrimony, and now the two were ready to speak their vows.

David watched Adam's sincere and caring expression as he spoke directly to Samantha, "I, Adam, take thee, Samantha, to be my wedded wife, to have and to hold, from this day forward; to love, honor, and cherish. . . ." The words seemed to float around David's head, and he fought the urge to weep.

Samantha's face glowed with intense happiness, and David felt a lump in his throat. She'd known way too little of joy before Adam came into her life. David was so thankful for the course that had finally brought his little sister to Mountain Lake, and so sorry for his own inability to find and rescue her himself. His emotions nearly strangled him as the two of them faced each other.

David took a deep breath and listened to Samantha's voice, soft and expressive, as she delivered the vows that would bind her to Adam forever. "I, Samantha, take thee, Adam, to be my wedded husband. . . ."

Samantha hadn't even let him bring up those awful years in Wisconsin with their drunkard father. "He's gone now, David," she had told him, "and we don't need to concern ourselves with the past any longer. Seeing you again, being with you here in Minnesota, has healed those memories, and you should not concern yourself any longer with what you might or might not have been able to do."

David noticed the expression in Adam's eyes as he held Samantha's hands and gazed at her while she recited her vows. David had no doubt that Samantha was loved by Adam and would be tenderly cared for by him. Tenderness is what Samantha needed. If he'd made the choice, he couldn't have found a more perfect mate for her. The thoughts were reassuring, and the smile he gave his sister as she turned with her husband to face the congregation was nearly as joyful as theirs.

After the announcement of "Mr. and Mrs. Adam Klaassen" to the congregation and their first public kiss, the newlyweds shared a hug, with Adam laughingly sweeping Samantha clear off her feet. But after he set her back down on the wooden floor, Samantha ran straight to David, throwing her arms around his neck to hug him.

David felt warm tears against his neck, and he pulled away to look into her face. "Hey, what's with the waterworks?"

Samantha laughed through her tears, wiping at them with shaking fingers. "They're happy tears, David, every one of them. My heart's just so full I can't contain all of it!"

David held her against his chest, fighting tears himself. He rocked his sister back and forth, pressing his cheek against her hair. "Always be this happy, Sammy. For me?"

Samantha leaned back to smile up at him. "For us both."

David nodded and released her to join her husband and greet the waiting crowd. Adam's family, by turn, embraced her, welcoming her officially into their fold. David stood off to the side, watching, battling his own mixed emotions. A hand tugged at his sleeve. He looked down to find Josie at his side.

"Adam will take good care of her for you, David." Josie's brown eyes held understanding and sympathy.

David swallowed and gained control before answering. "I know, Josie. I know Adam loves her—and she loves him. I know she'll be fine. It's just . . ."

Josie patted his arm, then clasped her hands together. "You feel as if you're losing her."

David nodded.

"But you know," she continued, "you're not letting her go forever. She and Adam will be right here in Mountain Lake, and so will you. You'll see her often, still be involved in her life. Samantha wouldn't have it any other way. She's worried about losing you, afraid you'll go back to Minneapolis now that she's married, instead of staying on with Uncle Hiram at the mercantile."

"She is?" David was rather startled at this news.

"Mm-hm." Josie went on in an earnest tone, "David, don't feel abandoned. Samantha will always have room in her life for you."

How on earth could such a young woman, barely more than a girl, possess such insight? That's exactly how he was feeling—abandoned. Foolish? Yes, but the truth. He stared at Josie in amazement. "Thank you, Josie. I needed to hear that," he finally managed.

"Come on," she said. "Let's chase the buggy, and shower them with good turkey red wheat kernels!"

David joined the other happy celebrants in sending the wedding couple away on the road to their new life together.

When Adam and Samantha disappeared around the bend in the road, everyone returned to the church to continue the celebration. Women had brought double-decker rolls called *zwieback*, preserves, cold meats, pickles, and assorted baked sweets for a light supper.

David filled his plate like everyone else and seated himself at a makeshift table in the sunny church yard. Weddings were cause for merry making, and the whole town had turned out to wish Adam and Samantha well. Adam's extended family—his parents, uncle and aunt, grandparents, all eight brothers and sisters, as well as the siblings' spouses and children—were all in attendance. They filled one plank table, plus most of another.

Although Josie had invited him to sit with the Klaassens, he got separated in the confusion and sat instead with a group of chatting townsfolk. Across and slightly kitty-corner from him was the dark-haired girl he'd noticed earlier in the church. What was her name? He frowned and tried shake it loose from his memory. Oh, yes, Priscilla, Priscilla Koehn, the only daughter of John and Millie Koehn. He'd heard rumors that Samantha had suffered some intimidation from that spoiled young lady.

David watched Priscilla out of the corner of his eye as he ate his meal. She was undeniably one of the most attractive women he had ever seen. Long, curling black lashes surrounded bright blue eyes, topped by arched brows that made a perfect frame. Her bowed lips were soft rose with a full lower lip, and her complexion retained its milky white color thanks to a wide-brimmed straw hat trailing an abundance of pink satin ribbon. Her glossy black hair fell in lovely waves down her slender back. Yes, she was definitely pretty.

Too bad she knows it so well. David watched her flirt expertly with a handsome young man on her left, who responded with equal proficiency. David knew who he was—Lucas Stoesz, the younger brother of Jake Stoesz who'd married Adam's sister Liz. Jake was a good, solid man. David had found little of the wholesomeness Jake possessed in young Lucas, who struck David as cocky and full of himself. No doubt a good match for the haughty Miss Koehn. He went back to eating.

"Mr. O'Brien?" he heard a feminine voice call from the other end of the table.

David lifted his head to see a coquettish smirk from none other than the subject of his observations. "Yes? Miss Koehn, isn't it?" He couldn't help but be pleased with his dispassionate tone and mock uncertainty.

The girl batted her eyelashes with practiced ease. "I wanted to say I thought it was a lovely service. Samantha was so pretty. And I'm sure you're just thrilled that she's managed to land the most handsome—as well as one of the wealthiest—bachelors in town!"

The hairs on the back of David's neck prickled. How dare she insinuate his sister was a gold-digger? "I can't be more delighted that Samantha is happy and married to the man she loves. That's all I could want for her."

Priscilla laughed—a laughter that held little gaiety—then pulled her face into a little pout. "Oh, my, I've managed to put my foot in it again." She rested her forearms on the edge of the white tablecloth and crossed her wrists. "Mr. O'Brien, I meant no offense. Now, it's no secret that I did fancy Adam. He is, as I said, quite a catch! But I wish Adam and Samantha nothing but the best." Tipping her head, she fluttered those long eyelashes again, the bright blue eyes wide and teasing.

David resisted rolling his eyes. "I'm sure you do, Miss Koehn."

"Oh, please, call me Priscilla." Her lips curled into a beguiling smile. "'Miss Koehn' sounds so stilted and formal."

David glanced down at his now-empty plate. He stood, nodding in Priscilla's direction. "Please excuse me, Miss Koehn. I'll be joining the Klaassens now. Have a good day. Good-bye, Lucas."

⌒〇

Priscilla watched in disbelief and annoyance as David O'Brien turned his back and walked over to seat himself beside Liz and Jake. He'd dismissed her! Just who did he think he was, marching off as if she was a nobody? Narrowing her eyes, she jerked around, quivering with indignation.

Lucas bumped her arm with his elbow. "Well, well, whaddaya know," he said with a smirk. "There's one man immune to your fatal charms."

"Oh, shut up!" Priscilla muttered and jumped up from the table. She stormed away, leaving her half-filled plate behind for someone else to carry to the washtub. Sending a murderous glare in David's direction, she silently vowed to get even. Priscilla would not be one-upped by anybody. Even someone as good looking as David O'Brien!

Chapter Two

"Mama, will you please hurry?" Priscilla shot a glance over her shoulder. "The store will close before we get there at this rate!"

Mama puffed along behind, her heels tap-tapping on the boardwalk. "I don't know why we can't just go to Hiebert & Balzer's, Priscilla. It's closer to home, and they have ready-made. No waiting for an order from the catalog."

Priscilla whirled around and stopped in the middle of the walkway. "I already told you," she said, gesturing with her hands. "I've seen their ready-mades, and I don't like any of them as much as the one in the catalog."

Mama's shoulders heaved with her sigh, and she pressed one palm to her breast and fanned herself with the other. "Why in the name of all things sainted do you need a new dress anyway? You've got three new dresses from last spring hanging in your wardrobe, and they're all perfectly fine."

Priscilla let out a little grumble of annoyance. *Why must Mama be so stubborn?* Hadn't Daddy already told them both that Priscilla could order a new dress? Whatever Daddy said was the order of the day, and that was that. Mama knew that as well as Priscilla. Tossing her curls over her shoulder, Priscilla spun back and hurried on, determined to complete her errand.

Mama followed, murmuring under her breath, but Priscilla ignored the disgruntled complaints. Mama's opinion didn't matter. Priscilla couldn't help her smirk, remembering Daddy's response to Mama's claims about a new dress. His chiding voice echoed in her mind. "Now, Millie, I see nothing wrong with Prissy picking out a new dress. After all, it is spring! A new season, a new wardrobe . . . Plus her graduation is coming. Take her down and let her choose a pretty dress from the Sears, Roebuck catalog."

Priscilla had wrapped her arms around her father's neck and squealed, "Oh, thank you, Daddy! You're the sweetest, most wonderful daddy in the whole wide world!" And he'd responded with a fond chuckle and a teasing, "Oh, get on with you, you little imp."

As the only daughter following the four Koehn sons, Priscilla had been pampered and cosseted by her father since birth. Although stern with her brothers, Daddy never used any kind of discipline on her. She supposed there were many who considered her a spoiled brat, but what did she care? As long as she got what she wanted, nothing else mattered.

Priscilla stepped daintily over the threshold of the Family Mercantile. She had given the screen door an extra hard push so the little bell hanging above the door jangled wildly. Mama stepped in behind her and moved directly to the counter, but Priscilla paused in the middle of the floor and glanced around the store. Where was David? Ah, there in the corner, stacking work boots on shelves. She stared at his back, willing him to turn around and look at her. But he kept working. With a little toss of her head, she joined Mama at the counter.

The proprietor's buxom wife, Hulda Klaassen, bustled from a door at the back, tugging at her apron. "Why, good morning, Millie! What can I help you with today?"

Mama released a tired sigh. "Priscilla would like to see the catalog. She's ordering another dress."

Priscilla laughed—deliberately high and tinkling, she hoped. But David still didn't turn around. "Now, Mother, you know perfectly well I have Daddy's permission. Don't sound so gloomy."

Priscilla ignored Mrs. Klaassen and Mama exchanging a meaningful look. Turning, Mrs. Klaassen called, "David, would you please bring out the new Sears, Roebuck catalog? Priscilla here would like to look at it."

"Certainly, Mrs. Klaassen." David disappeared behind a checkered curtain into the storage area.

Mama leaned forward and whispered to Mrs. Klaassen, "Is the young man here to stay?"

Priscilla toyed with the lace at her collar, pretending not to listen.

Mrs. Klaassen nodded, her extra chins quivering. "Yes." She whispered too. "Hiram has hired him as his assistant, and the young man plans to stay on. You see—"

The sound of a clearing throat brought both women up short, their lips pursed. David was standing at the end of the counter, and he held out the catalog. "Here you are, ma'am."

"Thank you," Mrs. Klaassen said, her cheeks pink. "Here, Priscilla, come take a look."

Priscilla made a deliberate circle around Mama so she could sashay past David, her nose in the air. She sneaked a peek in his direction, but he'd gone back to his boot stacking, seemingly unmindful of her presence. She seethed. Fat lot of good it was going to do to ignore him if he didn't notice her, one way or the other! Her mind raced, sorting through some means of capturing his attention. Mama always said one caught more flies with honey than with vinegar. Maybe Mama was right this time.

She swung her hair over her shoulder, angling a glance at the back corner of the store. "Oh, Mr. O'Brien, would you come here for a moment, please?"

Mama's eyebrows rose in an unspoken question. Priscilla tossed a scowl in her mother's direction, and Mama backed up a step. Priscilla pointed to one of the dresses as she turned a pretty expression of indecision in David's direction. "I just can't seem to make up my mind between this one"—she flipped two pages to point at another dress—"or this one." She paused, peeking out from beneath her lashes. "Which do you like best?"

"Priscilla!" Mama nearly sputtered. "How presumptuous, taking Mr. O'Brien away from his work to make a decision for you."

Priscilla raised her eyebrows innocently. "Well, a single lady must consider what a gentleman will find appealing. I'm simply requesting his opinion. There's nothing presumptuous about that at all, Mother."

Mama crossed her arms and frowned, her discomfort evident. Priscilla turned to David. "Well . . . ?"

David flipped the pages of the catalog back and forth, examining first one and then the other. Finally he pointed to a third dress—the simplest dress on either of the pages. Solid pale green with a plain rounded neckline—no collar or embellishments of any kind—and straight long sleeves. Ivory buttons fastened it from neck to waist. "This one is nice."

"That one?" The words came out in an unbecoming squeak. "Why, that's the ugliest dress I've ever seen!" Priscilla stared at the gown, then back at him.

David looked over at her. "Really?" He paused. "I thought it suited you."

Fire ignited in Priscilla's cheeks. She forgot about the vinegar-and-honey theory. Arching her neck, she planted her fists on her hips and glowered at David. "You are insufferably rude!"

David looked a bit startled, then arched a brow. "You asked for my opinion, and I gave it. If it doesn't please you," he said with a shrug, "you're free to choose something else." He looked briefly at Mrs. Klaassen. "Now if you'll excuse me, I have more boots to put away." He turned and moved back to his corner.

Priscilla sucked in a sharp gasp. He'd done it again! Stomping toward the door, she shot over her shoulder, "I do not wish to order a dress today. I'm going home."

Mrs. Klaassen let out a low chuckle, which further incited Priscilla's ire.

"Mama! Let's go!"

"Yes, dear." Mama scurried after her.

❧

David bit the inside of his cheek to hold back his smile as Priscilla darted out of the store. He supposed he shouldn't needle the girl. She was, after all, a customer, and his handling of the situation might convince her to shop elsewhere. And the Klaassens might wonder if he was good for business. But Mrs. Klaassen didn't seem at all upset with him. In fact, she winked and smiled. Grinning, he returned to boot stacking. Then the cowbell clanged again, announcing the arrival of another customer.

Josie Klaassen entered the store, but her gaze was aimed out through the screen door at the boardwalk. She gestured and asked, "What has Priscilla in such a dither?"

Chortling, Mrs. Klaassen came around the counter and embraced her niece. "Oh, you know Priscilla. When she doesn't get her way, she can get herself—and everybody else—all in a tailspin faster than a spring tornado." Holding on to Josie's hands, she said, "What brings you to town this morning?"

"Several things." Josie swung her aunt's hands from side to side, her smile bright. "Mother needs some baking powder, and Becky needs another writing tablet. This close to the end of the term, it seems a shame to buy another one, but she has to write on something."

David found himself sending surreptitious glances in Josie's direction. After the encounter with Priscilla, Josie's sweetness felt like a soothing balm. A grin tugged at his cheeks, and he gave a little wave when she looked in his direction. "Good morning, Josie. How are you today?"

A smile broke across her face, and she moved toward him. "David! I was just about to ask where you were."

Pleasure bloomed in his chest. He worked his way out from behind a stack of boxes. "Oh, and why is that?" For the first time he noticed that Josie had a spattering of pale freckles, and her clean, open face seemed refreshing and appealing.

"Mother would like for you to have supper with us Saturday. Samantha and Adam will be there, and she thought you might like to come, too."

David definitely wanted to come. Having grown up in their Wisconsin home with a widowed, abusive, alcoholic father, he and Samantha had both responded to the warmth and happiness and, yes, the faith exuded by the Klaassens. Even though he didn't really understand the faith part of it, when he and his sister had finally been reunited, he determined that she had been transformed from a timid little waif to a young woman who was lovely from the inside out—one most certain to capture the eye and the heart of someone like Adam Klaassen.

He followed Josie back to the counter while she waited for Mrs. Klaassen to get the items the needed. He couldn't help but note how different she was from Priscilla. Josie was too honest and sensible to engage in idle flirtation. He found Josie's simple, unassuming ways preferable to the beguiling Priscilla.

A blush warmed Josie's cheeks as she took a quick glance at David. She brushed a hand across her mouth. "Do I have some breakfast on my face?"

"No, not that I can see."

She gave a little chuckle at his confused tone. "Well, did you hear what I asked? About Saturday?"

David felt his ears grow hot. "Of course—you invited me to supper. Or rather," he corrected, "your mother did. And you can tell her, yes, I'd love to be there, especially since my sister is invited." But he wasn't sure if it was Samantha or Josie he wanted to see.

"Josie, here's your baking powder and a tablet for Becky." Hulda Klaassen pushed the items toward Josie's waiting hands. "Have you made arrangements to take the teaching exam yet?"

Josie nodded, her brown braid bouncing against her spine. "Yes. The day after graduation. Only three more weeks! I admit, I'm rather nervous about it—I want this so badly."

Samantha had told David that Josie was planning to be a teacher after she graduated from the community school. He thought she had the right personality to be a teacher—steady, even-tempered, unflappable. . . . But cute as a button, unlike some schoolmarms he'd sat under. No doubt the boys of all ages would have crushes on her.

"Will you teach here in Mountain Lake?" he asked.

Josie crinkled up her nose. "Probably not. The teacher who's been here for the past three years, Mr. Reimer, has given no indications of leaving. He's getting married this summer to a local girl, so I'm sure he's here to stay. He's very good at what he does, and we're glad to have him. I'll submit applications to all the area schools and wait to see what happens. I'm praying the right door will open up for me."

David had no response for that. He wasn't a praying person himself, although he knew the Klaassens and his sister believed prayers were important—that they actually were heard and answered. "Well, good luck to you. And I'll see you Saturday."

"Yes, Saturday," Josie said. She turned her smile on her aunt. "Good-bye, Tante Hulda. Have a nice day." She left to the clanging cowbell.

David glanced out the window as he headed back to his assignment, then paused a moment to watch Josie crossing the street to a waiting buckboard. A young man approached and took the purchases from her. Josie smiled at the dark-haired young man, who helped her up into the buckboard. The man stayed close to the wagon, his elbow draped over the edge of the seat. The two engaged in conversation.

David began his work and kept his tone conversational. "Mrs. Klaassen, I haven't met the man out there with Josie. Do you know who he is?"

The older woman walked to the window and glanced out. "Oh, that's Stephen Koehn." She paused, her brow furrowed in thought. "Hmm, I thought he was still in Blue Earth, helping his grandfather. Must be home again." She glanced over at David. "Stephen is Josie's beau—since Thanksgiving of last year. But he's been gone for a while. When his grandfather took ill, he had to go help mind the farm. Things must be better there."

"Stephen Koehn . . . Any relation to Priscilla Koehn?" he asked.

"Brother and sister," Mrs. Klaassen replied, shaking her head, "but as different as air and smoke. There are four Koehn boys, all older than Priscilla, which I suppose is why John Koehn has spoiled the girl. Why, she—"

"So Stephen Koehn is a decent fellow?" David cut in. He wasn't interested in hearing any more about Priscilla.

"My, yes. One of the most decent young men in town."

David's heart dropped with disappointment. He put the last pair of boots on the shelf. "Well, I've got that shipment of dried beans to inventory. Guess I'd better get to it."

Mrs. Klaassen clicked her tongue against her teeth and followed David into the storeroom. "Now, young man, I have a question for you." David turned to face Mrs. Klaassen as she folded her arms over her ample chest. "I'm going to ask you straight out. Do you have a shine for our Josie?"

Had he been so obvious? Heat filled David's face.

The woman tsk-tsked. "Now, David, I'm going to be very honest with you because I like you. You're a good worker, and both Hiram and I have found you to be an honest young man. But Josie is a Christian, and—"

"It's all right, Mrs. Klaassen." He shouldn't interrupt, but he couldn't bear to listen to all the reasons why he wasn't good enough for Josie. He knew more than anyone just how unworthy he was. "I'd better get to those beans before lunch. Excuse me please."

He moved quickly to the twenty-pound bags of beans, tossing them into a crate. It was just as well Josie had a beau, he decided as the last bag landed in its place. She deserved a steady, dependable man like Stephen Koehn instead of an unpolished fly-by-nighter like him.

Chapter Three

Saturday morning, while Hiram Klaassen readied the cash box, David opened the mercantile's front door and propped it open with an iron doorstop shaped like a sleeping cat. He paused for a moment on the front stoop, breathing in the fresh scent of a new spring. A sense of belonging filled him.

He loved his work, his place of residence, and the people of Mountain Lake. The Klaassens had accepted him as readily as they had Sam, and this evening he'd be enjoying supper with their family. Had he ever experienced such a feeling of "home" before? No. He could cheerfully live here forever.

"Good morning, Mr. O'Brien."

The voice, with its slight note of challenge, sent a prickle of awareness across his scalp. He turned to find Priscilla Koehn and a heavy-set, gray-haired man approaching on the boardwalk. David nodded his head in greeting.

"This is my daddy, John Koehn." Priscilla's blue eyes flashed, daring David to parry with her when her father was in attendance. "He came to order my dress."

"Well . . ." David cleared his throat. "Welcome." He nodded to Mr. Koehn as he held the door open. "You can ask Mr. Klaassen for the catalog." He went inside behind the two and quickly found something to keep him occupied in the storeroom. Just seeing the girl gave him the urge to throttle her. Her father certainly wouldn't stand for that. David would keep his distance.

His back to the curtained doorway, he bent over a recently arrived crate from Chicago and examined the contents. He felt a tap on his back. He jolted upright and spun around. Priscilla!

Irritation clenched David's chest. "Miss Koehn, customers are not allowed in this room." He kept his voice even and low so as not to attract attention, but his face burned. He couldn't believe this woman! He gestured toward the curtain. "You'll need to get yourself out there. Please."

Priscilla locked her hands behind her back and cocked her head. "I just wanted to let you know that I ordered a dress— the pink and white striped one I showed you the other day. My daddy says it will make me look as sweet as a candy peppermint stick. Mr. Klaassen told me the dress will be here in three weeks, and I'll want it delivered immediately. Please make note of it, as I assume you're the delivery boy in addition to your other duties here."

The way she said "boy" rankled. He spoke through clenched teeth. "Miss Koehn, that message could have been left with Mr. Klaassen. I can only presume, then, that your intentions are to insult me, get me riled."

"And have I succeeded?"

Her too-perfect face was set in a knowing smirk. What a shame all that beauty was wasted on someone so shallow. David balled his hands into fists and pushed them deep into his pockets. He'd never laid a hand on a woman, but at that moment he would like to have turned her over his knee for a sound paddling.

"It's not something of which to be proud, Priscilla," he finally said. "For the life of me, I can't figure out why you take such pleasure in aggravating people."

Priscilla laughed. "Oh, not just anybody, David." She emphasized his name, causing heat to flood his ears as he realized he'd called her by her Christian name. "You make it so easy for me. But really, now, you must learn not to be so suspicious. And you think so ill of me. What can I do to change your opinion?"

David drew in a deep breath, ready to let her have it with more than she'd wish to hear. Before he could speak, however, the curtain parted, and Priscilla's father stuck his head in.

"There you are, Prissy. Did you get the delivery for your dress worked out?"

"Yes, I did, Daddy." Priscilla answered sweetly, still holding David with those blue eyes of hers. "David says he'll be delighted to deliver my dress as soon as it arrives. Isn't that right, David?"

Apparently Mr. Koehn wasn't interested in David's response, because he didn't give him time to answer. "Well, come on then. I can't remain here all day."

"Of course, Daddy." Priscilla turned toward the door obediently. But before she stepped through the curtains, she sent one last look over her shoulder at David and waved two fingers.

David sat on the edge of the crate and ran a hand down his face. Mercy, that girl was a problem. Was she like this with every young man she encountered, or did she save it all up just for his benefit? Hard as he tried, he couldn't imagine what he'd done to earn this treatment. He pictured her as she'd stood in the storeroom, her hands locked primly behind her back, her lustrous hair trailing over her shoulders, eyes sparkling. She was an incredibly beautiful girl.

"An incredibly beautiful, obnoxious girl," he said as he stood up. He shook his head. That girl was trouble with a capital T. The less he saw of Priscilla Koehn, the better off he would be. Determinedly, he put Priscilla from his mind and got back to work.

⟿

David sipped a final cup of coffee while cheerful chatter swirled around either side of him. Samantha had once laughingly told him that mealtimes at the Klaassen home were always an adventure. With people everywhere, including unexpected guests at times, all kinds of subjects came up in conversation, and one never knew what new delight Laura Klaassen would prepare.

Tonight they'd feasted on *verenike*—cottage-cheese-filled dough pockets which were boiled and then smothered with ham gravy. Thick slices of ham straight from the Klaassen smokehouse, *zweiback*—which was delicious spread with Laura's strawberry-mulberry preserves—fried potatoes, and a sweet soup called cherry moos rounded out dinner. David concluded his sister was right: meals here were definitely an adventure and a most pleasant one, at that.

The part of the meal he enjoyed the most wasn't the food, though, but the company. To David's delight, he'd been seated next to Josie. The girl was intelligent and even opinionated, David discovered, but not off-putting at all. Her brown eyes sparkled as she joined in the conversation that flew around the table, asking David's input from time to time and making him feel included. He appreciated it, and he found himself admiring her more and more as the evening progressed. He fleetingly wondered where "Josie's beau" was tonight but not enough to ask.

When everyone had finished eating, Adam invited David to walk around the barn for some exercise. Although David hated to leave Josie's company, he wouldn't refuse time with Adam. This man had befriended Samantha—yes, rescued her—at a time when she was at her most vulnerable, and David felt a deep debt of gratitude. But he also admired Adam's level-head-edness and strength of character—attributes he believed were sorely lacking in his own life.

"Sounds good," David said over a chuckle. "I could use some exercise after that wonderful meal." He rubbed his belly, his eyes following Josie as she moved around the table, clearing dishes. He added, "If I ate like this every day, I'd be as big as your barn. Thank you for the invitation, Mrs. Klaassen," he called over to her as she stacked plates in the sink.

Laura Klaassen lit up, the corners of her eyes crinkling into her smile. "You're quite welcome, David. You feel free to come by here anytime."

"Thank you, ma'am, I just might take you up on that." He sent a quick glance at Josie, but she didn't look his way.

Adam said, "Sammy, honey, David and I are going to stretch our legs a bit." The two men turned toward the back door.

Samantha dashed across the kitchen, a dishtowel flapping from her shoulder. "Wait just a minute there, mister!" She turned her face upward for a kiss, and Adam grinned and placed his arms around her waist, dropping a light kiss on her mouth.

"Check on the sow, too, while you're out there," Adam's father, Simon—often called Si—called to them from the parlor. "She's due to farrow soon," he said, now standing in the kitchen doorway. He peered at them over his reading glasses and his *Farmer's Almanac*. "Remember, you and Samantha will be raising a piglet or two from this litter."

Adam saluted in response, then sent Samantha back to his mother with a teasing, "Now head over there and do your duty, missus." Samantha laughed and went back to his mother to help with cleanup.

As the men sauntered toward the barn, David commented, "Sam seems really happy."

Adam nodded. "There's no 'seems' about it. She is happy. And so am I."

"I'm so glad for you both." David put a hand on Adam's shoulder. "It means a lot to me, seeing her like this. Happiness was a pretty scarce commodity when we were growing up."

"Samantha's told a lot of it to me." Genuine sympathy colored Adam's voice. "I'm sure, though, there's a lot she hasn't shared yet. The memories are painful, as you know, David. But I'm doing my best to replace the unhappy ones with good ones. I hope you know that."

"I do." David gave Adam's shoulder a squeeze and dropped his hand.

"Keeping Samantha happy gives me the greatest joy." Adam's boots scuffed up dust as the men moved across the farmyard. "I plan to spoil your little sister rotten."

David laughed along with Adam. But then he slowed his step, turning toward his new brother-in-law. "Speaking of spoiled . . . I have a little problem."

Adam stopped in an attentive pose—feet widespread, arms crossed, face creased in concern. "What is it?"

David stroked his chin. "Well, it's a who rather than an it." He drew in a deep breath. "Priscilla Koehn."

"Ah." Adam grimaced. "What's she up to this time?"

David drew back. "This time? You mean she's generally stirring things up?"

Adam laughed. "You haven't been around long enough, my friend. Yep, our Miss Priscilla Koehn lives to get things into a turmoil of some kind. She's been a troublemaker since she was in pinafores, and none of us can figure out why John Koehn allows it. He's always been firm with his boys, keeping them in line. But Priscilla walks all over him." He snorted. "Let's face it—Priscilla walks all over everyone."

David fell back into step with Adam as the two ambled on in the direction of the barn.

"I guess it's because she's the only daughter," Adam continued. "Maybe I'd do the same with a little girl. I suppose even Ma and Pa have spoiled our Sarah, since she's the baby. Not to the extent of Priscilla, though. All I know is John has never enforced any kind of behavior standards with Priscilla, and the result is one spoiled, selfish young woman." He leaned against the corral fence, the hint of a grin on his face. "What's she done now?"

David ducked his head, embarrassed to admit he couldn't manage a girl seven years his junior. He cleared his throat. "Oh, I guess she's just managed to get my dander up by acting coy and then arrogant. And I've heard she's been spiteful toward Sammy." A rush of protectiveness washed over him.

Adam worked the toe of his boot against the ground. "My advice to you is to make sure she never knows she's getting to you. As I said, she loves to stir things up. If she thinks she's annoying you, she'll keep it up till you're ready to smack her one."

Remembering the urge he'd had earlier in the day, David gave a brusque nod.

"Keep a handle on your reactions to her needling," Adam advised, "and she'll soon tire of the game."

David sent Adam a sidelong glance. "I'll tell you something if you won't get big headed about it."

Adam shrugged.

"After your wedding, Priscilla mentioned she'd always had eyes for you—that she considered you 'quite a catch,' I think she put it."

Adam threw back his head and laughed. "I hate to say it, but that isn't news to me. Priscilla has chased me around for years. But I was always very careful not to be caught. Can you imagine?" He stopped his amused chuckle as realization seemed to dawn. He pointed a finger at David. "You know, that could be why she's giving you a hard time. She's jealous of Samantha because Samantha got something—or rather, someone—she wanted. Priscilla isn't used to not getting what she wants. I'm sure she knows how protective you and Sam are of one another. By trying to get under your skin about Samantha, she's upsetting you. Which invariably will upset Samantha. And me . . . well, you get the picture."

David considered Adam's comments. "That makes sense. Also makes me want to pound the dickens out of her."

Adam chuckled. "Get in line." Then he added more seriously, "But really, David, you can't let her know she's aggravating you. That will only add fuel to the fire. As much as is possible, ignore the girl. In time, if she can't rile you, she'll back off."

David blew out a big huff of breath. "I hope so. She's one persistent little female."

"That she is." Adam slapped David's shoulder and pushed off from the fence. "C'mon now, let's go check on that sow for Pa. Get our minds off of Miss Priss."

David grinned broadly. "That sounds good to me." As he followed Adam into the barn, he admitted to himself there was another young lady in Mountain Lake he'd rather think about. If only Stephen Koehn hadn't already staked a claim on her . . .

Chapter Four

When Adam and David returned to the house, David pointed to a buckboard hitched in front of the smokehouse. "You've got company."

Adam nodded. "Looks like the Koehn buckboard."

An uneasy prickle climbed the back of David's neck. Could it be Priscilla? The men entered the house, and David was relieved to see Stephen Koehn seated at the Klaassen's plank kitchen table. But his relief was quickly replaced by a stab of jealousy. The fellow looked as if he belonged there.

Samantha, Josie, Liz, Jake, and Laura also sat around the table, each enjoying a glass of cold milk and homemade oatmeal cookies. Samantha made room for Adam and David to sit beside her. Adam gave his young wife a kiss, then reached across the table to offer Stephen a firm handshake. "Have you met Samantha's brother, David?" he asked. After the introductions, Adam asked, "When did you get back, Stephen?"

The man grinned, showing one dimple. His face was square, with a prominent chin and broad forehead. His hair, as shiny as a raven's wing, brushed back from his forehead in thick waves curling up at the collar of his plaid shirt. He had an earthy kind of wholesomeness about him that David couldn't help comparing to Priscilla's undisciplined flightiness. He also found himself comparing his own ordinary features and tall, lean frame to Stephen's undeniably handsome face and muscular build. Small wonder Josie found Stephen attractive.

"I got back day before yesterday." Stephen's deep voice registered his pleasure at being home. "Grandpa's doing fine, and

I'm not needed anymore. So home I came." He reached for another cookie, then quickly looked at Laura Klaassen. They all laughed at his expression—like a boy caught with his hand in the cookie jar. Laura handed him one, her eyes twinkling.

"Well, it's good to see you," Adam said.

Josie nodded agreement, David noticed.

"Glad to hear that." Stephen shot Josie a quick smile before turning back to Adam. "I intend to make a regular nuisance of myself around here."

The Klaassens all laughed again, and Laura said, "Now, Stephen, you know you are never a nuisance! You're always welcome here."

Apparently the open invitation applied to every person who walked by out here. How deflating, realizing Laura's statement to him earlier was being echoed already to another young man who obviously held the same intentions David had been considering. He bit into one of Laura's oatmeal cookies, hardly tasting it.

Samantha reached across Adam to tap David's arm. "David, Adam and I will stop by the boardinghouse and pick you up for church tomorrow."

David raised one eyebrow. "Yes, ma'am, I'd be delighted to accept your gracious invitation."

Samantha's expression turned sheepish.

David offered a grin. "Does lunch figure into that invitation as well?"

"Of course!"

He'd never pass up the chance for lunch with his sister, even if meant sitting through church first. "I'll be ready." He stood. "Mrs. Klaassen, thank you once more for your kind hospitality. I think I'd better be heading home now."

Laura rose, too, reaching out to clasp David's hand. "You're very welcome, David, and please consider yourself one of the family. Come by anytime."

David got in a quick glance at Stephen. The man was studying him. "Yes, ma'am, that I will." Was Stephen as unflappable as he appeared? Some sort of deviltry made him want to find out. He turned to Josie. "Josie, it was wonderful visiting with you this evening. You are a pleasant dinner companion."

Josie's faint freckles disappeared beneath a flood of pink. "Now, David, you're embarrassing me." She covered her face with both hands. "Go on, now!"

David laughed. "Yes, ma'am," he drawled, smiling to himself at the look on Stephen's face. It gave him pleasure to rattle the other man a bit.

They all called their good-byes, and David received a tight hug from Samantha before he headed out to begin the ride back to his quarters on his borrowed horse. Not until he was half a mile down the lane did it strike him. By intentionally trying to nettle Stephen, he'd behaved in the same way he found so annoying in Priscilla.

What on earth had come over him to conduct himself in such a manner? Not too difficult to figure—the old green-eyed monster, jealousy. He was jealous of Stephen Koehn—of Stephen's handsomeness and position in the community as well as his familiarity with Josie. The realization gave David a bit of understanding about Priscilla's motives. Although he still couldn't abide her blatantly self-centered behavior, he could at least imagine how jealousy could make a person act in an undesirable manner.

And now that he'd recognized it in himself, he could do something about it. The next time he saw Stephen, he would apologize for his behavior at the Klaassen home. He could do something about Priscilla, too, he decided. The next time she pulled one of her attention-getting schemes, he'd let her know he understood by refusing to rise to the bait. Maybe a little consideration was in order there too.

Maybe . . .

⌒⊙

A tapping on David's door at nine-thirty Sunday morning announced the arrival of his ride to church. David swung it open to find his sister dressed in an attractive rose-print calico dress and a charming little straw bonnet perched atop her bountiful russet hair.

"Well, aren't you as pretty as a picture." He grabbed his brown bowler from the hook on the wall and placed it over his own unruly hair.

"You're very handsome yourself, David," Samantha returned, smiling up at him.

David snorted. "Handsome? Yeah, right."

Samantha touched his arm. "Yes. You're very handsome. The most handsome man in town!" Her expression turned impish. "Next to Adam, of course."

David laughed.

She tipped her head, giving him a speculative look. "Are you intending to turn the head of some special young lady this morning?"

An image popped into David's mind, but he pushed it aside. "In church? I think not."

Samantha teasingly knocked her shoulder against his as they made their way to the waiting wagon. "But there are lots of girls in church. That's where to find the nice ones."

David offered Samantha a hand up next to Adam. "That's the trouble, Sammy. Too many nice girls—but no girl for a not-so-nice man like me."

As soon as David settled himself next to her on the seat, she placed her hand over his knee and peered up at him with tears shining in the corners of her eyes. "Davey, please don't talk that way about yourself. I know Pa always told us we were worthless, but he was wrong. None of us are worthless. We're loved by God, and He has wonderful plans for us. Don't let Pa's senseless rambling hold you captive any longer."

David swallowed the bitter taste of that memory. He wouldn't argue with his sister. He loved her too much to hurt her. But he couldn't accept her statements about God. If God existed, He must not have much use for David O'Brien or He'd have made Himself known a long time ago. "We better get moving, or we'll be late," he said.

Adam flicked the reins, and the horses jolted forward. Samantha kept her hand pressed over David's knee, her eyes closed, on the way to church. David suspected she was praying. Praying for him. The thought put a lump in his throat. He set his jaw and tried to ignore the uncomfortable feeling.

David paid attention to little of what went on in the church service. He had to admit, Adam and Samantha, as well as most of the congregation, seemed to find it all interesting, judging by their rapt attention to the minister's words. But how did church—or God—benefit anyone? Pa had always said a man was responsible for himself. If people weren't able to be responsible for their own lives, then maybe believing Someone bigger and stronger had control would make them feel better. But David had a stomach full of his pa ordering him about. He didn't need anyone else—particularly God or even his beloved sister—telling him what to do.

He sat on the hard bench trying not to fidget, and he sneaked a surreptitious peek in Josie's direction. She sure had a pleasing profile. She kept her eyes on the minister, Reverend Goertzen, looking like she was completely caught up in what he was saying. Something about a man named Lazarus. David didn't know who that was. He gazed at Josie for a long time, hoping for her to return his look, but she remained focused on the front of the church.

Stifling a sigh and shifting his position, he glanced over his shoulder. He felt a jolt go through him when he realized Priscilla Koehn's dark blue eyes were pinned on him. She sat primly beside her mother, her hands resting palms up in her lap—the picture of piety and attentiveness. When his glance met hers, she turned her perfectly shaped nose in the air and pinched her lips together.

The same irritation shot through him again. Last night he'd resolved to offer understanding. But looking at her arrogant expression, he decided the resolution would be much easier made than kept. However, he did owe Stephen an apology, and he would do that just as soon as this service was complete.

After the closing hymn, David skirted past the parishioners pausing in the aisles to chat and trailed after Stephen. The other man was already halfway across the church yard. David cupped his hands around his mouth and called, "Stephen, hold up there a minute, would you?"

Stephen stopped and turned around. When he saw who had called him, he looked surprised but held out a hand. "Hello. It's David, right?"

"Yes." David gave his hand a shake then shoved his hands into his jacket pockets. "I need to talk to you, if you have a little time to spare."

Stephen shrugged, glancing around. "Sure."

David cleared his throat. He wished he'd planned his apology in advance. He now found himself searching for appropriate words. "Um . . . the other night at the Klaassens, I think I left you with the wrong impression . . . about Josie. About Josie and me."

Stephen pulled his mouth sideways. "Yes . . . ?"

David scraped the toe of his boot in the dirt. "I shouldn't have tried to mislead you. You see, I do find Josie interesting, and I guess I wished she would pay attention to me like she was paying you. So I intentionally made it sound like—well, like something it was not. I'm sorry."

A grin slowly curved Stephen's lips. "Wow, that's most interesting, David. And I can't say I'm not relieved."

David shook his head regretfully. "She's a sister to my brother-in-law, so I'm bound to see her now and then, but not the way you might have thought."

Stephen wiped a hand across his forehead and blew out his breath. "You had me worried, old man. After all, I was gone for almost four months. Josie and I hadn't made any promises, and a lot can happen in that amount of time. I thought maybe . . ."

David forced an answering grin. "No, nothing like that. I was just feeling a bit of the old Nick, I guess. I'm sorry."

Stephen clapped David on the shoulder. "No hard feelings at all, David. And thanks for letting me know."

"Letting you know what?" A female voice sounded from behind David.

He looked over his shoulder, then sighed. Priscilla. He exchanged a look with Stephen, noting the other man's lips pressed together in what looked like irritation.

"Well, aren't you going to tell me?" She placed her hands on her hips, glancing perkily between the pair of men. "What are you two whispering about over here?"

David started to answer, but Stephen moved a step forward and poked his finger against her shoulder. "You. We were trying to decide whether to tie you to that tree"—he pointed to the elm at the corner of the church—"or the tall oak next to the schoolhouse. Maybe keep you from sticking your nose in other people's business."

She slapped his hand away. "You are such an idiot. You know very well that's not what you were talking about."

"No, it's not, but it's all I'm going to tell you. What David and I were discussing is none of your concern. And your name did not come up. Not even once." Her brother seemed to take some delight in letting her know that.

Priscilla crossed her arms and leaned back at the waist, a too-familiar look of disdain on her face. "We'll just see about that, Stephen Koehn." She whirled away, her long hair swinging in a curtain behind her.

David watched her go and shook his head once. Understanding? Who could understand that girl. Certainly not him.

Stephen released a sigh. "Now it's my turn to apologize to you . . . for my sister. I'd like to say she isn't normally like that, but my mother taught me not to tell lies."

David chuckled. "Don't worry about it. I've had a couple of toe-to-toes with her, and I imagine she's just letting me know I'm not going to get away without a fight."

Stephen gave David a pensive look. "You've bumped heads with Prissy?"

David nodded, embarrassed. "I'm afraid so."

"And who came out the victor?"

David pulled at his cheek with a finger. "Well . . ."

Stephen chuckled low in his throat. "Don't answer, I can guess. I was hoping maybe she's finally met the man who can subdue her."

"Subdue Priscilla?" David held up his hands in defeat. "Don't look at me."

Stephen laughed loudly, then sobered. "What did she do to ruffle your feathers?"

David offered a shrug. "I guess maybe I ruffled her feathers, and she wasn't used to that. Then she came back at me, and I—."

"I'm not surprised." Stephen dropped his gaze for a moment. "My sister has a way of rubbing everyone the wrong way. She seems to think it's her God-given right." He met David's gaze once more. "I hope you won't judge all of us by Priscilla's actions."

David would be the last one to judge someone based on their relatives. He'd been on the receiving end of that treatment more than once in his life, with people shying away from him because of his father. "Don't worry about it. I admit, I might envy your friendship with Josie, but I sure wouldn't trade my sister for yours."

Stephen laughed good-naturedly, impressing David further with his even temperament. "I won't hold that against you." He paused. "You know, David, I'd like to get to know you better. Would you be able to come home with me, for *faspa*?"

David drew back a little, uncertain how to respond. He wasn't accustomed to friendly overtures—particularly when he'd set out to mislead the man just the evening before. Pleased yet puzzled by Stephen's invitation to the family's Sunday-noon meal, he recognized the beginnings of a friendship forming. But he had to decline this time. "Thank you for asking, but I've already got plans to go out to Adam and Sammy's and eat with them."

Stephen shrugged. "Maybe another time?"

David nodded. "Yes, I'd like that—especially if your sister has another event to attend." He grinned to take any sting out of the remark, and Stephen laughed too.

"All right then." He stuck out his hand, and David shook it. "I'll talk to you later."

David trotted over to Adam and Samantha in their wagon. Samantha greeted him with a little huff. "Finally! What were you two yammering on about over there? I didn't know you were friends with Stephen Koehn."

David climbed up beside her on the buckboard's front seat. "I'm not friends with Stephen Koehn—yet. But I think I will be. And as for what we were talking about—mind your own business. You're as snoopy as Priscilla."

Samantha gasped then gaped at him. "Well!"

Adam whistled. "Oooh, brother, them's fightin' words."

David laughed and threw an arm around Samantha's shoulders, pulling her against him in an affectionate hug. "Sammy, you are about as much like Priscilla as I am like Adam's Tante Hulda."

Imagining tall, slender David standing next to short, rotund Hulda sent all three into gales of laughter.

"All right, you're forgiven." Samantha relaxed against his shoulder. "Maybe I'll feed you after all."

"And there are at least two of us who are grateful." David bestowed a kiss on his sister's cheek as the wagon rolled out of the church yard. He kept his arm around her shoulders, grateful that she was nothing like Priscilla Koehn. What kind of life would it be with someone like that living under your roof, interfering in your every move? David shuddered. Lucky for him, he'd never have to find out.

scilla sat at the table, pushing the food around
the china plate but carrying none of it to her
mouth.

at's the matter? Finish your food," Mama scolded.

ed her eyes. "I'm not hungry." She inserted the
e into her voice, hoping Daddy would notice.

ross the table, Daddy cupped her hand. "What's
ssy?"

ot a look of pure venom at Stephen, who sat on
then hung her head, affecting a persecuted air for
enefit. "It's nothing, Daddy. I'm just a little upset,
be fine." She peeked up at her father, biting the
r cheeks to hold back a satisfied smile.

gaze went from Priscilla to Stephen and to Priscilla
yebrows pulled down sharply. "Has Stephen done
to upset you?"

hn," Mama interceded, "why must you assume . . . ?"
n look silenced her, and she turned her face to her
lips set in a grim line. Stephen slumped down in his
ing at his sister. Daddy patted Priscilla's hand. "Come
ssy. Let's have it. Tell me what's wrong."

cilla sighed. "Oh, Daddy, I don't want to cause prob-
eally, it's not important. But Stephen and that awful
)'Brien were talking about me after church today, and
, it's gotten me upset, that's all."

ldy turned his frown on Stephen. "What's this all about?"

Stephen slapped his fork onto to the table.
I were talking after church. It had nothing to d
She came up behind us and demanded to kno
discussing. I told her it wasn't her business." He
"And it wasn't. I should be able to have a conve
her sticking her nose in it."

Daddy turned to Priscilla. "Is that what hap

Priscilla brought up her head and pointe
Stephen. "He said he was going to tie me to the
the school!" She quivered her chin and blinked
the presence of indignant tears.

Daddy reared back. "Stephen!"

Priscilla ducked her head to hide her smirk.

Stephen blew out a noisy breath. "Of course
such a thing. I was aggravated and merely wante
her place."

Mama held out a hand in entreaty. "Yes, Jo
Stephen—"

"Stephen, you will apologize to your sister.
think it would be best if you did not spend time with
O'Brien. He upset your sister yesterday at the mer
his impudence. He doesn't seem to be the kind of
whom we need to associate."

"Oh, but, Pa—" Stephen tried.

"Apologize to your sister," Daddy commanded in a
ous tone.

Stephen's face glowed red. Priscilla pushed two p
and forth with her fork, waiting for her brother to follo
father's directive, the way he always did. Finally Stephe
tered, "Sorry, Pris."

His words emerged through gritted teeth, but I
tossed her head and offered her brother a sweet smile.

Daddy squeezed her hand. "There. He's apologized." He released her hand and pointed to her plate. "Now sit up there like a good girl and finish your food. Go ahead."

Priscilla picked up her fork and carried a bite to her mouth. Daddy beamed. "That's my girl."

Priscilla beamed back.

༄༅

Stephen smoldered, watching his sister out of the corner of his eye. So smug, her eyes sparkling with success. Why did his father cosset her so? He wasn't doing her any favors. Priscilla was the most self-centered, unfeeling person he knew. And others knew it too.

And how humiliating to be reprimanded like this at his age. Twenty-three years old and treated like a child. It was time to get away from his father's house. Suddenly he had the need to see Josie and bask in her goodness. Josie would restore his feelings of control.

He dropped his napkin onto the table. "Ma, will you excuse me, please? I'll be out for a while." Although he tried to be polite, he knew his voice sounded strained.

Pa shrugged when Ma looked to him. "Yes, Stephen, go ahead." Her eyes offered Stephen a silent apology.

Stephen leaned over and gave his mother a kiss on the cheek before leaving the room. He made a promise to himself to never treat his own wife in the demeaning manner Pa used with Ma. His wife would be a partner.

He took deep breaths to help calm his churning insides as he went out to the barn for the horse and wagon. During his ride across the countryside, the final tensions of his latest family argument faded away. He even found himself whistling a cheerful tune as he bounced along on the wagon's high seat. Spring was here, and with it the promise of new growth, new beginnings.

Stephen mulled over the possibility of his own new beginnings. The sun beamed down warmly in the west, baby birds poked their little noses out of nests and demanded their dinner, and wildflowers sprang from dried brown stalks, bringing a welcome splash of color. Stephen flicked the reins, clicking his tongue to hurry the horses. He could hardly wait to see Josie and find out if maybe spring was touching her the same way.

He parked the wagon in front of the Klaassen farmhouse, then trotted around to the back door, eagerness lightening his steps. Becky answered his knock and called out in a sing-song, "Oh, Jo-o-o-sie, it's your knight in shining ar-r-mo-o-or!"

Mrs. Klaassen scolded, "Becky, it's not polite to embarrass our guest." She held out a hand of welcome to Stephen. "Come right on in, Stephen. We've finished the kitchen cleanup, and Josie ran up to change her clothes. You can sit in the parlor with Mr. Klaassen until she comes down."

"Thank you, ma'am." Stephen removed his hat and hung it on a hook by the back door. "I bet you didn't know that when you offered to let me come anytime that I'd take you up on it quite so soon."

Mrs. Klaassen laughed and waved him through the kitchen. "I never say something I don't mean, and I did mean 'anytime.' Now go on in and visit with Mr. Klaassen. The boys went out right after eating."

Stephen passed through the kitchen and stepped into the parlor, greeting Mr. Klaassen with a handshake and smile. He felt better already, just being here.

"Sit down, Stephen, sit down." Josie's father motioned to the upholstered sofa. "What brings you out here this Sunday afternoon, as if I don't know?" His eyes twinkled with fun.

Stephen grinned, grateful for Mr. Klaassen's welcome and seeming acceptance of the friendship with Josie. "Well, I was hoping to take Josie for a walk, if that's all right with you."

Mr. Klaassen nodded his graying head. "Perfectly all right with me, but you might want to ask her. You might have already discovered she does have a mind of her own."

The two men chuckled together, and Stephen said, "That she does." She was no empty-headed, simple-minded, and overly agreeable "pretty face." Josie was unique, someone whose attractiveness was matched by her lovely nature. And Stephen couldn't help but be hopeful.

The men discussed the recent headlines—the end of the war, which pleased everyone; the outbreak of the Spanish influenza, which concerned everyone; and local news, which certainly would never make the headlines but affected everyone in the community. Stephen was leaning forward, making a case for the importance of changing to motorized farm implements, when Josie appeared in the doorway.

Stephen quickly finished his sentence and stood up. "Hello, Josie. I hope I'm not disturbing . . ." He paused and started over. "Well, I'm wondering if you'd like to take a walk."

Josie moved across the room at the same time he did. As they met in the middle, she said, "It's nice to see you, Stephen. And yes, I would like a walk."

After the dreadful scene at his home table, Josie seemed like a breath of fresh air.

Ever respectful, Josie looked past him to her father. "Is that all right with you, Papa?"

Mr. Klaassen waved a hand at them. "Certainly, long as you're home before suppertime so you can help your mother."

Stephen assured him, "I'll have her home well before then, sir. Thank you."

Stephen held the door, and as Josie slipped by him he caught a clean, attractive scent. Halfway across the yard, he reached for her hand. When his fingers closed around hers, she drew to a halt, peering up at him inquisitively. He suspected he knew what had brought her up short. He lifted her hand between them. "Do you mind?"

Josie pursed her lips, looking thoughtfully at the clasped hands. "I'm not sure, Stephen. It seems a bit . . . well, too friendly—"

"Aren't we friends?" Stephen asked in mock hurt.

She laughed. "Of course we are, but I'm friends with lots of fellows. I wonder how you would feel if I allowed one of them to hold my hand."

David O'Brien immediately surfaced in his mind. The idea of David holding Josie's hand did not sit well, no matter how much he appreciated the man's honesty and apology. Yet Stephen hadn't staked his claim, so to speak, where Josie was concerned. She had every right to be friendly with other young men if she desired. His heart pounded with his frustration and uncertainty. He had been gone for four months, and maybe his expectations were not the same as hers.

Still holding her hand, he led her to the wooden swing beneath the crabapple tree in the middle of the Klaassens' yard. He guided her into it, then sat on the tender shoots of grass near her feet. He pulled one tiny blade of grass free from the earth and watched it as he twirled in his fingers.

When he looked up he saw the new green leaves above Josie like a canopy, and the spring flowers around them created a heady backdrop of scent and color. Josie was dressed simply in a dress of blue cotton, only a small ruffle at the neck and sleeves. Her sandy brown hair, pulled into its usual single braid, swung across one shoulder. The light spattering of freckles across her nose gave her an innocent, fresh appearance that Stephen found most alluring. And there was much more to Josie than her pleasing appearance. She was intelligent, caring, and moral—the perfect choice for a lifelong mate.

He stared into her face. Was this the time to let her know? Had her question about whether he wanted her holding hands with another man been some kind of a hint? Females could be so confusing. . . .

"Stephen, what are you thinking about?" Josie's voice cut into his thoughts. "You have the oddest expression on your face."

He squinted into the setting sun between the branches of the tree. "I'm sorry. I didn't ask you to come out here so I could stare at you." He grinned and added, "Not that staring at you isn't a pleasant pastime." Her blush pleased him. She was so open and innocent.

"Now don't start that, Stephen Koehn," she said and chuckled, "or I'll get up and go back in the house." Then she sobered, an earnest look crossing her face. "Really, I do want to know what you're thinking. Please tell me, Stephen. Something is on your mind."

Stephen rested his elbows on his knees and tossed aside the little blade of grass. "Did you miss me while I was in Blue Earth, Josie?"

"Well, of course I did. I've known you forever. Why wouldn't I miss such a good friend?"

"That's all?" he asked, his heart sinking. "You missed me as a friend?"

Josie frowned. "Well, shouldn't I think of you as a friend, Stephen?"

Stephen shifted his position. "Well, yes, I hope you think of me as a friend." His voice came out sharper than he intended. He softened his tone. "But isn't there—well, something more?"

"Like what?"

Frustration pressed at Stephen's chest. Was Josie purposely making this difficult? Why did he have to spell it all out for her? "I'd been calling on you for two months before I left for Blue Earth. I wasn't calling on anyone else, and I haven't called on anyone else since. I thought we might have . . . well, an understanding."

"No one else has called on me, Stephen."

A wave of relief washed over him. Stephen scrambled to his feet and pulled Josie out of the swing. "Come on, let's walk."

But Josie stood in front of him without moving a step. "I'd rather finish this conversation before moving on to something else. You definitely have something on your mind, Stephen, and I hope you trust me enough to tell me about it. If you don't, then I think there's something important lacking in our relationship."

He clung to that last word. "Do we have a relationship, Josie?"

"I thought we did." Impatience colored her tone. "But I'm starting to wonder what your intentions are. If you can't even express them, then—"

He halted her words by grasping her shoulders and placing his lips against hers. When he pulled back, she was staring at him with wide eyes. "Why, Stephen!"

He couldn't help his amusement at her reaction. "Do you know what my intentions are now, Josie?"

She took a big breath and let it out. "Does this mean it would bother you if I held hands with some other man?"

He growled menacingly. "Just let someone try it, and see how the fur flies."

She giggled. "I've been warned." Then she sobered. "But, Stephen, we still need to talk. Just kissing me doesn't tell me what I need to know."

Stephen cupped her shoulders with his hands. "What do you want me to say, Josie? When I was in Blue Earth, I missed you desperately and couldn't wait to return to Mountain Lake. To you. When I think of starting a family of my own, you are always at the center of those thoughts. Last night when David O'Brien thanked you for your attention during supper, I was shocked and near green with envy." He paused, his hands tightening on her shoulders. His voice dropped to a near whisper. "Josie, I want to marry you. I want you to be my wife."

Josie took in a sharp breath. "M-marry me?"

Stephen chuckled, then stopped when she did not join in. "Well, yes, you silly girl. You didn't think that kiss was for nothing, did you?"

"No, and I don't take kisses lightly either, but . . ."

"But . . . ?" He ducked down and peered into her face.

Josie turned her head away, sucking on her lower lip. "But I'm not sure . . . I'm not sure we're ready to think about getting married."

Stephen's hands dropped slowly from her shoulders, and he took a step backward, his gaze still fastened on her face. His arms hung limply at his side. "Why not?"

Josie twisted her hands together, a pleading expression on her face. "Stephen, you kissed me and told me you want to marry me, but there's something you haven't said."

Her tone was kind, but Stephen caught the undercurrent of disappointment in her eyes. He lowered his head. "What do you want to know?"

"You said you think of me when planning to start your own family, you missed me when you were away, you were envious of the attention I paid to David. . . . But you didn't tell me you loved me. Shouldn't that be said before a marriage proposal is made?"

Stephen lifted his head. "I'm sorry, Josie. You're right. I should have said that first." But he fell silent.

Josie tipped her head and looked him straight in the eyes. "Do you love me?"

"I care for you deeply, Josie, you know that." He glanced down again.

"Yes, I do know that, but that isn't what I asked." She stepped forward, reaching out to place a tentative hand on his forearm. She repeated very softly, "Stephen, do you love me?"

Stephen swallowed. Hard. "I think I do." He met her gaze, both anguished and bewildered. "I've never felt about anyone the way I feel about you. I want to be with you every day, every hour. Does that mean I love you?"

Josie turned away slightly, giving him a view of her profile. "I don't know. Only you can answer that."

Stephen held out a hand toward her. "Josie, are you saying you won't marry me?"

Josie sighed. "No, Stephen, I'm not saying I won't marry you; someday, maybe we will be married. But I think some misplaced sense of jealousy or spring fever or seeing me again after your time away—or something has caused you to step over an important part of getting to truly know each other. Of knowing your heart—and mine . . . Unless you are sure you love me, we shouldn't even be discussing this."

She was right, but he wasn't willing to admit it. His ego felt bruised. He turned away in frustrated silence.

"I think we need some time, Stephen," she went on in a calm, sensible tone. "I would like to continue seeing you, but I don't think either of us is ready to make plans for a future together. After all, I plan to take the teacher's examination, and you aren't sure. . . . Maybe we both need to rethink where we're going with this."

Stephen stared at her, dumbstruck. He'd come out here intending to sweep her off her feet—maybe even ask permission of her parents to make their engagement official before he left—and here she was, sweetly as you please, telling him that he should think about it more and that she was still planning to go off somewhere and teach.

"Well, all right then," he blustered, his chest tight, "if you want to think, then fine. Take all the time you need to think. And when you're done thinking, you know where to find me." He whirled away.

Josie's hand shot out, catching his arm and holding him in place. He glowered at her, and she frowned. "I'm only trying to be sensible, Stephen. One doesn't make an important decision like getting married without giving it serious thought. There's no reason to be angry."

He jerked his arm free. "I'm not angry."

"You must be angry, because you're yelling."

"I'm not yelling!" he yelled. Then he fell silent. His head drooped, his chin nearly touching his chest. It was springtime, and he'd been all ready to take the young lady of his choice to be his wife. It wasn't supposed to be this difficult.

Josie stepped close to him again, and he raised his head to meet her gaze. A shimmer of tears brightened her brown eyes. He hadn't meant to make her cry. He swallowed his anger and reached out to brush her cheek with one finger. "Maybe you're right. Maybe we should take a little more time and . . . and think this through before making a commitment."

She nodded. The crestfallen expression on her face tore at Stephen's heart. "I still want to see you, Stephen." She sounded sad yet hopeful.

He managed a reassuring smile. "I want to see you, too. Shall we plan on meeting next Saturday? Maybe go on a picnic?"

A slight smile appeared. "I'd like that. Should I pack a lunch?"

"No, this time it's my treat. I'll have Ma throw some sandwiches together."

Teasing glinted in her eyes. "Sounds as if it's your mother's treat."

He gave the expected chuckle. "Yeah, well, I don't cook so good. . . ."

Josie looked toward the house. "I'd better go in now, Stephen. I'll be praying about what you asked me. I want to do what's right. What's right for both of us."

He nodded. "Me, too."

She paused. "I'll see you Saturday."

"Yes, Saturday." Stephen slipped his hands into his pockets. "I'll pick you up before noon, and we can drive over to Goose Pond."

She began backing away, her hands clasped behind her back, the braid still over her shoulder the way Stephen liked. She smiled tremulously. "Saturday . . ." At Stephen's nod, she spun and ran to the house, disappearing inside.

Stephen stood in the yard, staring after her. *Well, Lord, I sure messed that up.* The brightness was suddenly missing from spring.

raduation Day for the Mountain Lake Community School senior class of 1918 took place on a golden afternoon in late May, right outside in the school yard. Josie sat with the other graduates on the raised platform built for this occasion, facing the audience. As her gaze roved across the sea of familiar faces, it wasn't hard to imagine that at least half of the people on hard benches beneath the bright May sun were there just to see her receive her hard-earned diploma.

Josie's grandparents and oldest brother, Daniel, had traveled with his family clear from Minneapolis for her big day. The biggest surprise of the day was what had carried Daniel, Rose, and their two little girls to town—a brand-new, black shiny Model T Ford. It was the first automobile to chug down the cobblestone streets of Mountain Lake, and it caused quite a commotion. Josie smiled to herself as she recalled some of the stunned expressions when Daniel chugged to a stop beside the horse-drawn buggies and wagons that had brought the others to the graduation.

Her smile faded, though, when she confirmed one important face was missing from her group of supporters this morning—Stephen's. Ever since their talk when she had gently declined his marriage proposal, he had been cool and distant. Although they had gone on the picnic that Saturday a few weeks ago and had gone walking together after church on Sundays since, the old ease of being together had slipped away.

Could he be holding himself aloof to punish her, to force her into bending to his will?

Irritation mounted as she mulled it over. He knew she had her own goals—mainly, of teaching. Why should she have to give up her dream simply because he decided he was ready to settle down with someone? Especially when he couldn't even say the words I *love you* to her. Josie realized she should wait until her own head and heart were in agreement before making a life-changing decision like getting married. One would think an intelligent man like Stephen would be that sensible, too.

But she was going to ruin this day for herself if she didn't think of something positive. Determinedly, she turned her attention elsewhere. A baby gurgled somewhere in the throng, and Josie twisted in her chair and spotted one of Liz and Jake's twins, little A.J., with a grip on his Uncle Adam's nose. She covered a smile with her hand when she saw that the tyke wouldn't let go. Beside Adam, Samantha shook with silent laughter as she tried to wrestle the baby's chubby hand downward, but A.J. chortled loudly and flapped his dimpled hands at his Auntie Sam. David sat next to Samantha, smiling at the little boy's antics. The Klaassens considered David an honorary member of the family, but until recently he'd kept himself a bit at arm's length. Josie had made sure her parents invited him to the graduation, but she hadn't expected to see him. He sat grinning at Adam and Samantha as they tussled with A.J. Then he turned his head and caught her watching.

He smiled, lifting a hand to wave briefly. Her cheeks went hot. She nodded, flustered. Would he think she'd been staring at him? She didn't have much time to worry about it because the ceremony began.

Reverend Goertzen stepped onto the platform and asked the congregation to rise for an opening prayer. Josie stood nervously and squeezed the hand of Tessie Jost, seated on her left. It gave her some assurance that Tessie seemed to be just as nervous as she was, considering the girl's moist hand.

The graduating class of 1918 had only five members—four girls: Josie, Tessie, Mary Wiens, and Priscilla Koehn; and a lone male, Joseph Enns. Their teacher, Mr. Reimer, gave a brief address, instructing the graduates to fulfill their dreams and look above for guidance in the pathways their lives followed.

The school board president, Mr. Arthur Neufeldt, solemnly shook the hand of each graduate as he handed them the rolled piece of parchment that signified their successful completion of school requirements. Josie had to hide another grin as she took hers; sweat poured from the poor man's bald head like water from a sieve. Josie turned toward her family and flashed a beaming smile. Each member returned it a hundredfold from across the audience.

The rest of the school's students gathered in a group at the front and sang the hymn "Jesus, Gentle Shepherd." Then Reverend Goertzen prayed once more, bestowing a final blessing on the young people, and it was over.

Josie hugged each of her classmates in turn, even briefly embracing Priscilla who offered her cheek with her usual condescension. Then Jodie stepped off the platform and bounded over to her family in an unladylike manner, waving her diploma over her head. "Now to take the teachers' exam, and I'm all set!"

Congratulations floated around her as she moved from one person to another, receiving enthusiastic hugs and kisses. She turned from Adam's hug to find herself face to face with David. The warmth ignited in her cheeks again.

"Congratulations, Josie." David held out his hand rather than opening his arms. Self-consciously, she took his hand and felt his long, hard fingers close tightly around her own. "I have a gift for you." And he held out a small square package bound in brown paper and tied with string. "I couldn't find a better wrapping . . ." He seemed embarrassed by its plain appearance.

Josie beamed at him, trying to put them both at ease. "Why, thank you, David." She took the package and held it against her graduation dress of mint faille. "You didn't need to do that. Just coming today is all the gift I need."

David shrugged and ran a hand over his unruly hair. "Well, it's not much. But graduations are special, and I was grateful to be invited. I'm proud of your accomplishment."

Josie's eyes widened in surprise. She'd never have imagined him saying something like that. And he was pink around the ears himself.

"Josie, come on." Sarah tugged at Josie's sleeve. "Mama baked a big ol' white cake with strawberry icing! Let's go eat it!"

Josie laughed at her youngest sister's eager face. "All right, I'm coming." She paused, looking back at David. "Are you . . . coming too?"

Ma stepped up and slipped her arm around Josie's waist. "Why, yes, David, do come out. The party wouldn't be complete without you."

A smile crept over David's narrow face, lighting his pale blue eyes. "Thank you, I will." He fell into step behind them, his long shadow falling across Josie's frame. She hurried her steps, suddenly uncomfortable but uncertain why.

Josie's graduation party turned out to be a raucous affair. The children dashed between the legs of the adults, earning reprimands but slowing not a whit. Laura Klaassen provided enough food to keep a whole army fat and happy. The womenfolk carried things from the kitchen into the yard for a good fifteen minutes. The men gathered in clusters to discuss the things males liked to discuss, and frequent bursts of laughter resounded from their ranks. David mingled in their midst, treated as if he belonged. It warmed him. How wonderful to fit in somewhere after all those lonely years.

When bowls of food filled the plank-and-sawhorse tables, Si Klaassen gave a whistle and motioned everyone to gather around. "Children, it's time to settle down," he admonished. When they had finally done so, he looked around the table at the sea of faces. A smile crossed his face when his eyes found Josie, and he held out his hand to her. "Come here, Josephine."

Josie tucked herself beneath her father's arm, grinning up at him.

"Josie—" Si lifted his voice for all to hear—"we're all very proud of you, and we want to wish you God's richest blessings for what lies ahead. Graduation is the finish of school, but it's just the beginning of everything else to come. And I know great things are in store for you." A hint of moisture brightened Si's eyes, and his arm tightened around her.

Josie blushed, laughing as Si put his other arm around her in a tight embrace. "Thank you, Papa."

"Let's pray," Si said, and all around the long table bowed their heads. "Lord, we're together as a family to celebrate Josie's graduation from high school. You know her heart and the hopes she has to become a teacher. We ask that you bless her desires and open the doors to let her fulfill those dreams. Be with all of us as well. Now bless this food and the hands that prepared it. Amen."

"Amen!" echoed more than a dozen voices, and Liz and Jake's nine-month-old twins hollered in unison, "Amaah!" Laughter erupted, and the eating commenced amidst much talking and more joyful merrymaking.

David found himself sandwiched between Frank and Arn in the middle of the table. Josie sat at the head, Si having given her the seat of honor with a dramatic wave of his arm to more laughter.

David thought back to Si's prayer, specifically the words "We're together as a family," and his heart expanded at the feeling those words evoked.

Samantha sat next to Adam, helping Liz with one of her twins, laughing over her shoulder at something Adam whispered in her ear. She looked as if she were born to this world, as if she'd never known anything else. David envied her the ability to let go of the past. How had she managed to do it? In all likelihood, Adam's love had brought her around. The love of someone as special as Adam would be enough to change anyone.

His heart hammered at the next thought. Could someone special possibly fall in love with him and bring the same change in his life? His eyes wandered to Josie. She was definitely her brother's sister. Both were self-assured but not overbearing, each in possession of a contentedness that David couldn't imagine ever experiencing. His heart lifted as he watched her, the center of attention and thoroughly enjoying every minute of it, but still managing to allow everyone to share in her happiness. Yes, Josie was definitely a very special person.

All the Klaassens had those qualities, and David marveled at the legacy the Klaassen grandparents had handed to their offspring. Quite different from the self-loathing and uncertainty that David and Samantha's alcoholic father had bestowed on his children. Samantha had broken those chains, thanks to Adam. Would it be possible for David to throw off his cloak of despair with the help of a special woman?

He rested an elbow on the edge of the table, his chin on his fist, and gazed in Josie's direction while questions filled his mind. Why wasn't Stephen here? He'd noticed the man at the graduation ceremony standing at the back of the school yard, gazing at Josie, but he hadn't approached her. Did it mean they were no longer seeing each other? Was she free to accept the attentions of someone else? Maybe his attentions . . . ?

"Hey, brother," Adam called, interrupting David's thought. "Are you going to sleep over there?"

David sat up, his face heating. He quipped, "Not a chance with all this racket."

"Well, I'm glad," Laura joined in, "because it's time to watch Josie open her graduation gifts. You won't want to miss out on that."

David smiled and nodded. He most definitely would not want to miss watching Josie, no matter what she was doing.

The two youngest Klaassen offspring, Sarah and Teddy, brought Josie her gifts. First she opened a fabric-backed journal and pen from Daniel and Rose. Josie grinned appreciatively at her oldest brother and his wife in a silent expression of thanks. When she opened a box holding lace-edged handkerchiefs and a small glass decanter of perfume from Frank and Anna, she immediately touched the stopper to her wrist, sniffed, and proclaimed, "Mm! Delightful!"

Similar expressions of gratitude accompanied each package, and David's admiration of the young woman grew with each happy exclamation. His ears went hot when little Teddy laid the next gift into Josie's lap. He sat in anxious silence, his heart pounding, as she pulled off the plain brown paper and opened David's gift. She ran her fingers over the pale-pink stationery and matching envelopes, fastened together with a ribbon. "Oh, thank you, David! This is wonderful. Now I'll have nice paper to write letters home on when I go away to teach."

David didn't dare ask whether she would write to him too. "You're welcome," he managed, and everyone's attention went to the next package.

Grandmother Klaassen had crocheted a beautiful shawl in shades of burgundy, wheat, and palest pink. Josie buried her face in its softness. When she emerged, tears were flowing. "Oh, Grandma, it's just beautiful! And you did this with your poor fingers."

Grandmother Klaassen pooh-poohed Josie's exclamation with a dismissive wave of an arthritic hand. "You surely do not think I would reward an occasion as important as this with some store-bought trifle! As long as I am still breathing, I will continue my needlework."

Josie darted around the table to give her grandmother a long, heartfelt hug.

From her seat next to Grandmother Klaassen, Hulda Klaassen called, "Now open ours."

Josie eagerly reached for the next package, a small one, and lifted a beautiful cameo pin from its velvet-lined box. "Oh, this is too much!"

"Not at all." Hulda pulled her face down until her extra chins formed a perfect double-U beneath her chin bone. "Graduations come once in a lifetime. We want you to remember this one."

"Oh, I will," Josie breathed, awe in her eyes. "Thank you so much."

David, observing the bright eyes and love glowing on the women's faces around the circle, felt a lump in his throat. He'd never forget this day, either.

Teddy thumped the next package onto the table. Josie peeled back the paper and squealed. "A dictionary! My first teacher's book! Thank you, Liz. You too, Jake!"

Little Andy banged a spoon on his high-chair tray, and Josie added seriously, "Oh, you, too, Andy and A.J. I'm sure you helped your mama and daddy pick this out." Everyone laughed, and both babies cooed and slapped their hands against their trays as if they knew they were being included.

Only two more packages remained—one round hatbox, and one rectangular box of substantial size. Josie rested her hands on the top of the second one, glancing impishly at her mother out of the corner of her eye. "Given Mother's penchant for practicality, I hope this isn't underwear."

Laura jumped up, laughing. "It would serve you right if it was!" She rounded the table and rubbed noses with her daughter. Then Laura ordered, brows furrowed into a mock scowl, "Open it up, you ungrateful child."

Josie tugged the top off the big box, then paused, her mouth hanging open. Slowly she reached in and lifted out a beautiful dress of deep garnet organdy. She stood and held it against herself and stared down its length. Although David didn't consider himself a fashion connoisseur, he recognized the sophisticated cut of the dress. The frock gave Josie a maturity that he found most fitting—and irresistible.

Frank joked, "Somebody reach over and close my sister's mouth for her before she starts drawing flies."

The whole group burst out into more laughter, and Josie twirled in a circle with the beautiful garnet dress held in place at her shoulders. "Oh, Mother, Papa, this is the most wonderful, unexpected present. Oh, it's just perfect! However did you manage it?"

Samantha leaned forward, her eyes twinkling. "It wasn't easy. Mother Klaassen and I have been working on it at our place so you wouldn't find out about it. Adam says you are the worst snoop."

"Oh, I know I am," Josie cheerfully admitted. "But this is a wonderful surprise. I'm so glad it isn't underwear!" she said to more chuckles.

Her father shoved the hatbox under Josie's nose. "See what's in here now."

Josie carefully placed the dress in its wrappings, touching it briefly with a trembling hand before turning to the hatbox. When she lifted the lid, she squealed once more. A beautiful store-bought hat—the exact shade of garnet as the dress—appeared, and Josie perched it on her head, beaming at them all from beneath the dipped brim. A tiny cluster of satin ecru ribbon and pearl buttons attached an ostrich feather fit snugly into the dip. Josie placed both hands on the edges of the hat to hold it in place and swung around once more. "I'll be the best-dressed teacher in Minnesota!"

Teddy pulled a slender box from beneath his jacket and thrust it at his sister. "This goes with it. It's from me, Arn, Becky, and Sarah."

Sarah bounced in her seat. "Open it fast, Josie. I can't wait!"

The ostrich feather bobbing, Josie grasped the box in both hands and slid the lid up with her thumbs. She let out a squeal and held a hatpin aloft. A good twelve inches in length, the gold shaft was tipped with a deep-red center stone the size of a man's fingertip. Josie went over to the line of siblings, hugging each. She finally returned to her place at the head of the table, glowing with brightness and joy. Her ostrich-feather hat was still on her head with the hatpin angled artfully across it. Happy tears shimmered on her eyelashes. "This has been the most wonderful day. Thank you, all of you, for your gifts and sharing this day with me. I'm so glad you all belong to me." And then she covered her face with both hands and burst into tears.

The women surrounded her, patting and laughing and crying a little themselves. Even the men looked misty eyed. And David experienced a deep desire to be a permanent part of this happy circle. He wanted what his sister had found with Adam— love and acceptance and peace. And, he decided with sudden resolve, Josie was the key. *Somehow, Josie must be mine.*

Chapter Seven

*J*osie passed the teachers' exam a week after graduation and received her teaching certificate bearing the seal of the state examiner. She floated for days on a cloud of anticipation as she sent out letters of application to every school within a hundred miles of Mountain Lake. Pa and Ma suggested she was pushing herself out a little farther than was necessary, but when Josie assured them she'd prayerfully consider any offer before accepting it, they gave her their blessing.

Stephen continued to sulk. At least, that's how Josie saw it. He made no effort to seek her out, and it wasn't her place to go chasing after him. Josie missed his company—although Stephen seemed uncertain of his feelings for her, she knew that she did love him. She had since she was just a little girl in pigtails. But she couldn't tell him so—not when he was uncertain about his feelings for her. So she busied herself at home, helping her mother put in their huge garden, sewing two more dresses appropriate for a teacher to wear—praying as she stitched that they would be put to good use, and hand feeding a little calf that had been rejected by its mother. Although her days were full, she thought of Stephen often and wondered if she might get a note or if he'd show up and surprise her.

Samantha came over the day they planted corn. She and Adam lived in a dugout that had been built by Adam's grandparents when they immigrated to America almost fifty years before. The little dwelling was near the fields Adam's family planted with wheat, but there wasn't a plot for a garden. So Samantha helped with the large garden at Si and Laura's home in return for some of the harvest. Josie and Samantha worked side by side in the sun, dropping the seed corn into furrows and tamping the dirt down. Planting was a long, tedious chore, and by midafternoon both needed a break.

They collapsed in the shade of Josie's favorite crab apple tree. Becky brought out glasses of lemonade, cooled with ice from the Klaassens' own icehouse. After taking a long swallow, Samantha placed the sweaty glass against her equally sweaty forehead and sighed. "Ah, that feels good."

Josie planted her palms in the grass behind her and let her head hang back, gazing at the bright leaves overhead. "If it's this muggy already, what will it be like in July?"

"Unbearable," Samantha predicted. She drained her glass dry, then rattled the ice chips in the glass. "Josie?"

Too tired to even respond, Josie sat in silence.

A bare toe poked at Josie's leg.

Josie sighed and looked at Samantha. "What?"

Samantha grinned. "Can I be nosy?"

Josie released a soft chortle. "Yes, to my experience, you can be very nosy."

Samantha grimaced. "Spoken like a true teacher. *May* I be nosy?"

Josie crossed her legs and leaned her elbows on her knees. "You've never bothered to ask permission before. Go ahead—but I reserve the right to refuse answering."

"Fair enough." Samantha set the glass aside, wiped her forehead with a grimy hand, and asked, "What's happened between you and Stephen?"

Josie groaned and buried her face in her hands. "Oh, I don't want to answer that."

Samantha reached over and clasped Josie's hand, her expression sympathetic. "Adam and I have been worried about you. Did he stop seeing you because you want to teach?"

Josie looked up. "I'm not sure he's stopped seeing me—for good, I mean. He's a little upset with me right now." She cocked an eyebrow. "He asked me to marry him, and I said not now."

Samantha sighed her understanding. "I see."

Josie pulled free from her friend's touch and shook her head. "No, I don't think you do. I love Stephen, and I want to marry him. But when he asked me, he couldn't even tell me if he loved me. Why would a man propose marriage to someone he's not sure he loves? And how could I say yes to a man who isn't sure he loves me?" She took a deep breath, raising her eyes to the tree branches overhead for a moment, then looked back at Samantha. "And then there's my wanting to teach. Stephen knows I've wanted to teach since—well, since I was a little girl. I see no reason why I can't teach for a year or two, then get married. I know by my age lots of girls get married and start a family, but I'm not ready for that. I don't think that means there's something wrong with me. Do you?"

"Of course not!" Samantha squirmed around to face Josie. "Does Stephen think there's something wrong with you?"

"I don't know." Josie forced out a frustrated breath. "Maybe not wrong, exactly, but he's not sure what he wants. When I told him I thought we needed to think some more about getting married before we became engaged, he got angry and stomped around. I'd never seen him act so high-handed. I didn't like it. Things haven't been the same between us since."

Samantha scooted close and put her arm around Josie's shoulders. "I'm sorry. Can I do anything to help?"

Josie smiled sadly. "It's helped some to get it off my chest. Thanks for sticking your nose in. This time, at least."

They both giggled and shared a quick hug. Then Samantha looked over at the garden plot. "Well, should we finish up the corn? We could probably get the cabbages in, too, if we hurried."

Josie stretched her arms over her head with a groan. "Why not? If my hands are busy, my mind doesn't run so much."

Samantha stood and held out her hand. "Come on." Josie allowed herself to be pulled to her feet. But then Samantha just stood still for a moment, holding Josie's hand, her head tipped and brows pulled low. "You say you know you love Stephen?"

"Yes, I do." Longing washed through Josie's middle. "He's the only one I've ever even considered spending my life with. Why?"

Samantha dropped Josie's hand. "No reason." Yet Josie suspected something else was on Samantha's mind. Before she could ask, however, Samantha brushed the back of her skirt and headed for the garden plot. "Come on, let's go get our hands busy."

～⌒◯

The pink and white striped dress arrived at the mercantile the last week of May. When Hiram pulled it from its shipping box, he turned to David and raised bushy eyebrows. "Well, Mr. Delivery Man, are you ready for this?" By now it was no secret that David and Priscilla got along about as well as two tomcats in an alley.

David shook his head and blew his breath out. "I really do not want to see that girl, Mr. Klaassen. She gets my goat worse than any female I've ever met."

"I've noticed," Hiram said wryly. He folded the dress neatly and put it back in its box, then shoved it down the counter close to David. "But I can't afford to lose any customers, so I'd appreciate it if you would try to keep a handle on your tongue when you make this delivery."

The two men—one tall and lean, one short and wiry—faced off. David did not want to do it, but delivering was part of the job he was hired to do, and Hiram would never give in. David reached for the box.

"I'll make a deal with you." Hiram placed a bony hand on David's shoulder. "You make this delivery to the unpleasant Miss Koehn without causing a ruckus, and when you return, I'll send you out to Si and Laura's with that old trunk of mine Josie asked to use."

David perked up. "Trunk? Did she get a teaching position somewhere?"

Hiram snorted. "Nah, not that I've heard—yet. But that girl has got to be organized. She wants to be packed and ready when the call comes."

David smiled. That sounded like Josie, all right. He grabbed up Priscilla's dress. "Mr. Klaassen, you have yourself a deal. I promise—no trouble this time."

His resolve faded fast when Miss Koehn herself answered his knock and her lips turned immediately into a familiar, arrogant smirk. "Well, well, well . . . If it isn't the Klaassens' dependable delivery boy."

David held out the box. "Your dress arrived this morning, Miss Koehn."

Priscilla feigned a pout and twisted a silky black lock of hair around her finger. "Now we're back to 'Miss Koehn,' are we? I thought we'd gone beyond that . . . , David."

David formed a sharp retort, but he'd promised not to rise to her bait. He cleared his throat. "Do you want me to leave the package here, or shall I bring it in for you?"

Priscilla pushed the door open, inviting him in with a flamboyant swing of her arm. "By all means, bring it right in."

David stepped into the Koehns' parlor and couldn't help but gawk. He'd been in several homes in Mountain Lake, but this was much more ornate than any other he'd seen. The windows were dressed with tasseled curtains of heavy peach jacquard, and each piece of furniture held a patterned throw or was stacked high with fringed pillows. Every bit of wall space held framed photographs or actual oil paintings of flower arrangements or landscapes. A heavy carpet covered the wood floor, and bric-a-brac of every variety covered any available surface. David stood with box in hand, his gaze moving from one cluttered area to another. Where should he lay the box?

Priscilla swished past him, motioning for him to follow. He trailed behind her down a darkened hallway with doors opening off in both directions. At the end of the hall, she stopped and pointed into the last room. "Put it in there." She didn't even pretend to be courteous.

A four-poster rice bed, bearing a flowered appliqué quilt, filled the center of the room. A delicate china doll dressed in satin and lace leaned against the ruffled pillows. A maple dresser and washstand of the finest quality stood against the wall. The woodwork was white, and the walls were covered with a vines-and-flowers wallpaper in soft pastels. A large cheval mirror stood prominently in one corner. He nearly snorted at the sight of the mirror.

Suddenly it struck him that the house was awfully quiet. "Miss Koehn, is your mother here?"

She crossed her arms with a meaningful grin. "What's the matter? Do you feel the need for protection? A big, brave man like you?"

Anger smoldered beneath the surface, and he wished he could drop the box. Forcefully. On her head! But that wouldn't do. He stepped into the room and placed the box on top of the appliquéd quilt and turned to leave. But Priscilla stood in the doorway, blocking his exit.

He stopped three feet away from her. "Excuse me, Miss Koehn."

Priscilla locked her hands behind her back and tipped her head in a cocky manner. "I prefer to be called Priscilla."

David bit down—literally—on his tongue. For ten interminable seconds he held it tightly, painfully, between his teeth. Then he relaxed his jaw and spoke carefully. "Miss Koehn, I have other deliveries to make. Now if you will kindly step aside—"

"Oh, gracious sakes, go!" Priscilla stepped back and gestured as she had before, with dramatic flair. "Run along, Mr. O'Brien, and make your deliveries. Don't let me stand in the way of your very important business."

David shouldered his way past her and back up the long hallway to the front door. Just before his hand closed around the cut-crystal doorknob, Priscilla darted in front of him, placing her back against the door and holding up her hand, nearly putting it against his chest.

"Miss Koehn, I need to be leaving." Only the promise he'd made to Hiram kept him from moving her bodily out of his way.

Priscilla held her head high, glaring at him with narrowed eyes. "But I haven't tipped you." Her condescending tone made the blood rush to David's face.

He gritted his teeth. "I do not require a tip, Miss Koehn. Delivery of purchased goods is part of the service the mercantile provides."

Her face twisted in an odd expression, her eyes flickering with some emotion he couldn't read. She lifted the heavy strand of hair that fell across her shoulder and swished it back and forth. "Did you read that in a book somewhere?"

Impatience got the best of him. "Miss Koehn, you are by far the most irritating young woman I've ever encountered. You are spoiled and willful and so full of yourself there isn't any room for anyone else." Suddenly he remembered his vow to be agreeable, and he shut his jaw so forcefully his teeth clacked together.

Priscilla's expression hardened, but she spoke very sweetly. "I simply offered to tip you. I fail to see why that should make me irritating and spoiled and willful and full of myself." She extended a finger for each description David had mentioned. "It seems to me that it makes me generous."

She flounced from the door, her head high. When she was several feet away from him, she spun around and gestured to the now unblocked doorway. "Well, go ahead—leave. But don't expect me to give a glowing report on your far-from-cheerful service."

What he wouldn't give to reach out and shake the arrogance out of her. David grabbed the doorknob and wrenched it open, nearly throwing the door against the parlor wall. As he stepped out into the May sunshine, he felt a light tap on his shoulder. He looked back to see Priscilla stepping back safely behind the screened door.

"I've decided to excuse your impertinence this time, given your rather unpleasant upbringing. I suppose instead of being insulted, I should feel sorry for you. So I forgive you for your unwarranted attack on my honorable intentions."

The impudent little upstart! To save face, he said, "That's very mature of you, Priscilla." But she'd won. She'd managed to make him drop his guard and call her Priscilla. He could have kicked himself.

"Good-bye, David." She shut the door but not before sending him off with a satisfied grin.

David stood a few seconds on the Koehns' front porch, stifling the urge to pound on the door and . . . and what? That girl was some piece of work. He stormed toward the mercantile, dirt rising with every step, his mind trying to comprehend the reason behind Priscilla's terrible behavior. He had suspected jealousy was what motivated her, but now he wasn't so sure.

His steps slowed as he pictured her as she had looked just minutes before, standing in her bedroom doorway, her long dark hair falling in beguiling waves across her shoulders, her huge blue eyes sparkling with some emotion he couldn't recognize. She had a face that could stop men in their tracks, a beauty that would evoke admiration or jealousy from other women. Now that he'd seen her home, he knew she had all that money could provide. Of what could she be jealous? She seemed to have everything, didn't she?

Except happiness.

He stopped short right in the middle of the street, reminded of his father. Burton O'Brien had been filled with bitterness and anger. With all that unhappiness inside, what could come out but hatefulness and spite? Could it be that Priscilla was reacting to her own inner unhappiness?

But why should she be unhappy?

He shook his head. Why bother trying to figure out Priscilla Koehn? In all likelihood, the only thing wrong with Priscilla was a father who had spoiled her shamelessly instead of teaching her proper behavior or any manners.

He set his feet in motion again. He'd get that trunk and take it out to Josie. Time with her held a lot more anticipation than thinking about Miss Priscilla Koehn's problems. But for some odd reason he didn't pretend to understand, he had a hard time shaking from his mind the image of Priscilla and her unreadable, incredibly intriguing, bright blue eyes.

Chapter Eight

*D*avid gave the reins a gentle tug to the right, and the horse pulled Hiram's wagon onto the Klaassens' yard. Squinting against the sun, David spotted three gardeners busy in the large plot east of the house, all wearing skirts and shirtwaists along with floppy straw hats on their heads. As the wagon lumbered on toward the barn, the trio turned in his direction, and the middle one—Samantha—pulled off her hat and waved it over her head.

"David!" Samantha tossed the hat aside and hop-stepped out of the garden area as David pulled it to a stop next to the barn. She lifted her arms for a hug the minute David leaped down.

David pulled away and held his nose, wrinkling up his face. "Phew! I hate to mention it—"

"It's just good honest sweat!" Samantha pushed at him, laughing. "What could smell better than that?"

"I can think of lots of things," David retorted, but he left his arm draped around his sister's shoulders as they walked around to the back of the wagon. Josie and Becky, carrying Samantha's discarded hat, joined them.

"Hello, David." Josie approached slowly, her lips curved into a hesitant smile. "What brings you out this afternoon?"

David's stomach did a funny somersault at her unusual reserve. Coming up with a cheerful smile himself to make up for the one she lacked, he flapped his hand at the wagon's bed. "Take a peek."

All three women stepped forward and peered over the high side. Josie's reticence disappeared in an instant. She clapped her hands and let out a squeal of delight. "Oh, my trunk!"

David swung it out, grunting a bit with the effort of clearing the side of the wagon. "Yep, it's all yours." The trunk against his thighs gave him an awkward gait as he headed toward the house. "Where shall I put it?"

Becky opened the back door for them, and Samantha and Josie followed David in, Josie sticking particularly close in her excitement. She clasped her hands together. "Could you please take it up to my room? I'm afraid there are no other men around here right now."

David looked down into her face. Strands of hair, pulled loose from her simple braid, clung to her sweaty cheeks and neck. Her nose was sunburned, her freckles stood out boldly, and a smudge of dirt decorated her right cheek. David grinned. She sure was cute.

"I think I can handle that." He pushed the trunk a little higher with one knee. "But everybody get out of the way in case I fall—or drop it. I don't want to hurt anyone."

The girls obediently cleared a path, dashing upstairs to the far edge of the landing. They watched, wide-eyed, as David made his way to the top of the stairs. He couldn't see his feet, and once he almost missed a step, causing the girls to gasp, but he quickly regained his balance and arrived with his burden.

"Whew!" Josie offered a broad smile, which gave David's heart a lift. "You made it."

"Which room?" His arms were starting to ache.

Josie pointed to a door on his left, and he turned sideways to get through it. He set the trunk down carefully at the foot of the bed, careful to keep from scratching the hardwood floor. He straightened and pushed a hand against the small of his back with a little groan.

"Heavy?" Samantha asked.

"Nah." David shook his head. "But I'm not offering to carry it down when you've got it all filled up with your female frippery."

"Female frippery, huh?" Josie, hands on her hips, grinned and then shrugged. "Very well. I guess you've done your part." She turned to her younger sister. "Is there any of that lemonade left?"

Becky nodded. "Sure, at least one glassful."

Josie sent a look in David's direction. "Does that sound like a fair reward?"

David gave a quick nod. "That sounds wonderful." Becky hurried downstairs.

He turned in a circle, taking in the simple furnishings of the room—the green-painted iron bed with its homey patchwork quilt, the tall, unadorned *schrank* that probably held Josie's entire wardrobe, and the washstand with its plain white pitcher and bowl beside the door. The walls were plastered and painted but unpapered, and the single nine-over-nine pane window bore simple homemade curtains of yellow gingham.

On the floor beside the bed rested a bright rag rug, obviously handmade. The only unnecessary fixture in the room was an oval photograph with a domed piece of glass protecting the picture beneath. David bent closer to see it more clearly. No doubt a wedding picture, the man and woman standing side by side in their best suits of clothing, somber expressions on their faces. David smiled to himself. From the looks of them, marriage wasn't such a pleasant undertaking.

He tapped the glass. "Who's this?"

Josie inched up behind him and touched the picture with a finger still holding dirt from the garden. "My grandmother and grandfather Klaassen, on their wedding day."

He glanced down at her, grinning again as he spotted the unbecoming smudge on the glass. "They look pretty serious."

Josie shrugged, her forehead wrinkling briefly. "I suppose. But, then, marriage is a pretty serious business."

David turned from the photograph and let his gaze rove over the room once more. He mused aloud, "This is the second young lady's bedroom I've seen today."

"Where else have you been today?" Samantha demanded. Even Josie looked up at him expectantly.

David wished he'd kept his mouth shut. "I made a delivery to the Koehn house with a package for Priscilla. She wanted it in . . . in the bedroom." Heat blazed his ears when he recalled the visit. He'd spare the girls the details. "Her room is sure different from this one."

Josie nodded her agreement. "Oh, I know it. I've been in Priscilla's house." She headed for the stairs, and David and Samantha followed. "Millie Koehn has the best of everything. They were the first family in town to get indoor plumbing, and John Koehn spares no expense on decorating."

When they reached the kitchen, David accepted the iced lemonade from Becky with thanks.

Josie went on, "But I'd rather have my house. It might not be fancy, but it's homey. The Koehn home is—" She frowned, as if seeking the right words. Then she lifted her shoulders in a sheepish shrug. "Well, it's kind of cold, impersonal. Of course, I might be a little biased."

David chuckled. "You might be biased, but I think you're right. This home is definitely warmer and more inviting." He took another sip of his lemonade, then decided to add, "You're also marked."

She drew back, startled.

David reached over and touched Josie's cheek with the tip of one finger. "Right here. You have a dirt smudge."

Flushing, she spun around, her hand rubbing at the spot he'd touched. "Sam, why didn't you tell me?"

"I'm sorry, I didn't notice." Samantha burst out laughing. "Josie, you aren't helping it a bit. Look at your hands."

Josie held her dirt-coated hands in front of her and groaned. She'd masked her freckles under a smear of dirt. She headed for the stairs, calling back over her shoulder, "Please excuse me. I'm going to wash up."

Becky followed, and Josie's indignant voice trailed behind them down the stairs. "Why couldn't someone tell me my face was dirty?" David and Samantha shared a grin at her expense.

Samantha examined her hands and grimaced. "Oh, my. I need to do the same." She pumped water from the kitchen sink into a pan.

David leaned against the work table and finished his lemonade, watching Samantha. "Did you get the garden all in?"

Samantha turned, rubbing her hands dry with a towel. "Gracious, no. We've still got beans, carrots, tomatoes, okra, turnips—"

"You needn't say more." David held up his hands. "A farmer's wife's work is never done, right?"

Samantha nodded, looking content. "But I wouldn't have it any other way." She hung up the towel and turned back to David. "The potatoes have been in for a couple weeks, and we got the corn and cabbage done today. We're well on the way."

David nodded, and glanced around. "Where are Laura and the youngest two?" The house was uncharacteristically quiet without Sarah and Teddy running around.

Samantha linked arms with David and guided him toward the porch. "Mother Laura took the youngsters into town to visit some friends who had a baby last week. They should be back before supper time." The two settled themselves on the porch swing, and Samantha set it into motion.

David rested his arm across the back of the swing, shifting sideways so he could look at Samantha while they talked. "I imagine you and Adam will be having callers for the same reason before too long."

Samantha's cheeks grew pink. "Oh, I'd like that. I wouldn't mind having a baby right away, and neither would Adam. He's used to a big family, and we both want lots of babies. But Mother says we're young, and there's plenty of time, that we should enjoy each other for now. She's probably right."

David peered over at her, pleased by the relaxed expression on her face. "It sounds funny, hearing you call someone Mother."

Samantha's brow puckered. "I've never used the title before since our mother died when I was born. I like having someone I can call 'mother.' But . . . does it bother you?"

"Not at all," David assured her, "it just seems a bit odd. I'm happy you feel so close to Laura Klaassen. But since I remember our mother, I can't imagine calling someone else that name."

Samantha leaned against him lightly. "You remember our mother well?"

"I do." David's heart caught. "I still see her often." Samantha drew back with a puzzled look. David settled her against him. "In you, Sammy. I see her in you. Your hair, your eyes, the way you hold your mouth when you're thinking hard about something. You even have her ears." And he flicked one small ear-lobe with a finger.

She covered it with her hand and laughed softly. "Oh, you're teasing—you don't remember her ears."

David nodded, serious. "Yes, I do, Sam. She had small ears, with small lobes, just like yours. And she wore her hair up in a tight coil during the day, but at night she'd take it down and brush it out, and it glittered red in the lantern light. Even then, I thought she was beautiful with her hair down." He broke off, staring ahead.

Samantha placed her hand on his knee. "David? She was a good person, right?"

David nodded, his gaze still aimed into the distance. "She was a wonderful person. We had a very kind, very special mother." Against his will, other thoughts clouded his mind. Of their father, who could never be described as kind or special. And there were so many more memories of him. Of his drunkenness, his wild ravings, his punishing fists . . . Pa had controlled David completely with the man's fearful, incomprehensible anger.

"David?" Samantha's worried voice cut through David's recollections.

"W-what?"

"You don't have to think about him." Her voice was gentle, understanding.

How could she have known? But of course she'd know. She'd suffered at Pa's hands too. He hung his head, shamed that he'd damaged their time together.

Samantha's hand tightened on his knee. "He's gone, David, and he has no hold on either of us anymore. Not unless we let him. You have to let go of the unpleasant memories and put your trust in a heavenly Father who loves you and wants you to be His own. With Him, you'll find all the love and acceptance you need."

Despite his sister's kind tone and sweetly beseeching expression, David experienced a rush of anger. After escaping Pa, he had no desire to call anyone else father. He started to tell her so, but before he could speak Josie stuck her head out of the parlor door, her face clean and shiny and her hair neatly combed.

"Sammy, I'm going to start supper now. Are you two planning to stay?"

Samantha rose from the swing. "I can't. I promised Adam I'd be home before then. If it's time to fix supper, I'd better get going."

David wanted to stay, but responsibility called. "I still have some work to do at the mercantile, and I've frittered away enough of the afternoon." He looked at Samantha. "Do you need a ride home?"

Samantha shook her head. "I rode Pepper over here. He'll get me home again."

David gave her a hug and took a step toward the porch stairs.

Josie dashed over and gave David a brief, impetuous embrace that set his heart thumping. Before he could wrap his arms around her, she shifted backward with a pink-cheeked grin. "Thank you for bringing my trunk, David. I'll need it when I get my teaching job. And now I can have it all ready to go."

David forced his shoulders into a nonchalant shrug. "It was no problem. I—I hope you get to use it." His conscience panged. He'd just told a fib.

Josie beamed, swinging her arms. "Oh, I do too! I've been praying about it, so now I just have to be patient and wait."

Praying again . . . David set his lips in a firm line and stepped aside as Samantha and Josie shared good-bye hugs and their next gardening plans before disappearing into the house.

David reached for Samantha's arm, and they walked around the house to the barn where he had hitched the wagon. The horses nodded lazily in the late afternoon sun. He saddled Samantha's horse and hooked his fingers together to give her a leg up. "Good luck with the garden, Sammy," he told her with a pat on her leg.

She waved and laughed. "You'd better wish me more than luck, brother. I reckon you'll be eating some of the fruits of my labor too."

He grinned and patted his belly. As he turned toward the wagon, Samantha called to him. "David, will you think about what I said . . . about Pa?" She peered down into his face, tears winking in her eyes. "God can wash the hurt away, and when you're empty of the pain, you'll be open to new loves, just like me with Adam. That's what I want for you, Davey."

Something tight wrapped itself around David's chest. "I'm glad you've found happiness believing in God, Sam. But I don't need Him. I don't want Him. And the sooner you accept that, the better off I'll be." Steeling himself against her stricken expression, he strode toward the wagon, climbed in, and aimed the horse toward town.

Chapter Nine

One mid-June morning, Josie met Arn in the yard, and he handed off the family's mail before trotting on toward the fields. She flipped through the few envelopes—and discovered one addressed to her from the Winston School superintendent. Closing her eyes for a moment, she prayed for the strength to face yet another rejection. "You know I want Your will, Lord," she finished as she often did.

Three other letters had arrived, each one a thank-you-but-we-are-not-in-need-of-teachers-for-this-term variety. Polite, but disappointing. So she had little hope as she peeled back the flap and removed the letter typed on official stationery. But when she read the opening lines—"Dear Miss Klaassen, We have received your letter of application, as well as a high recommendation from Mr. Joel Reimer, so it is with pleasure that we ask you to consider the position of teacher for the first-, second-, and third-grade students of Winston School . . ."—she gave a shriek of delight.

Letting the screen door slam behind her, she raced for the stairs. "Ma! Ma!" Josie took the steps two at a time, tangling herself in her skirts and tripping on a step. She rubbed at her shins and scrambled the rest of the way upward, calling, "Ma! Mama, come quick!"

Laura emerged from Teddy and Arn's room, her arms full of sheets and her face pale. "Josie, what on earth—?"

"I got a letter! From Winston!" Josie wrapped her arms around her mother, sheets and all, and spun them both in a circle. She laughed and tried to talk at the same time. "They want me to teach first through third grades!"

She paused in her ecstatic dance to hold the letter in front of her nose, her hands shaking so badly the words bounced on the page. She read it again, interpreting for Ma. "They got my letter, then contacted Mr. Reimer to ask about me, and they were impressed with his recommendation, and they want me!" She hugged the letter to her chest, her heart pounding so fiercely her ribs ached.

Ma dropped the sheets and embraced Josie, her eyes shining with pride. "Oh, Josie, I'm so happy for you." After a brief laugh, she said, "I can't help but be happy for Pa and me, too. Winston is close enough that we can go get you for weekends. I didn't want you very far from home, especially for your first year."

Josie paced back and forth, unable to stand still. "I'm supposed to be there by the second week of August, he says, and I'll be staying in a rooming house where the other single teachers stay, and school will start the third week of August, and— oh, Ma! This is so wonderful."

Laura caught Josie around the waist, forcing her to stand quietly for a moment. "Is some kind of reply in order?"

"Reply? For what?"

"To the superintendent. What was his name?" She pointed at the return address. "Benjamin Kleinsasser. Are you supposed to let him know you accept?"

Josie slapped a hand to her forehead. "Oh, my goodness!" She laughed. "Of course I need to reply." She headed for her bedroom. "I'll just ride into town right now and wire a telegram." She grabbed a comb and smoothed errant wisps of hair into place as she continued her planning. "And while I'm there, I'll stop by the mercantile to tell Uncle Hiram and Tante Hulda and check to see if any new fabrics are in, because I really should have one more dress and I might as well wire the boardinghouse, too—the name of the owner is in my letter—and let her know I'll be taking the room that's available. . . ."

She had run out of breath and returned to the landing, where Ma waited, a smile on her face. Tipping her head to the side, Josie said, "What else should I do, Mother?"

Ma picked up Josie's braid and flicked her chin with the curled tip. "Do you think maybe Stephen might want to know?"

Josie's excitement flickered. She bit her lower lip for a moment, then offered a slow nod. "Yes, I suppose I should tell him too. I just hope he'll be nice about it. He's been so unpredictable lately."

Ma gave Josie's cheek a soft pat before scooping up the sheets. "I imagine he's concerned about being separated. You can't blame him for that."

Josie sighed. "I suppose not. But he's known forever that I planned to be a teacher. Why does he have to make it so hard on me?"

Ma headed for the stairs with Josie following. "Because men like to be first in a woman's life," Ma said over her shoulder. "Oh, they might act tough and self-reliant, but underneath they all want to be needed. I'm guessing that Stephen feels threatened by your desire to teach and be on your own for a while. He probably thinks it means you don't need him or that he's not as important to you as teaching is."

"But that's silly," Josie countered. "He has other interests—his job at the mill, hunting, even playing checkers at the mercantile on Saturdays. I've never felt threatened by any of those things."

Ma dumped the sheets on the table in the kitchen and turned to face her daughter. "No, I'm sure you haven't. But as I said before, men like to be first. Before children or hobbies—or the desire to teach." Ma's soft smile helped soothe the edges of Josie's frustration. "That doesn't make you wrong or him wrong, it just means you have different opinions on this. It will be a challenge for both of you to respect one another's viewpoints. But if you plan to spend a lifetime together, it's very important to begin building the groundwork of respect now. And respect goes two ways."

Josie considered Ma's comments. Stephen was so head-strong! Would he be able to respect her decision to accept this position? Or would there be another display of temper? She loved Stephen and wanted to be with him, but there were other desires in her heart requiring attention also. The desire and ability to teach were God-given gifts and shouldn't be ignored. Could Stephen accept her desire to use those gifts without feeling he was less important? Somehow, she'd have to make him understand.

Josie leaned forward and kissed Ma's cheek. "Thank you. I'll see Stephen after I send my wire."

"Good girl."

Josie crossed to the door and then paused, sending her mother a thoughtful look. "Ma, did you have to give up any dreams to marry Papa?"

Ma gathered the sheets to her chest, a contented smile creasing her gently lined face. "Your papa is my dream, Josie. Being his wife and the mother to his children was all I ever needed."

Josie frowned, biting the inside of her cheek.

Ma added, "But that was me, Josie. You are you, and you must do what you feel is the right course for your life. You're an intelligent, rational young woman, and I know you've prayer-fully considered becoming a teacher. Teaching is right for you, and your father and I support that decision. We wouldn't try to change you, Josie—for you are you, not me."

Josie dashed across the room to throw her arms around Ma with the bundle of sheets getting most of the hug. She gave her mother a boisterous kiss on the cheek before pulling back and winking through grateful tears. "Thank you, Mama."

"You're welcome, sweetheart." Ma gave her a gentle push. "Now go send your wire and see your young man."

Josie laughed, waved over her shoulder, and headed for the door.

The cowbell above the mercantile door clanged wildly, and David turned from organizing bolts of fabric. When he saw Josie skipping over the threshold, her face ringed with joy, his heart gave a happy flip. He hadn't seen her since delivering the trunk to her home, trying to keep his distance in an attempt to forget his attraction to her. But his reaction to the sight of her smiling, freckled face told him his plan hadn't worked.

"Good afternoon," Hulda Klaassen greeted her niece, delivering a kiss on Josie's flushed cheek. "Look at your eyes all sparkling. You look sea *schaftijch*."

Josie hunched her shoulders and giggled. "I am very happy, Tante Hulda. I came in to buy fabric for a dress, because I just sent a letter to Benjamin Kleinsasser in Winston accepting the position of first-, second-, and third-grade teacher for next term!" With each syllable, her voice rose in volume and pitch—and speed as the words tumbled over each other. As her excitement built, David's diminished.

Hiram bustled around the counter and stood beaming at his wife and niece as Hulda threw her arms around Josie. Hulda crowed, "Your first teaching job! What a joy!" The two rocked back in forth in a lengthy hug, both laughing, and then Hiram extracted Josie from Hulda's embrace and aimed Josie toward the fabric display. "Come right over here now. We've got in a new shipment of fabric only yesterday, and there are some very nice choices."

David dropped the bolt of cloth he'd been holding and backed away as Hiram and Hulda propelled Josie across the floor.

"But don't choose for just one dress, Josie," Hulda said. "You choose for two! Then go to the millinery shop and have another hat made to match as a congratulations present from your uncle and me." The pair smiled at Josie as if they were second parents.

"Oh, but you just bought me a graduation gift, and—"

"And that was for graduating. This is something entirely different." Hulda shook her finger at Josie. "And if you argue with me, I will consider you to be impertinent and disrespectful." Her extra chins quivered in mock indignation.

Josie glanced at David helplessly, and when he had nothing to contribute to the discussion, turned to her aunt and uncle and shook her head, another smile lighting her face. "All right, you've won—and thank you. It would be nice to extend my wardrobe a little bit."

David rounded the display, hand outstretched, battling the desire to hold tight when Josie placed hers in his. "This is what you wanted, isn't it?" He shook her hand and hoped the sadness filling his chest didn't reflect in his eyes.

"Yes, it is." She giggled, the sound melodious. "I'm so excited I was dancing jigs at home."

"When do you leave?"

"In two months—mid-August."

David sucked in a breath. So soon . . .

Josie turned to Hulda. "Do you think there will be time to get two more dresses made, and a hat, too?"

"Ask Sammy to help you," David suggested. "You know how she enjoys sewing, and I'm sure she'd be delighted to give you a hand."

Hulda bobbed her head in agreement. "My, yes, and she does such a nice job. As for the hat, just take a snippet of fabric over for Emma to use for matching ribbons and such. She won't need a finished garment."

"You're right." Josie sighed her relief. "Here I am planning to teach, and I can't even think straight."

"Oh, you're just excited." Hulda wrapped her heavy arms around Josie's slight frame and squeezed. "And you have every right to be." She pulled back. "Have you told Stephen yet?"

David took quick breath and waited for her answer.

Josie shook her head. "No, not yet. I'm going over to the mill next. I'm not sure how he'll take it."

So Stephen didn't want her to teach. David busied his hands smoothing a rumpled bolt of cloth, keenly attune to the women's continued conversation.

Hulda gave Josie's shoulder a consoling pat. "Now you listen here, young lady. Don't let that stubborn young man talk you out of doing what you know is best for you. The good Lord opened that door for you, so you need to walk right on through it."

"Your aunt is right," Hiram added. "If Stephen is too hard headed to see that, then you just tell me, and I'll thump him over the head with one of his own flour sacks!"

Josie laughed, and David swallowed a grin at the thought of wiry, gray-haired Hiram tussling with young, stocky Stephen.

"You are a woman worth waiting for, Josie," Hiram added, "and don't you forget it."

Josie's brown eyes misted over with tears. "I won't forget it, Uncle Hiram." She gave the older man a quick hug then made her fabric selections. Only minutes later, she left the store, her steps light and her face glowing with excitement.

David watched her go, a confusion of emotions tangling him in knots. He didn't want to see her happy mood disintegrate. Yet if Stephen reacted negatively she might end the relationship with him. She might turn to another man. Maybe even . . . him. His heart skipped a beat at the thought, and he tried to squelch it. Still, it niggled in the back of his mind as he returned to work. Sometimes all a man had to cling to was a dream.

Chapter Ten

At a tap on his shoulder, Stephen glanced up at his brother Matt, who pointed toward the mill door. Stephen's pulse tripped into double beats, competing with the noise of the flour mill. Josie . . . Was he dreaming? No, there she stood, hands clasped behind her back, braid falling sweetly over her shoulder, her face holding a pensive expression.

His heart leaped. Certainly she'd come to tell him that she'd changed her mind—that she'd given up this silly idea of teaching somewhere and would marry him now, before the summer was over. He slapped Matt on the shoulder and bellowed over the noise of the grinder, "Gonna take a break."

Matt nodded and grinned, and Stephen loped across the flour-spattered floor. The sound of the gears and steam engine would make conversation impossible, so he guided Josie through the mill with a hand on her back, opened the wooden rear door for her, then sealed the noise behind them. They stood under the summer sun with only the breeze to keep them company. He took hold of her shoulders and released a heavy breath. "Josie, I've been hoping you'd come."

"I've missed you, Stephen." Josie brought up her hands to hold on to his forearms. "It's been very lonely without you."

He tipped his head forward to kiss her, but she turned her face slightly. He frowned. "What's the matter?"

"I came to talk, not spoon."

"Can't we do both?" He smiled, moving his hands to her upper arms and squeezing gently.

"Stephen, please." She took a backward step, ducking from his grasp. "This is important."

He pushed his hands into his overall pockets. Maybe she wasn't here for the reason he'd thought. "What's so important?"

She removed a folded square of paper from her pocket and held it out to him. "This."

After a moment of hesitation, he took it and unfolded it, his eyes on her. She angled her head to the side, biting on her lower lip. Trepidation made his mouth go dry. He read the letter once, then again. A weight settled in his middle. He slapped the letter against his pant leg, drawing her attention.

"I bet you're happy." He refolded the missive and thrust it at her. "It's what you wanted."

She tucked the folded square into her dress pocket. An apology glimmered in her eyes. "It's not what you wanted, is it?"

"No, it's not." He honestly tried not to sound curt, but his tone came out sharply anyway.

Palms pressed to her bodice, she implored him, "Can't you be at least a little bit happy? For me?"

He faced the hedgerow that separated the yard of the mill from the yards of the houses behind it. He searched his heart for a hint of happiness, but only disappointment swirled through his chest.

Josie stepped closer to him, one hand extended but not touching him. "Stephen, I'm going away to teach because it's what I've always dreamed of doing. I'm not going to get away from you."

Stephen spun toward her, anger rising. "What about my dreams, Josie? My dream is to get married and start a family. I can't do that all by myself. What am I supposed to do while you're off fulfilling your dream?"

"I'll be back. I'm not leaving forever."

He snorted. Her reasonable tone did little to placate him.

Josie folded her arms over her chest, eyes now snapping. "And to be quite honest, Stephen, I couldn't marry you right now even if I wasn't planning to take this job. You said you thought you loved me—not that you knew you loved me. Even as much as I love you, I can't marry you when you aren't sure."

She loved him! He'd heard her admit it. He turned to her, hope rising in his chest. "You love me, Josie?" She couldn't leave him. Not if she loved him.

Josie hung her head, her shoulders slumping. "Yes, Stephen, I do love you. I've known that for some time now. But I can't marry you until you can honestly tell me you love me and mean it with all your heart."

"So you're going."

She nodded.

Frustration again boiled in Stephen's gut. He muttered, "I don't see how you can say you love me, then say you're going to leave. I don't understand that at all."

"You left me for four months to go to Blue Earth after claiming to care for me."

He sputtered, "I went because I was needed. My grandfather was ill. And it wasn't for a year—only a few months."

"Well, the truth is I'm going where I'm needed, too. And it's not a whole year—just nine months. Besides that, I'll only be gone a week at a time. I'll be home every weekend. We'll be able to see each other almost as often as if I was home."

Her calm reasoning only served to incense Stephen further. "Someone else could certainly teach at that school." He pointed a finger at her. "You aren't the only one who could do the job, but I was." He shoved his thumb against his own chest for emphasis.

Josie sighed, shaking her head. "Stephen, I can see you aren't going to give an inch, so there's no point in continuing this conversation." She blinked quickly. "My mother told me two people have to respect one another's opinions if they are to have a good relationship, and obviously that's something we can't do. Not on this, anyway." She squared her shoulders. "In two months I will be leaving to teach. I would rather go with your support, but if you can't give your blessing, I'll simply have to go without it." Her voice got a little wobbly, and she stopped and took a deep breath. "In the meantime, I'm going to pray you will come to understand this is what's right for me now, and that doing what's right for me doesn't take anything away from you." She turned and walked away, her back straight and shoulders stiff.

Stephen, watching her go, could tell she battled tears. His heart demanded him to go after her and set things to right, but stubborn pride held him in place. He was the man. He shouldn't be the one to give in. Giving in would be exhibiting weakness, and a man couldn't be weak. He'd learned that much from his father. John Koehn never backed down from his convictions just because a female had other ideas.

Turning his back on Josie, he stared at the hedgerow, his thoughts tumbling. He was twenty-three years old, and he wanted to move out of his father's house to start a family of his own. What was wrong with that? Absolutely nothing! It was perfectly natural at his age. These crazy ideas Josie had about needing to be more than a wife and a mother were the unnatural ones.

Why did she have to be so set in her ways? He'd invested the better part of a year in courting Josie, and now she was leaving after refusing his marriage proposal. He kicked at a clump of new grass, sending the bright green blades scattering in an arc across the ground. He didn't want to start over with another girl—besides, there hadn't been any other girl but Josie since he was twelve years old. He only wanted her. And she was leaving for a whole year.

His stiff shoulders slumped. His dreams were turning to dust.

⌘

David stepped out of the post office just as Josie came charging into the doorway. With her head low she plowed directly into him, her toe catching against his foot, and with a squeal of surprise she fell forward. David dropped the mail and caught her around the waist, setting her back on her feet. She looked up at him, her eyes wide.

"Are you all right?" David asked. "I'm sorry—you could've taken a tumble."

Josie wiped at her eyes with trembling fingers and smoothed her blue cambric skirt. In the white blouse and plain skirt, she looked every bit the schoolmarm. "I'm fine. Just clumsy. Thank you. You saved me from adding some extra bruises to my shins."

"Extra bruises?" David frowned and reached out to raise her chin, looking directly into her eyes. Her red eyes and blotchy face told him she'd been crying.

She forced a chuckle. "Yes. I bruised my shins this morning when I stumbled on the stairs." She looked away and sighed. "This just hasn't been my day. . . ."

After the undeniable cheerfulness she'd exhibited earlier, her sorrow pained him. Things must not have gone well with Stephen. Although David had other errands to run for Hiram, he decided taking care of Josie was more important. Hiram would understand. In a deliberately playful tone, he asked, "Not your day, huh? I seem to recall you thinking otherwise just a little while ago. Let's go for a walk, and you can tell your ol' uncle David what happened to spoil it for you."

Tears shimmered in her brown eyes, but Josie held her chin erect. They took a few steps, and then she flapped her hands in aggravation. "It's men. Why must men be so *stekjsennijch*?"

David couldn't help but laugh. He knew she wasn't trying to be funny, but she looked so endearing standing there with her arms crossed, her lower lip in a pout, and those cute freckles dancing across her nose—complaining about men. She looked no more than twelve years old. "So what does that mean? You know, *steksenick*, or whatever you said."

Josie glared. "Hardheaded—you know, stubborn. Men are so stubborn."

"Men?" He raised one eyebrow. "Or one particular man?"

Josie's anger faded, and she pursed her lips, clearly uncertain. Before she might choose to dart away, he caught her elbow and guided her to a bench on the boardwalk in front of the jewelry store. He nudged her onto it, then seated himself next to her. He would like to have laid his arm across the back of the bench, but he decided that would not be wise. Not in her current emotional turmoil.

He smiled encouragingly. "Now, tell me what's wrong, and maybe I can help. Sometimes it takes a man to make another man's viewpoint understandable."

Josie took in a deep breath, then released it, ruffling her fine, airy bangs. She looked at him out of the corner of her eyes. "You're right. It is just one man. It's . . . Stephen."

"Ah." David injected great meaning into the simple word. "He didn't take your news well?"

"I should say not!" Josie grimaced. "He doesn't want me to teach." She paused. "Well," she said, her tone softening, "I guess that's not entirely true. It isn't the teaching he opposes so much as my going away for the next school year." She looked at him sideways again, pink stealing up her cheeks. "I hope you don't mind my telling you this. You see, a few weeks ago, he asked me to marry him, but I want to wait. I think he's still a little mad at me about that."

David narrowed his gaze, thinking. "Stephen is older than you, isn't he?"

"Five years. He's ready to settle down. But . . ."

"But you're not?"

She shook her head, then turned to him once more. "It's not that I don't want to marry him. I love Stephen—I really do. But our desires right now are different. He wants to get married and start a family, and I want to be able to spend some time as a teacher before settling down. He knew when he started seeing me that my plans were to teach, but I guess he figured I'd change my mind once he proposed marriage."

She averted her gaze and went on almost as if to herself. "If only he'd been able to tell me that he loved me, maybe I would have changed my mind. But I can't change courses based on a maybe."

David sat quietly and sorted through what he'd just heard. So there was some question in Josie's mind about Stephen's true feelings for her. But why would the man propose if he wasn't sure he loved the girl? That didn't make sense. Unless he simply wanted to settle down, and Josie was available. David studied Josie's profile—the high forehead, the brown eyes that usually sparkled with openness, the pert chin now angled downward as she struggled with hurt feelings. She deserved a man who was willing to give her his whole self, not just a halfhearted proposal based on his own selfish needs.

David's ire rose as he considered Stephen's bullheadedness. The fellow meant to intimidate Josie into bending to his will. If Stephen knew upfront what Josie's intentions were, he shouldn't act put-out now when she was seeing those plans through. On the other hand, he could understand how Stephen felt. If Josie was his girl, he'd have a hard time letting her trot off on her own for any length of time.

He swallowed and carefully chose words he hoped would offer her some comfort. "Have you heard the old adage, 'Absence makes the heart grow fonder'?" He waited until she nodded, then said, "I'll bet when you've left for Winston, Stephen will come to his senses and realize what your Uncle Hiram told you is true: you are a woman worth waiting for. Wait and see. Things will work out for you."

"Do you really think so, David?" Her brown eyes begged him to be right.

David reached over for her hand and squeezed it. "Yes, I do. Don't let his fear of letting you go put a damper on your happiness or make you let go of your dream. If you do, you'll regret it, and you'll resent Stephen. We men can be *sheck . . . schteksennyick . . .* you know, that." He smiled at her chuckle. "But somehow you women always manage to turn us around."

Josie's smile lit her face. "Thank you, David. I'll try to be happy. And as I told Stephen, I'll keep praying that he'll come to understand I had to do this, for me." Then, unexpectedly, she leaned forward and delivered a little kiss on David's cheek.

The moment her lips touched his skin, David went stock-still as if he were cut from stone. She jerked away, color flooding her face. Before he could say a word, she bolted to her feet, ran down the boardwalk, and disappeared around the corner.

David remained on the bench for several long minutes, his errands forgotten. He sat, the spot on his cheek burning as if lit from within by the gentle touch of her lips. His heart pounding fearfully in his chest. Feeling things he had no business feeling for a girl who had just admitted that she loved another man. But feeling them just the same . . .

ednesday evening while his sister and brother-in-law attended services in the little church in the valley outside of town, David pulled the straight-back chair in his room to the open window. He sat, then propped his feet on the windowsill and leaned the chair back on two legs. Hands locked behind his head, he rocked. And thought.

Although his eyes were aimed at the line of sparrows fluttering along the top of the false-front of Koehn's & Sons Milling across the street, his mind's eye held an image of Josie as she sat next to him on the bench in front of Nickel Jewelry. He smiled, remembering how her brown eyes flashed when she had announced that men were hardheaded. But then when she'd confessed that she loved Stephen, the look in her eyes had been soft and forthright. David didn't doubt her sincerity. But then . . .then she had kissed him. Confessed that she loved Stephen, but kissed him—David.

He dropped his feet from the windowsill and the chair come down with a bang against the wooden floor. The sparrows scattered. He squeezed his fingers together at the back of his neck, frowning. From the way she'd turned bright pink and escaped, he was sure she hadn't planned to give him that kiss. He was equally certain that she rued her impulsiveness before she'd even stood up to flee. But her moment of recklessness had been his moment of reckoning.

David was hopelessly attracted to Josie. He was, he admitted, falling in love. He sighed, stood, and moved to the oval mirror above the washstand. He had to lean down a bit to see himself, and grimaced at the image of his round-shouldered reflection. He wished for the hundredth time that he was a handsome man. He was too tall, too lanky, with a face that was too narrow and too freckled—and his hair. What woman could possibly look twice at a man who had a mop of waves that refused to lie down and couldn't even be described with one color?

When he pictured Stephen Koehn—wide-shouldered, raven-haired, chisel-featured—he gave a snort of disgust and spun away from the mirror. Comparing a scarecrow to Adonis. When up against someone like Stephen, he didn't stand a chance. And it wasn't just in physical appearance that he lost out.

David threw himself down on the bed hard enough to make the springs twang. He recalled Adam telling him about the turmoil he'd gone through when he'd realized he was falling in love with an "unbeliever," as he'd put it. Samantha's conversion to Christianity had allowed Adam to confess his love for her openly. No doubt Josie too placed importance on a man believing as she did. And Stephen was a churchgoer. Probably a Christian, too, or Josie wouldn't have been seeing him.

David's heart sank. He lost in every category—looks, personality, religion. No matter how much he might care for Josie, she wouldn't reciprocate those feelings because he was an unbeliever. Church and her faith were important to her.

So now what? He was falling in love with a Bible believer who might be available but who loved someone else. He groaned. What a mess. He never did anything right. He buried his face in his hands, battling self-recrimination. Just as Pa always said, he was a complete failure. The way he had it figured, he had two choices: he could give up on Josie, or he could start going to church regularly and try to understand and accept what was taught there.

He sat up on the edge of the bed, pressing his palms hard against the mattress. The first choice was out of the question. His heart wouldn't allow him to give up on her. But the second choice wasn't easy, either. He wasn't interested in religion. But he was interested in Josie, and her religion was a big part of her. Should he go—for her? It seemed deceitful, attending church to impress a girl. Church was considered of great importance to many people who mattered to him, and he felt guilty for even considering going there simply to win Josie's favor.

There was something else to think about, too. He'd been awfully adamant when turning down invitations to church in the past. What would Sammy think if he suddenly showed up on a regular basis? She'd probably think her prayers had been answered. And—the thought hit with physical force—maybe his ponderings right now were the result of Sammy's prayers.

He shook his head and crossed to the window. Although he couldn't see the church from this distance, he imagined the clapboard building with its bell tower. Inside, Samantha and Adam—and Josie—gathered with others in the congregation. Were they praying for him right now? Praying that he'd come . . .?

With a snort, he spun from the window. What a silly notion. This was his own idea, not some subconscious thought planted in his mind by a Superior Being. Still, regardless of the origin, becoming a churchgoer was the best way he knew to win Josie's trust—and maybe her heart.

Starting Sunday, he'd go. He'd listen and try to understand. But he would do it for Josie, not for himself.

∽◦

David sighed as he dusted the narrow shelves behind the counter at the mercantile. Each slim bottle of medicinal cures had to be picked up and placed on the counter. Using the feather duster, he'd sweep clean the empty shelf area and, finally, wipe each bottle neck and top with a soft cloth before returning them to the shelf. Such a tedious task.

The simple repetition left plenty of time for contemplation of other subjects. David's favorite thoughts were, of course, of the young woman whose heart he was trying to win. He smiled to himself, thinking how pleased Josie had been when he'd started attending church. He whistled softly between his teeth as he worked, picturing her straight back and interested expression, her face properly aimed toward the front. He went early so he could sit on the bench right across the aisle from her familiar spot. He would have preferred sitting beside her on the same bench, but for some reason he didn't understand, the women all sat on one side and the men on the other. There were a lot of things he didn't understand about church yet, but one thing was clear: his attendance pleased Josie—and Sammy.

Why, Samantha had almost shouted her joy the first time he had shown up without an invitation. She all but glowed during services, she was so happy to have him there. She had assumed he'd come because of his interest in the teachings rather than his interest in Josie. Guilt pricked. But, he assured himself, Sammy wouldn't mind what brought him, as long as he was there.

So he would sit across the aisle from Josie and Samantha— his two favorite ladies, he called them, making them giggle— and assume an attentive pose. Oddly enough, the longer he sat there trying to appear to be listening, the more he actually heard. And he even caught himself reflecting on some of it afterward. Samantha had told him his reflecting was the Holy Spirit knocking at his heart's door. He thought it was probably idle curiosity.

There was one other young lady—the one David thought of as the thorn in his side—who also took notice of his attendance. More than once, he'd sensed someone watching him, only to turn and find Priscilla Koehn fixing him with a pensive look that sent prickles of awareness up his spine. How on earth could that girl have attended church for her entire life and not taken any of the lessons to heart? The minister spoke of kindness, of treating others the way one would like to be treated, of emulating God's love through word and deed. . . . Hadn't Priscilla been listening at all? David was relatively new at all this being-like-God business, and already he possessed—without effort, he thought smugly—more Christian qualities than Priscilla Koehn.

As usual, thoughts of Priscilla created a tumult of aggravation within him, and he slammed the last bottle down on the shelf a little more firmly than was warranted.

"Be careful, David," came a female voice from behind him, "or those glass bottles might break."

He whirled around to find the object of his annoyance standing primly on the other side of the counter, a small beaded purse held against her ribcage with two white-gloved hands. He nearly groaned. Why hadn't he heard the cowbell? And why couldn't she have come at a time when David wasn't minding the shop on his own? Hiram had run to the bank, and Hulda had gone home complaining of "the vapors," leaving him alone. He couldn't escape and let someone else see to Priscilla's needs.

Stifling a sigh, he placed the feather duster beneath the counter. "What can I do for you today, Miss Koehn?"

"I've come to buy a birthday present for my daddy." She held up the little purse. "This is not to go on his account; this will be my own purchase."

She'd been there two minutes and hadn't said or done anything to rile him yet. Surely a record. He could be polite for as long as it lasted. David offered a tentative smile. "Did you have something in mind?"

Priscilla nodded. "I would like a pair of suspenders, and a bottle of shaving cologne. He prefers the kind that smells like sandalwood—the shaving cologne, not the suspenders." She smiled at her own little joke.

My, wasn't she in a good mood today? David couldn't decide what to make of her unusual affability. With some apprehension, he moved toward the flat, glass-covered display case at the end of the counter. "The suspenders are over here, and the shaving lotions and colognes are behind the counter. I'll see if I can locate the type you requested while you choose a pair of suspenders." He lifted the glass cover for her, then returned to the safety of the high wooden counter.

As he searched through the selection of bottled shaving colognes, he kept a covert eye on Priscilla. She lifted each elastic suspender in turn, giving each a thorough examination before laying them gently back in their wooden display box. A slight smile graced her face, and she hummed softly, seemingly enjoying the prospect of choosing something special for her "daddy." To his surprise, he discovered when she wasn't sniping at him she was almost pleasant to have around.

At last she returned to the counter, a pair of blue and brown striped suspenders in hand. "I like these. I think Daddy will too." She placed the suspenders on the countertop with a delicate flourish. "The blue is for his eyes, and the brown for his hair." She laughed, a tinkling sound, and covered her mouth. "At least, the color his hair used to be. It's not brown anymore."

David considered telling her the gray hair probably came in after her birth. But somehow it didn't seem appropriate, given her thus-far amiable treatment of him. Instead, he held out for her approval of the bottle of shaving cologne he'd selected. "I think this is what you want. Take a sniff of it and see."

Priscilla took the bottle, uncorked it, and sniffed deeply, her face a study in concentration. A smile broke across her face, stunning in its sincerity. "Oh, yes, that smells just like my daddy." She pressed the cork back down firmly and set the bottle on the counter next to the suspenders. Her bright eyes met David's with happy expectancy. "Can these be wrapped?"

"Certainly." David reached beneath the counter for paper and string. "One package or two?"

Her expression changed to puzzlement. She tipped her head. "Why are you being so nice today?"

Startled, David shook his head. He hadn't treated her any differently than he would any customer and started to say so. But then he realized, much to his embarrassment, he'd never before carried on a civilized conversation with the girl. Heat blazed his face. "Well, um, that's my job, isn't it?"

Priscilla continued looking at him with that same questioning look in her eyes, her head angled to the side. And then, abruptly, she said, "Two. That way, he'll have more things to open."

It took David a moment to realize what she was talking about. He wished he could ask her the same question. This genial behavior was certainly out of character for her. Maybe the act of giving was bringing out a positive change in her attitude. Or maybe she'd discovered a new way to rattle him. More than likely it was the latter. Whatever the reason, he'd be wise to keep quiet and pretend this was normal between the two of them.

He put her purchases in two conveniently sized boxes, wrapped them with plain brown paper, and tied them with pink ribbon in place of the string. Somehow, pink suited the prissy young woman on the other side of the counter. As he tied the bow on the first package, he realized she was wearing the pink and white striped dress he'd delivered to her house. And she did looked as sweet as a peppermint candy stick in it.

Much to his chagrin, his hands began to tremble. He pushed aside remembrances of previous encounters and concentrated on the task at hand. When he'd finished wrapping, he slid them across the counter, figured the total on a notepad next to the tin cash box, and announced the amount due.

"Let's see . . ." She dug through her ridiculously small purse. At last she extracted several coins and placed them in his extended palm. Her gloved fingers rested against his palm momentarily.

A fresh rush of heat ignited David's face. He rattled the coins into the money box. "Y-your change." He slid a nickel and two pennies across the wooden counter. "Thank you," he said as he did to all the customers, "and come again."

A sweet smile graced her face. She glided toward the door, her gaze aimed at him over her shoulder. When she reached the doorway, she paused, and her long eyelashes dipped against her cheek. "Good day, David."

David's head bounced in a jerky nod. "Good day, Miss Koehn."

The cowbell clanged as she left—he heard it clearly this time—and he broke out in a sweat. The pleasant Priscilla was almost more difficult to deal with than the patronizing, haughty one had been. He pondered the reason, then decided one couldn't be certain of her motives. Without doubt, that young woman had something up her pink and white striped sleeve. And he was sure it was only a matter of time before she lowered the boom.

But she was gone now. Heaving a sigh of relief, he returned to dusting.

riscilla made her way toward home, maintaining her graceful carriage—chin up, shoulders back, tummy in. She smiled and nodded to those she passed on the street, completely aware of—and at ease with— the lingering looks from the men and the raised eyebrows on the women. She was accustomed to attracting attention with her natural beauty, and she relished it. Was there any better place to be than the center of attention? Of course not.

She smiled to herself, thinking of the clerk at the mercantile— poor David. She didn't quite know what to do with him, which was certainly an unusual state of affairs. Her usual feminine wiles seem to be wasted on him—or worse, had sent him the other way.

Goose bumps rose on her arms, and she released a dreamy sigh. David O'Brien . . . Images filled her mind's eye. So tall—a good two inches taller than any other man in town. And his hair! The color of maple leaves in late September—not red, not gold, but a gentle blending of the two. A lustrous color. Oh, how she'd like to stick her finger in one of those curls and discover if they were as soft as they looked. She even found his freckles attractive, scattered as they were across his narrow, serious face.

But serious—what a sourpuss! She wrinkled her nose, envisioning his somber expression. Today he'd come close to smiling, though. How his mind must be churning, wondering about her recent placid demeanor. Well, drastic measures were needed; he seemed absolutely immune to her charms. If employing a spoonful of sweetness would turn his head, she'd give it a whirl.

If it hadn't been for the kind of attention she'd received from other men, she might wonder if there might be something wrong with her. But, no, it had to be him. Oddly, the more he resisted her, the more she wanted to win his favor. So far she'd managed to keep him off-kilter by being flirty, then strident. But that had only turned him away. It was the positive variety of attention she wanted from him now.

She swung her little purse by its gold chain, shaking her head. Seeing him in church had certainly been a shock. But his attendance there would make him more acceptable to Daddy, and she did so want to please Daddy. After all, she needed her father to keep her in clothes and baubles, defend her from those false accusations of selfishness—and on center stage.

A satisfied smile crossed her face. If there was one man she could manage without even trying, it was her daddy. It seemed she'd spent her whole life controlling him and consequently the rest of the household. And what did that say about her family, that a mere girl ran roughshod over all of them? She gave a little snort of derision, then shrugged. She wouldn't complain. She always succeeded in getting her way, and that was what she liked, wasn't it?

A sudden picture of David, his nose only inches from hers, his pale blue eyes snapping, flashed through her mind, and a chill of delight raced up and down her spine. Now there was a man she wouldn't be able to control easily. And for some reason even she couldn't grasp, that made him all the more appealing.

When she reached the corner of her street, she saw Mama on the front porch, hanging paper streamers from porch post to post. Priscilla gave a little hop-skip to speed herself along and bounced up the steps. Priscilla took in the red streamers that looped across the porch and waved in the gentle breeze, making soft crinkling noises. "What are these? What are you doing, Mother?"

The woman stepped back to survey her work. "I'm decorating for your father's birthday. This is his sixtieth, you know. That's quite a milestone. I think it deserves some extra attention, don't you think?"

Priscilla wrinkled her nose. "Daddy doesn't seem the paper-streamer type to me."

Mama's brows dipped together. "I only want to please him." She clasped her hands together nervously. "He is a bit hard to second-guess, but surely he'll see this as a sign of how much I want to make his day special."

"Well, maybe . . ." Priscilla swished by her mother into the house. Inside more streamers swung from the brass chandelier outward to window casings. Mama had cleared the low, claw-footed table in the center of the parlor of its usual collection—an urn of peacock feathers, a stereoscope with a selection of photographs, and the clutter of small porcelain birds, china bowls, and tatted doilies. Now the table wore a Battenberg lace tablecloth, linen napkins of deep green, Mama's finest china dessert plates, silver forks, and the biggest cake Priscilla had ever seen. She peered at the cake in wide-eyed wonder.

Four layers high, covered with creamy white frosting, and decorated with painstakingly shaped roses. What a cake! Mama surely must have spent half the day baking and decorating it. Priscilla placed her gifts on the corner of the table with two other wrapped packages.

Suddenly Mama hurried through the front door. "Your father is coming—I saw him. Oh, I told Stephen to keep him at the mill until four o'clock, and it's only three-forty! I'm not ready for him yet!"

Priscilla hid a smile at Mama's nervous twittering. She couldn't recall ever seeing Mama so excited. She walked over to her mother and offered several consoling pats on her shoulder. "Calm yourself, Mama."

"But I wanted to change my clothes yet, and my hair—"

"Your hair is fine." Priscilla rolled her eyes as her mother worriedly inspected herself in the hall mirror. "Besides, when Daddy gets a look at all this, he'll understand why you're still in your everyday clothes." She suddenly grinned as a devilish thought struck. "Let's peek out the window and watch his reaction to your streamers." Priscilla could pretty well guess what his reaction was going to be—if she was right, the fur was going to fly.

Priscilla followed her mother who crept on tiptoe to the bowed parlor window. The woman peered furtively between the lace panels. Stephen and Daddy were striding up the cobblestone street side by side, apparently deep in conversation. Daddy was gesturing broadly about something when he suddenly stopped in his tracks, his arms locked in a widespread position. Priscilla had no doubt he'd spotted the streamers. Even from this distance, she knew he wasn't smiling.

"Oh, dear," Mama murmured, touching trembling fingers to her lower lip. She dashed for the door, Priscilla trailing.

⁓♡

Stephen looked into his father's dumbstruck face, then ahead. Bold red strips of crepe paper created a spider's web of color on the front porch, matching the angry slashes on Pa's whiskered cheeks. Stephen cringed.

Boots clomping, Pa stormed toward the house. Stephen trotted alongside him, scrambling for words that would pacify his father's temper. "Pa, don't—"

"Help me get these things down!" Pa yanked at the streamers, filling his arms with snarls of the red paper. Ma and Priscilla darted onto the porch. Pris took one look at Pa's stormy face and headed back inside, but Ma rushed to his side and caught his arm.

"John, I—"

"Good heavens, woman, what are you trying to do? Make me the laughingstock of the neighborhood?" Pa reached for a streamer dangling over his head. "I'm a grown man, not a child."

Ma wrung her hands. "I'm sorry, John. I just wanted to make your birthday a bit more festive. I didn't think—"

Pa thrust the tangled wad of torn paper into her hands. "You didn't think, all right." He pointed to the house. "Get that nonsense inside before anyone else sees it."

Trembling, Ma skittered for the door. Pa thumped in behind her, and Stephen followed Pa, his chest tight. Why must Pa overreact to everything? Ma's gaze circled quickly around the parlor, and her shoulders seemed to sag with relief. Stephen caught a glimpse of Priscilla darting down the hallway, one strip of red paper stuck on a heel. Apparently Ma had decorated inside too. Stephen sent a silent thank-you to Pris for saving Ma another tongue lashing.

Ma offered a penitent look in Pa's direction. "I'll dispose of this." She bobbed her chin toward the paper in her hands. "Sit down, and we'll have some cake when I get back. I'll only be a minute." She disappeared down the hallway to the kitchen.

Stephen stepped fully into the parlor, and Pa passed him to glare down at the monstrous cake. Hands on his hips, Pa snorted, "Good heavens."

Stephen couldn't stay silent, even if it did mean risking Pa's ire. "Ma was only trying to make your day special, Pa. You shouldn't be angry. She's gone to a lot of work . . ."

Stephen didn't continue as Pa blustered under his breath, but his face slowly faded to its normal shade. He shot a sour look at Stephen "She should have more sense. Streamers and cake . . . parties are for children."

Ma returned on the last comment, and Stephen's heart lurched when he saw her blanch. She moved hesitantly toward her husband and touched his sleeve. "I'm sorry, John. I thought you would appreciate the festiveness, considering that this birthday is such an important one. I didn't mean to offend you. Will you forgive me?"

Pa pushed out his lower lip, leaving his wife to suffer for several pained seconds. Finally he blew out his breath. "Yes, of course I forgive you. Just try to remember that I am a respected member of this community. I will not abide being made to look the fool."

Ma nodded meekly.

Pa waved his hands at the cake. "But would you remove those garish roses? It looks like a wedding cake, for good-ness' sake."

Ma wilted. "But it took me so long to—"

Pa glared.

Ma sighed. "Of course, John." She carefully lifted the dozen roses from the cake and placed them on a linen napkin. Her steps plodding, she carried them out to the kitchen.

Pa looked down at the cake, nodding in satisfaction. "That's better—except for those gaping holes. Looks as if it's been overrun by mealy worms." He laughed at his own joke.

Stephen bit down on his tongue lest he be disrespectful. When Stephen's brothers and their wives arrived a few minutes later—at the time Ma had specified, four o'clock—Pa told them about the paper streamers that he had mutilated and the silly, girlish roses that had circled his massive cake.

Matt's wife, Sadie, said, "I think Mother Koehn had a lovely idea, trying to make your birthday special."

Matt shook his head at his wife. "You'd do well to listen and learn. You women and your female notions are a tremendous bother to us men. I would react in exactly the same way if I came home to find paper streamers and sugary roses waiting for me. It's an embarrassment, Sadie. And men do not respond well to embarrassment. I hope you'll remember that."

Sadie blushed, lowering her gaze.

During the afternoon, Stephen sat back and observed Ma and his sisters-in-law waiting on their husbands like servants to their masters. The women seemed to anticipate every need of their men and jumped up to fetch and serve before a request was even made. None of the males had to refill a coffee cup, carry a plate to the kitchen, or even wipe up a crumb. The women were there, waiting and ready to take care of everything. Although the attitudes of the men were overbearing at times, Stephen had to admit the women were eager to please.

Unlike a certain young woman . . .

When Pa had finished his cake and coffee, he sat back in his overstuffed chair, and Priscilla handed him his presents one at a time. Stephen noticed that, ironically enough, Priscilla's gifts to her father were tied with pink ribbon—not a masculine color choice at all. But the man didn't rant and rave at his daughter. He laughingly said, "Why, these ribbons match your dress, Prissy. What a clever idea."

Priscilla beamed. "That nice clerk at the mercantile—David—helped me."

Pa gave Pris a speculative glance but didn't comment. He held the suspenders at arm's length. "Well, now, that's a good-looking pair of braces. And I'll need them after today." He patted his belly, chuckling. "After all that cake, I'll require some help keeping my britches up." It was the closest he would come to complimenting his wife.

He opened his other gifts, gave cursory thank-yous, and set them aside. Then he stood and stretched. "Well, I've had a birthday worth remembering. And since Stephen is going to go back and close down the mill for me, I believe I'll retire to my bedroom and take a little predinner nap. Millie, try to not clink dishes together too much so I won't be disturbed."

"Of course, John," Ma agreed.

Mitchell turned to his wife. "Mary, give Ma a hand here. I'm sure Sadie, Lillian, and Priscilla will help, too."

Stephen's sisters-in-law followed Ma to the kitchen without a word, but Priscilla crossed her arms over her chest. "I already did my part by pulling down Mama's ridiculous streamers in here before Daddy could raise the roof. I intend to go to my room and read."

Mitchell glared at his sister, but he waved his hand. "All right, then, Miss Pris, go read. But be quiet." Priscilla stuck her nose in the air and flounced away to her bedroom. Mitchell looked at Stephen. "She'll never change, will she?"

Stephen shrugged. "Why should she? She's got Pa wrapped around her little finger, and she knows it."

Stanley shook his head. "I pity the poor sap that ends up married to her. Can you imagine?"

Matthew shuddered. "It would be a life sentence of misery." The brothers shared a laugh, then Matthew turned to Stephen. "So when will you be tying the knot, little brother? Heaven knows you're old enough. I'd already been married three years by the time I was your age."

Stephen ducked his head as frustration rolled through his gut. "I reckon I've got time yet."

Mitchell said, "Ma said you were seeing one of the Klaassen girls—Josie, I think. How old is she by now?"

"Eighteen." Stephen set his jaw. Old enough to be married, that was for sure. . . .

"Good age," Stanley mused, smoothing his mustache hairs with thumb and forefinger. "Old enough to know how to take care of things, young enough to be trained."

Stephen shot his brother a startled look, but before he could question Stanley's meaning, Mitchell cut it with a hard laugh.

"You're forgetting that Priscilla is also eighteen, but she's way beyond training."

Stanley rested his elbows on his knees. "But Pris is a special case. You can bet the Klaassen girls were never pampered the way Priscilla has been. Surely that girl—Josie, you said?—is ready for marriage." He turned back to Stephen. "Isn't she?"

Stephen crossed his leg, resting his ankle on his knee and patting the shank of his boot. "So tell me about that horse you bought last week, Stan. Still happy with it?"

Matt shouted out a guffaw. "What's the matter, little brother? Did the girl turn you down?"

Stephen bristled. His brothers could be as annoying as Priscilla when they wanted to be. "Maybe she did. How does that concern you?"

Matt held up his hands in mock surrender, while Stanley and Mitchell chuckled. Mitchell said, "Now, don't get mad, Stephen. Each of us has a good marriage. We want the same for our brother."

"That's right." Stanley nodded. "Come on, talk to us. If there's a problem, maybe we can help."

Stephen looked at the three with narrowed eyes. They were older, and each certainly seemed to be content with the relationship he had with his wife. If they'd set aside their teasing, maybe they could offer some advice on how to deal with Josie's independence. He wasn't sure he wanted to admit that his marriage proposal had been declined, but he could benefit from their experience.

He sighed. "Well, there is a problem." He sent a hesitant glance across their curious faces. "Josie wants to be a teacher instead of getting married right away."

"A teacher?" Stanley gawked at Stephen. "Teaching is for men and old maids. What's a young girl like Josie want with something like that?"

Stephen shrugged. "She's wanted to teach since she was little. Now that she's old enough, she's planning to go to Winston and teach."

Matt asked, "Have you tried to change her mind?"

"Sure I have." Frustration welled again as Stephen remembered his conversations with Josie on the subject. "I asked her to marry me, but she said no, she wants to teach for at least a year first."

Matt shook his head. "That's rough, brother."

Mitchell frowned. "I hope you didn't just give in to her."

Stephen frowned. "What do you mean?"

Mitchell blew out a breath. "I hope you made it clear what you want her to do," he said sarcastically. "Women get funny ideas sometimes, but if the man is firm with his expectations, they always come around. After all, the man is supposed to be the head of the house. Surely Josie knows that."

Stephen swallowed a grim chortle. If Josie knew, she sure didn't indicate it to him. He said, "Josie knows what I want. But she's still going to teach."

Matt slapped his thigh. "Then cut her loose. You don't want to be married to a demanding woman. You'd be battling her all the time. Since you've given in on this point, she'll expect you to give in on the next conflict, and the next, and the next. Pretty soon she'll be running over you just as badly as Pris overruns Pa. Is that what you want?"

Like Pris and Pa? Stephen shuddered. "No, but—"

"No buts," Matt said. "Find yourself a girl who's willing to let you be the man. You'll be better off all the way around."

Stephen sank back on the sofa. In his mind, he reflected on the subservient attitudes shown among his brothers' wives and his mother. Is that how he wanted Josie to be? He didn't think so. But these men had the experience. . . . He sighed. "Maybe you're right."

"Sure he's right." Stanley leaned forward, his expression earnest. "You've never seen Pa kowtowing to Ma, have you? Or us to our wives? Absolutely not. And that's the way it should be. God named woman to be man's helpmeet, and Scripture clearly says she is to respect and honor her husband. It sounds to me like Josie wants to be the one in charge. I say, if that's what she wants, then good riddance. You're better off without her."

Mitchell added, "That's right, Stephen. Remember what Pa always says—living with a rattlesnake is easier than living with a bossy woman."

Stephen weighed his brother's comments against his own conscience. Something didn't set quite right, but he couldn't figure out the source of his unease. With another sigh, he pressed his hands to his thighs and rose. "Well, thanks, brothers." But as he stepped through the kitchen to see his mother and sisters-in-law tiptoeing around in their carefully silent cleanup duties, he wondered whether their mindless submission was preferable to Josie's self-assuredness. His brothers seemed pleased with their situations, but why wouldn't they be? What did the womenfolk think about it? He couldn't imagine expecting such servitude from Josie.

But wouldn't it be easier for both of them if she wasn't so set in her ways?

Confusion sent him out the back door and across the yard, taking a familiar shortcut to the mill. His thoughts continued to roll, snippets of his brothers' advice colliding with the images of the women in his mind. The Bible taught that the man should be the head of his household, but the way his brothers and father ruled their wives . . . An uncomfortable feeling nibbled at him. Was their way the way God intended? Still, he wanted to be the leader in his own home, as Scripture instructed. If Josie was going to be a part of that home, then she was going to have to make some changes—the main one being putting Stephen first.

Stephen stepped into the mill and went through his normal closing-down routine. As he turned the last crank, he made a decision: he'd give Josie the rest of the summer to stew and wonder if she'd managed to lose him, then he'd offer one more chance to give up this silly notion of teaching and become his wife instead. If she still saw teaching as more important than being with him, so be it. He'd let her go.

He squared his shoulders and headed back toward home, his jaw thrust forward. But halfway there, his determination sagged. *Can I really let Josie go?* The day she'd shown him the letter from the school in Winston, she'd indicated she would pray for him to understand that what was best for her took nothing away from him.

Stephen's steps slowed, his heart heavy. *Lord, I don't know how to pray except to ask . . . don't let her leave me. What would I do without her?*

Chapter Thirteen

*J*une and July melted away beneath the punishing summer sun. Minnesota lakes were a source of great pleasure and beauty, but during the hottest months, they were a source of high humidity and contributed to an onslaught of mosquitoes. Josie battled both as she stooped over time and again, plucking gritty green beans from their hiding places within the leafy plants. She stood, swishing her hands around her head in aggravation at the swarm of whining insects that tormented her, then placed a hand on her back and stretched. Mercy, it was hot.

Across the patch, Becky stood straight as well and swept her hand across her forehead and its shimmer of perspiration. "Can we take a break? I'm miserable, Josie."

Josie shot back, "Well, so am I, but standing around bellyaching won't get the beans in. Let's just get it done."

Becky's lower lip poked out. She bent to her task, mumbling, "Don't know why we bother. We'll just have to start all over again tomorrow. Dumb beans multiply like bunnies."

"Don't be so crude, sister. You know better."

Becky glared across the garden, mimicking Josie's grouchy attitude. "And I don't know why Sarah can't be out here helping. I picked plenty of beans when I was her age."

Josie huffed an impatient sigh. "You know she's helping mother wash and peel tomatoes. Those've got to be canned, too."

"I know, I know." Becky grabbed beans off the vines with rising fervor. "But it seems like she always gets the easy jobs."

Josie didn't respond further to Becky's complaints. What could she say? They all had jobs to do, and one was as unpalatable as another as far as she was concerned. All of the family was short-tempered from the hot, humid, long days of work. Well, everyone except her mother.

Josie's head ached from the blast of the sun's heat and the constant stooping. She reminded herself how good the beans would taste boiled with new potatoes, and how welcome they would be during the long winter months when fresh vegetables were unavailable—thoughts that had always managed to change her negative attitude in the past. But this time nothing helped. Josie's positive outlook on life seemed to have disappeared with spring's departure into summer.

If only the summer hadn't proved so disappointing. She'd imagined her last summer at home would be filled with social gatherings and long visits with the people she'd soon leave behind. But Stephen stubbornly avoided her, even at church, and there hadn't been time to get together with schoolmates. Summer was a time for work. So, mostly, she worked.

Foolish, she admitted, to have expected a carefree summer. If anything, her plans to teach had created more tasks to be accomplished—extra clothes to sew, purchases to make and box away for her trip, countless details requiring attention. In only two more weeks, she'd leave for Winston, and she hadn't enjoyed one single evening of fun just for fun's sake. Sweat dribbled into her eyes, stinging as fiercely as the disappointment that stung her heart. She sighed. Becky was right: she needed a break. But a much bigger one than simply a respite from picking beans.

Dropping her basket between rows, she knelt in front of it. Maybe kneeling for a while would relieve her aching back. Her hands were buried deep in the prickly leaves of a bean plant when a shadow fell across her pathway. She looked up, shielding the sunlight with one grubby arm angled above her eyebrows. Slowly her squinting eyes managed to focus. To her surprise, Stephen was looking down at her. She settled back on her heels and gawked at him, her arm still blocking the sun.

"Hello, Josie." The sun sent bluish glints off of his dark, dark hair and lit his deep blue eyes. He'd left the top two buttons of his cotton shirt unfastened, and his tan extended to the exposed wedge of skin. His sleeves were rolled up, revealing muscular forearms and their covering of dark hair. A sheen of perspiration made him glow as the sun beat down. Despite the casual appearance, Josie found him undeniably attractive. But she stayed on her knees. She didn't have the energy to greet him enthusiastically. Once bitten, twice shy . . .

"Hello, Stephen." Her dry throat made her voice sound raspy. She swallowed. "I wasn't expecting to see you."

Stephen shrugged sheepishly and lifted his chin, as if studying the clouds, before looking back at her. "Yeah, well, I guess I've been missing you."

The heat and sweat and her pounding headache combined to result in her sharp retort. "You guess you missed me. . . . You tend to guess about everything, don't you, Stephen?"

Stephen shook his head, pursing his lips. "At it already . . ." He squatted down next to her, picking up a plump green bean from her basket and twirling it between thumb and forefinger.

She dropped her arm. "What brings you here, Stephen?" The question came out on a disinterested sigh.

He bit the inside of his cheek, then said to the bean, "You. I need to talk to you one more time, try to make you understand."

Josie released a great huff of breath. "I don't mean to be rude, but I think I do understand. I understand that what you want right now and what I want right now are two entirely different things. Unless one of us has changed his stance, I don't see any point in dredging it all up again."

It looked like he clenched his jaw so tight the muscles bulged. "I notice you said 'his stance.' You still think I'm in the wrong, don't you?"

Josie met his gaze steadily, brown eyes boring into blue. "Yes, I do."

Stephen lurched to his feet, flinging the green bean back into her basket. He balled his fists and blew out a noisy breath. "Honestly, Josie, I sometimes wonder why I bother. You are by far the most stubborn female I've ever encountered. You just will not give in, will you?"

Josie was on her feet in an instant. "First of all, I am not stubborn. I simply know what is right for me, in here." She thumped her chest with a fist. "And why do I have to be the one to give in? I needed more than that halfhearted proposal from you. All you could give me was a list of 'I want' and 'I think I feel.' I'm supposed to change the plans you know I've been working toward since I was a little girl, based on a maybe? Well, I can't!"

"You mean you won't," Stephen retorted. He flicked a glance at their audience—Becky—listening from the other side of the green-bean patch. He lowered his voice. "Can't we go somewhere private to talk?"

Josie looked at her sister, who gaped unashamedly back at her. She turned to Stephen and shook her head. Tiredness made her head spin. "As I said before, Stephen, I don't see the point. All we'll end up doing is arguing more, and I simply don't have the time or the energy."

Stephen held out his hands. "But, Josie—"

"No." Josie pushed a strand of hair from her eyes. "I've told you how I feel, and that hasn't changed. I love you, but I won't give up my plans to teach because you can't seem to decide if you love me. Until you know for sure, one way or another . . ." Swirling emotions tangled her insides into knots. "I wish you would just leave me alone."

Stephen's voice was hard. "That's what you really want? For me to leave you alone?"

Josie shook her head once, meeting his eyes. "No, Stephen, it's not what I want, but I think it's what is best. If you care for me at all—even a little—please try to stay away from me. When you come, you give me hope, and then you can't say what I need to hear, and that makes things so, so hard for me. So please don't come around here, trying to change my mind, until you can look me in the eyes and honestly tell me you love me."

Stephen stared at her, something in his face making her look away. "Truthfully, the feelings I have right now are far from loving."

His words delivered such pain, he might have slapped her. Josie ducked her head, blinking against a rush of tears.

He went on in a low, grumbling tone. "All right, then. You win . . . for now. Go off to Winston. Go play teacher. But when you're ready to stop chasing silly dreams and come back to reality, don't be surprised if I'm not sitting around waiting for you. After all, turnabout is fair play."

He whirled away, but Josie stepped quickly forward and grabbed his shirtsleeve. "Is that all this is to you, Stephen? A game of comeuppance?"

"Of course not." He yanked his arm free. "I'm not a child."

Josie shook her head slowly. He wasn't a child, but sometimes he behaved like one. He must have read her thoughts, because his face flushed red. He took a giant backward step.

"Good luck to you, Josie. I hope you'll be very happy with your decision. I hope teaching meets your every need." He'd kept his voice quiet—friendly even—but the undercurrents were there. He was making his position abundantly clear.

Josie kept her voice on the same even track he had taken. "Thank you, Stephen. I'm sure everything will work out for the best."

Stephen stomped off, raising his feet high as he stepped through the green-bean patch and made his way to his waiting horse. Josie watched him go, a lump in her throat that felt like it would choke her. He mounted his horse and spun away without a glance back in her direction.

So that's that. Her heart hurt worse than it ever had in her whole life.

"Josie?" Becky's tone held love and sympathy.

Josie turned to face her sister.

"Do you want to go in and . . . I don't know—rest or something?"

Josie sighed. She swallowed hard, trying to dislodge the lump that clogged her throat. She wished she could crawl into a corner somewhere and bawl for an hour or a day or a week, but there was work to be done. She lifted her chin. "No, I don't. Let's just get the beans picked."

Becky used the hem of her dress to wipe the sweat from her forehead and sighed. "I reckon if you can concentrate on picking green beans after losing your beau, then I don't have any right to complain, either." She went back to plucking beans from their vines.

Josie returned to the task as well, but her trembling fingers lost their ability to grasp the beans. With a strangled sob, she pushed to her feet and raced from the patch. She'd enjoy a lengthy cry in the barn. Then maybe she'd be able to work.

On Josie's last Saturday at home, Pa and Ma hosted a large party in her honor. They invited the entire congregation of the Bruderthaler Mennoniten-Gemeinde, and half of the church members attended. People wandered everywhere in the yard and house, drinking lemonade, eating watermelon and crullers, and enjoying an afternoon of pleasant conversation.

Priscilla Koehn and her parents were in attendance, but to Josie's enormous disappointment, Stephen didn't come. Even though their last conversation had gone very badly, she still had hoped he would come for old time's sake. His mother made shamefaced apologies for him, with the excuse he was needed at the mill. Josie suspected the truth, but she wouldn't let Stephen's stubbornness spoil her day.

She'd fixed her hair in a puff that resembled half a donut strung from ear to ear on the back of her head, donned one of her new "teacher" dresses—the green watch-plaid skirt and ruffled blouse, and pinned the cameo at her throat. Becky claimed the grown-up dress and hairstyle added years to Josie's look of maturity and professionalism, and she felt sophisticated and confident as she moved among the circles of family members and friends in her fine clothes and fancy hairdo.

As the afternoon progressed, a few wispy tendrils of hair worked themselves loose from the hairpins and waved in the breeze. She was pushing at one strand that continually drifted across her face as she tried to carry on a conversation with David.

He laughed at her attempts to keep the hair out of her eyes. "Here, let me help." Josie stood still while he tucked it back into its place. "There. That's got it."

"Thank you, David." Josie shot him a bright smile. "Goodness, my hair just never wants to behave."

"Well, then, your students better not take their cues from their teacher's hair." They both laughed, and David added,

"Actually, it never looks ill-mannered to me. This style is particularly becoming on you." He surveyed the loose puff with exaggerated interest. "How do you do that, anyway?"

Josie's chuckle was short and rueful. "By standing on my head, almost. A braid is sure easier, but I guess now that I'm the teacher, I'll need to look like more than a farm girl."

"Well, the teachers I remember pulled it straight back into a tight little bun, put a pair of glasses on the end of their noses, and looked at all of us like this." He lifted his chin, arched his eyebrows high, and made a prune face.

She burst out laughing. "But I don't wear glasses."

David shrugged and dropped the pose. "Forget it, then. It wouldn't be effective."

Locking her hands behind her back, Josie swayed in place, enjoying their teasing banter. Over the recent weeks in Mountain Lake, David had gradually lost his reserve, and she enjoyed seeing this relaxed side emerge. She wouldn't mind visiting with him longer, but other guests required attention too. With a reluctant sigh, she started to excuse herself, but he spoke first.

"You know, Josie, I'm going to miss you." No hint of teasing colored his tone.

Warmth filled Josie's cheeks. She flicked a glance at his sober face. "I—I'll miss you, too, David." She realized she meant it. "You've become a friend. A good friend."

A smile lifted the corners of his lips, but something akin to disappointment lingered in his eyes. He said, "You'll have to make sure you look me up on the weekends and let me know how your teaching is going. I'll bet I get only good reports, though. You're bound to be a wonderful teacher."

How she appreciated his words of affirmation! "Thank you, David. Thank you very much. And I will be sure to let you know.

I'll see you at church on Sundays, and as always you'll join us for Sunday dinner from time to time."

"That sounds good."

She took a deep breath. "Well, I guess I should—"

"I ought to let you—" he said at the same time.

They both laughed. He motioned with his hand. "Please, ladies first."

"I guess I should see to my other guests."

He offered an elegant bow. "And I ought to let you."

She flashed David a smile of farewell then moved toward two women from church. She couldn't resist sending a glance over her shoulder, and she caught David standing still as a statue, gazing after her. Something in his expression made her pulse hiccup. The look of longing in his eyes lingered in her memory as she moved among the crowd.

avid watched Josie joining a group of older women, who welcomed her with hugs and immediately included her in the conversation. He shook his head, marveling. Josie was so charming and caring, she fit with young or old, male or female.

How many heads would she turn when she arrived in Winston? He couldn't help but feel uncomfortable with that idea. Samantha had confided that Josie and Stephen had suffered a falling out that appeared to be permanent, which left the door open for him . . . but only if no one else came along. How could he keep himself in the forefront?

An idea struck him.

David headed out across the yard to corner Adam, who was visiting with a gray-haired man in striped bib overalls. David interrupted them midsentence. "Adam, how—?" Realizing what he had done, he apologized and stepped back.

The man with Adam lifted a hand in farewell. "I guess I'll go get myself something to drink. See you later, Adam."

"I'm very sorry—"

"No problem." Adam clapped David on the shoulder. "I was ready to move on to another topic anyway. You can only discuss the fertility problems of swine for so long." Both laughed and ambled toward the table that held the watermelon. Adam asked, "What were you going to say?"

"I was wondering how Josie will be getting back and forth from Winston." He was pleased at how casual he'd kept his tone.

Adam picked up a huge knife and whacked off a slice of watermelon, halved it, and handed one piece to David. "We're all taking turns—Pa and Frank and me—and maybe Jake or Arn once in a while," Adam said around a mouthful. "With harvest in full swing, it'll be tough working it all out. But if we alternate, it shouldn't put any one of us out too badly. Why do you ask?"

David leaned over and held the dripping watermelon well in front of him. "Would it help if I volunteered to make the trip each weekend?"

Adam eyebrows shot high, and he spit out two seeds. "Are you serious?"

David took a bite of his own slice of watermelon, trying not to appear too eager. "If it would help, I'd be glad to." He waved the melon in the air. "I'm always done at the mercantile by two on Fridays, so I could go then and have her home by supper time. Then I could run her back on Sunday afternoons. It wouldn't be a problem for me."

Adam chewed the inside of his mouth, his brow puckered in thought. "Well, it sure would free us up. At least on Fridays . . . Sundays we wouldn't be working anyway, so you wouldn't need to go both times."

"Well, suit yourself, but I wouldn't mind." David nibbled at the slice of watermelon, his heart pounding with hope.

Adam said, "I'll talk to Pa about it, if you're sure it wouldn't be an inconvenience for you."

An inconvenience? Four hours every weekend with Josie? His pulse doubled its tempo at the pleasurable thought. He continued his light tone. "It would be no trouble at all. And I'd enjoy the chance to get out a bit. I'm pretty confined to the store most of the time."

"As I say, I'll mention it to Pa, and his will be the final word. But I'm sure he'll appreciate your willingness to help out. We do need to be in the fields this time of year, and any daylight hours are valuable." Adam flung the rind of his melon into a big barrel and wiped his hands on his pants legs. "Thanks, David. And Pa will let you know if it will work out."

David smiled. "Sure thing."

An hour later, as the crowd was thinning, Simon Klaassen caught up with David. "Thanks for offering to take Josie back and forth to her teaching job. I'd be glad to pay you for your trouble."

Time with Josie would be payment enough. "That's certainly not necessary—"

"Well, we'll settle that later. I'll make sure either Arn or Teddy is available to ride along too." Si sent a glance around the yard at the people gathered in small groups, then gave David an apologetic glance. "Not that I don't trust you, David, but it's best not to open the door for idle gossip. We don't want people to get the wrong idea."

David hadn't considered the propriety of the situation. The thought of a chaperone took a bit of his anticipation down a notch, but he'd tolerate the extra company to keep unpleasant speculation at bay. "That sounds fine."

"I'd already asked Jost about renting one of his buggies; he has some comfortable two-bench ones that would work well. Can't spare my wagon for the length of time it'd take you to drive there and back. But if you're sure you don't mind committing so much of your weekend, we'd like to accept your offer."

David sucked in a breath, holding back his shout of elation. He gave a little shrug. "I'm sure, and I appreciate it."

"All right then. It's settled. Thank you, David." Si whacked David lightly on the shoulder and sauntered off.

David jammed his hands into his pockets before he socked the air in jubilation. His chest expanded, joy exploding behind his ribs.

Josie, our friendship will blossom into something more. I just know it. Life is grand!

⌒◌

David drove Jost's finest buggy—a Cabriolet Phaeton usually rented by wedding parties, which he thought had some nice implications—to the Klaassen farm Sunday afternoon. He felt like a prince seated on the tufted leather seat with the carriage's brass lanterns gleaming in the afternoon sunlight. He, Josie, and Teddy would ride in style for the twenty-mile drive into Winston.

As Arn and Si loaded Josie's trunk and woven satchel on the backseat of the buggy, Josie hovered near, clasping and unclasping her hands in excitement. She wore her new garnet dress and the ostrich-feather hat, held in place with her graduation hatpin. Her hair was pinned into the puff that David had admired. It provided a perfect setting for the fashionable little hat. "Leave room for Teddy," she admonished. She shook her head, looking at the narrow gap remaining between her items. "It's a good thing Arn isn't the one going this time. He'd never fit back there."

As soon as Si and Arn stepped back, Teddy clambered into the buggy and wedged himself into the seat with a chuckle. "Just right," he called out, his grin wide. "Let's go!"

David stood on the left side of the buggy, watching Laura hug Josie long and hard, rocking her back and forth. "Take care, *liebchen*," he heard her say.

Josie whispered, "I will, Mama. Don't worry about me." Josie moved from Laura's embrace to Si's, and David looked away, feeling a bit like an eavesdropper as Si murmured last-minute endearments and cautions against Josie's hat.

Becky gave her sister a quick hug accompanied by an impudent grin. "Goodie—with you away, I get my own room. I won't have to sleep with Sarah anymore."

"That's what you think," Josie retorted, pinching her sister cheerfully on the end of her nose. "I'll be back every weekend, and I intend to be in my own room."

"Yeah," Sarah said, sticking her tongue out at Becky. She squeezed Josie tight around the middle. "I'll miss you, Josie."

"I'll miss you, too, imp."

Arn offered a manly handshake, but Josie laughed at him and hugged him anyway, sending color flooding his cheeks.

She stepped back and hunched her shoulders, reminding David of a little turtle trying to shrink into its shell. "Well . . . I said good-bye yesterday to Adam and Sam, Liz and Jake, and Frank and Anna at the party, so I suppose that means I'm ready to go." But she didn't move toward the buggy.

Teddy bounced on the backseat. "So come on and get in. What'cha waiting for?"

Josie, shoulders still high, gave a small chuckle. "I don't know. I've been looking forward to this day for years, but now that the moment of leave-taking is upon me, I—I don't want to go." Another giggle ended in a strangled sob. "I suppose—I suppose dreams up close look different than when they're just . . . dreams." She turned to Laura and burst into tears. "Oh, Mama!"

Laura wrapped Josie in her arms another time. "Now, now . . . It's a big step, honey, leaving home for the first time. You're bound to be a little scared, but you'll be just fine. We're only twenty miles away, and we'll see you again in less than a week, so you aren't leaving forever."

"I know." Josie sniffed against her mother's shoulder. "I feel so silly."

Laura pulled a handkerchief out of her pocket and gave it to her daughter. "I'm going to need it back if you don't stop it," she said with another hug and some chuckles around the little circle.

David was touched more than he could fathom. What must it be like, to feel such bittersweet emotions at leaving one's home? He could only imagine.

Si stepped in and guided Josie gently toward the buggy. "You're not silly, Josie. You're getting butterflies, which is to be expected. But your mother is right. You will be fine. We've watched you grow up, and you've got the gumption to see this through. You've also got all our love and prayers going with you. And to come home to."

Josie dabbed at her eyes. "Thank you, Papa. That's everything I need." She fell against him, wrapping an arm clear around his neck. He squeezed back, then helped her up into her seat.

David climbed in beside her. Si held Josie's hand while looking at David. "Have a safe ride."

"We will, sir." David smiled at Josie. "Are you ready?"

Josie took in a big breath, determination glowing in her brown eyes. "I'm ready." David brought down the reins and the horse started forward.

The family waved and called, "Good-bye, Josie! Good luck! We'll see you soon!" as the buggy pulled out of the yard and into the lane. Josie and Teddy turned completely around, waving and calling back.

When they had rounded the bend, Teddy began a close examination of this fancy new mode of travel. David glanced at Josie and saw unshed tears glittering in her eyes, and she was back to clasping and unclasping her hands in her lap.

David tried to think of a way to distract her from her worries. Finally he asked, "Want to hear something funny?"

She turned her face to him, but no interest lit her face.

"Back there, when you were saying your good-byes, I felt kind of envious."

Josie's eyebrows rose. "Envious? Why?"

David offered a self-conscious shrug. "Because it was so hard for you to leave your family, even for such a short while. It must be wonderful to love them so much when it makes you so miserable to leave."

"Oh, David, I'm so sorry you didn't feel that way when you left home." Her eyes were full of sympathy.

David chuckled. "You're sorry I wasn't miserable?"

Josie made a face. "You know what I mean. And I'm not exactly miserable right now—not really. More just nervous . . . and contemplative. Even though I'll be going back on the weekends, I know it will never be the same. I'll never live at home full time again, and I won't be Mama and Papa's little girl anymore. As exciting as it all is, it's rather scary too."

David nodded. "I know what you mean. But you're ready, Josie. Your whole life, your parents have been preparing you for this day, by teaching you to be independent and to think for yourself." He paused. "And I've got news for you. No matter how grown up you get, to your folks, you'll always be their little girl. I can tell."

Josie smiled and placed a hand on his knee for just a moment. "Thank you, David."

"For what?"

"For making me feel better. You really are a good friend." She gave him a dazzling smile that lit his insides clear to his toes.

"Hey, guys—I saw a doe and two fawns!" Teddy called from behind them. "They must have been born last spring. . . ." and on the boy went in his excitement.

David had a hard time concentrating though. The feel of Josie's hand on his knee, and the sincere appreciation in her eyes, remained in the forefront of his mind as they trundled on toward Josie's new life.

Chapter Fifteen

*T*hose feelings of acceptance and appreciation carried David through the week. He worked industriously at the mercantile, cheerfully waited on customers, and efficiently delivered the orders, opened crates, and put away arriving stock. And all week he looked forward to Friday, when he would drive to Winston for Josie.

Jost had promised to have the buggy ready and waiting for David on Friday afternoon. When three o'clock rolled around, all David had to do was wait for Teddy to trot from the schoolhouse to the mercantile, and the two of them would walk to the livery.

Mr. Jost offered a friendly howdy, but David didn't waste time on chitchat. He gave Teddy a boost into the front seat, then climbed in beside him and headed for Winston.

Although well into September, the day held a summer-like feel. Trees were green and full, a cheerful playground for chattering squirrels and raucous blue jays. A grainy scent from cut wheat filled the air, and the marigolds continued to bloom on each side of the road. Teddy's head was lifted to the sky. David flicked a glance upward and caught sight of a circling hawk high up, no doubt looking for his supper.

The horse's hooves landed briskly against the dirt road, sending up tiny puffs of dust. Each clip-clop brought him closer to Winston. Closer to Josie. A perfect day.

David drove directly to the school building rather than the boardinghouse. Josie had told him she'd stay there and correct papers until he arrived, then they would go together to the boardinghouse to collect her bag for the weekend. He pulled up in front of the tall, square brick building and set the brake. Just as he hopped down, Josie emerged from the building and ran down the wide concrete steps.

"David, you're here!" She nearly knocked him off balance with her welcoming hug. Then she whirled on Teddy, capturing him a in hug that lifted him from the ground. "Hey, little brother! It looks like you grew!"

Teddy wriggled loose and gave his sister an impish grin. "Did you make the kids mind?"

She laughed. "You bet I did."

"You must have had a good week. You sure sound—and look—happy," David commented.

"Oh, I had a wonderful week, David! I can't wait to tell you about it, but first I need to collect my things from my desk, and I'd like you to meet the other teachers—oh! and come in and see my classroom. I've already had the children hang some of their pictures on the walls to cheer up the room. Come on!" She caught Teddy's hand and David's arm, tugging them both toward the school building.

Josie was bubbling with excitement as she pointed out the cloakroom, her classroom, and the others in the building. The three teachers were still in their rooms, so she introduced them in turn—Miss English, a bookish-looking woman who appeared to be somewhere in her forties and taught the fourth through sixth grades, Mr. Tompkins, the seventh- through ninth-grade teacher who sported a thick beard that compensated for his thinning scalp, and Mr. Isaac, who taught the oldest students and looked as if he might have swallowed a persimmon.

In comparison, Josie appeared thirteen years old, but she didn't seem to be fazed by it. She chattered constantly as they made their rounds, and as she left the building she called out gaily, "Good-bye, everyone! I'll see you on Monday."

"So, what do you think?" she asked as they headed for the boardinghouse, side by side on the front seat while Teddy draped his arms over the backrest.

David nudged Teddy's hand, winked at him, then joked to Josie, "So you mean you're going to let us talk now?"

Teddy snickered and Josie grinned. "Sure. It's your turn now. What do you think?"

David couldn't take his eyes off her. I *think you're adorable* hovered on the tip of his tongue, but with Teddy hanging over the seat between them, he didn't dare. "I think you've found your niche. You love it, don't you?"

"Oh, I do. I am so glad I came! And I have so much to tell you."

Josie talked nonstop all the way to the boardinghouse, then instructed David and Teddy to wait in the parlor while she put her books away and grabbed her satchel, informing them in a whisper, "Mrs. Porter doesn't allow male visitors in our rooms. Even if one of them is my brother."

Teddy roamed the room, openly curious, while David sat on a camelback sofa that smelled of mothballs, staring at a ticking grandfather clock. He couldn't get over the change in Josie. She'd always been cheerful, but now—why, she glowed. She didn't talk, she bubbled. She didn't walk, she bounded. She didn't merely smile, she beamed. It was as if a cocoon had been split and a butterfly had been released, flitting and winging its way through a bright new world.

A clattering on the stairs caught his attention. Josie, wearing her bright smile of happy abandon, skipped into the room. She put down her satchel and aimed a finger at him. "I'll be right back," she said on her way past. She disappeared through a door at the rear of the parlor, and he could hear her voice coming from somewhere down a hallway.

"Mrs. Porter, I'm leaving for home. I'll be back Sunday afternoon." Another voice answered something David couldn't catch, and then he heard Josie's soft laughter before she added, "Yes, that's true. Well, good-bye now."

Then she was back, still seeming to float, still with shining eyes. "Well, fellows, are you ready? Yes? Then let's go." She ushered Teddy out the door. David trailed on their heels with the satchel.

She clambered aboard without assistance. David swung the satchel into the backseat, and Teddy immediately curled against it, looking like he might be getting ready for a nap. David stepped in beside Josie, who sat on the edge of the front seat, hands on knees and arms straight, holding herself erect. With her chin angled high, she seemed almost to be drinking in the air. David couldn't stop marveling.

The instant the reins touched the horse's broad back and the buggy squeaked into motion, Josie sat back and began talking. She told him how nervous she'd been when first faced with the roomful of giggling youngsters; how she'd broken the piece of chalk while trying to write her name on the board; how she'd played ball with the children at recess and hit a homerun, endearing herself to the third-grade boys; how one little boy named Bradley had run up to her excitedly on the first day.

"He was so cute, David!" she enthused. "He has all this spiky red hair sticking up and freckles all over his face and no teeth in the front—just the cutest little boy—and instead of saying hello he tells me, 'My papa made me a coathter wagon for my birfday an' that thing jutht goeth like heck. Mebbe you can come thee it thometime an' I'll give you a ride.'" She'd repeated the child's words verbatim in a little-boy contralto, even including his lisp. "Oh, I fell in love on the spot."

"Hmm," David mused, finally getting a word in. "So only a week away from home, and you already have a beau, huh?"

Josie laughed. "You betcha. Bradley's one of my first graders. I must admit, I like the littlest children the best, but they'll never hear it from me. I treat them all equally." And she went on to tell story after story, needing no encouragement from David to continue.

David was enchanted as her happiness spilled over in every word and gesture. Would she be this happy at the end of every week? He hoped the joy wouldn't wear off when teaching was no longer new. Then he had a worrisome new thought. If she was always this happy—if teaching fulfilled her completely—she wouldn't feel the need for anything else . . . like a home and family of her own.

He pushed the niggling worry aside as selfish of him and determined to enjoy riding with her beneath a cloudless sky, listening to her happy chatter and basking in her joy.

They finally rattled up the lane that led to the farm. She had suddenly quieted, straining for a glimpse of her home. He gave her a sidelong glance and asked what he'd wondered about since they left the boardinghouse. "What was true?"

She shot him a mystified look. "What?"

"Back when you were telling your landlady good-bye, I heard you laugh and say it was true. What was true?"

To his amazement, Josie blushed crimson, the color spreading from her collar clear to her hairline. She turned her face forward. "She—um—she said something, and I just agreed."

What could have created such a reaction? Curiosity got the best of him, and he couldn't help but push the issue. "What did she say?"

Josie cleared her throat and suddenly became very interested in a hangnail on her right thumb. "She said—she merely said, 'That's a handsome young man sitting in my parlor.'"

David held his lips against a delighted smile. "And you said, 'That's true'?"

She nodded, still bright pink.

Now it was David's turn to blush, but from pleasure, not discomfort. She had agreed that he was a handsome young man, and he wanted to crow in celebration. But with embarrassment staining her cheeks, he didn't intend to put a damper on her cheerful spirits.

"Well," he said, keeping his tone light, "that was a polite thing for her to say. But actually, I thought your parents had taught you to be honest."

Josie peeked at him out of the corner of her eyes. Slowly her lips curved into a grin, and her eyes snapped with mischief. "She did, and stop your fishing for more compliments."

"Agreed," David answered around his own grin.

Teddy roused, blinked around, then leaped out of the buggy as it rolled to a stop. He dashed across the yard, bellowing, "Ma! Ma! Josie's home!"

The back door flew open and Laura emerged, arms outstretched, followed closely by Sarah and Becky. Josie hopped down and into her mother's waiting embrace.

"Josie, it's so good to have you home!"

"Oh, Mama, it was just wonderful! I have so much to tell you. The children . . ."

The two women had linked arms and were headed for the house with Becky and Sarah trotting along on their heels. David swung Josie's satchel from the back of the buggy and gave it to Teddy. He grabbed it and ran to catch up with his family, the bag banging against his knees as he ran. When the women reached the stoop, Josie turned back and waved at David.

"Thank you for coming for me, David!" And then her attention returned to her mother and siblings as they entered the house together, shutting the door behind them.

David stayed where he was for a few minutes, absorbing the wonder of the day. The joyous hug of greeting, the cheerful chatter, the admission that he was thought to be a handsome young man . . . And the homecoming. What he wouldn't give to be welcomed home as readily and joyfully as Josie had been.

He turned toward the buggy. Before he took two steps, Teddy came pounding across the yard. "Hey, David, Ma says come on in and have some supper with us."

More time in Josie's company? He wouldn't turn down the opportunity. He clamped a hand around the back of Teddy's neck. "That sounds just fine, Teddy. Thanks for the invitation."

The two walked back to the house where David got to sit across from Josie, whose beaming face and more endless chatter filled his senses. He ate Laura's wonderful cooking but tasted not a thing. No one else got a word in—Josie's stories filled every minute of conversation. David had heard them once already, but he didn't mind a repeat performance. He had decided somewhere between Winston and the Klaassens' dinner table that he wouldn't mind listening to Josie for the rest of his life.

Chapter Sixteen

*A*fter the first weekend of transporting Josie, David established a routine. He'd retrieve the buggy from the livery at three o'clock Friday afternoons with Teddy in tow, drive to Winston, enjoy a pleasant two hours of private conversation with Josie while Teddy drowsed or read in the back, then stay for the evening meal with the Klaassens before returning the buggy to Jost's. After church Sunday, he'd go out to the farm for *faspa* and a couple of hours of relaxation before driving Josie back to Winston once more.

By the time October arrived, the ride was cool enough for a quilted lap robe, the leaves had changed from green to gold, and Josie and David had developed an easy friendship that made both look forward to their weekly drives.

Casual sharing of the week's activities gradually changed to serious conversations covering a variety of topics, some of them rather heartfelt. David slowly opened up, dropping the air of indifference he carried with most people and giving Josie rare glimpses of what his life had been like before he had come to Mountain Lake and was reunited with Samantha.

In turn, Josie began to share her deepest thoughts and feelings. It was only natural that in time, some of those feelings would involve Stephen. After all, he'd been a big part of Josie's life, and both of them knew it.

David, though, was unprepared for the turn their relationship would take when Josie told him about Stephen's position in her life and heart.

On the third Sunday in October, Josie was commenting on the beautiful colors of the leaves. "I particularly like the maples." She pointed to a stand along the road. "Look at the variety of color. Orange, gold, red . . . It's as if an artist painted them for his own personal pleasure."

"They are beautiful," David agreed.

"I think I'll take the children for a walk to gather leaves, and then we'll make printings with them. Have you ever done that?"

David shook his head. "No, I guess not. How's it done?"

"Oh, it's simple." Josie pulled the lap robe a little more snugly around herself. "You brush a light coat of paint on the back side of a leaf, then press it down on paper. When you lift it up, the imprint of the leaf will remain. You can overlap several colors, and it makes a wonderful collage." She pantomimed her instructions as she spoke.

David shot her a quick grin. "Sounds pretty. Did you come up with that yourself?"

"Oh, no, a teacher I had when I was a child showed us how." She sat for a moment, then laughed to herself, as if remembering something. "You know, it was the day we did leaf prints that I first really noticed Stephen."

David felt like his heart stopped temporarily. He gave the reins a little flick and forced a casual tone. "Is that right?"

"Uh-huh." When Josie turned sideways in the seat, bending her knee to fold it up underneath her, it grazed his thigh beneath the lap robe. "I must have been a second grader then. A tooth-less, freckled wonder!" She gave a brief snort of laughter that David echoed before she continued. "The whole class gathered up leaves, and then we made these leaf prints. I was so proud of mine. I thought it was the most beautiful work I'd ever done.

"Well, even back then, Priscilla was a spoiled brat and troublemaker! After school, I was waiting outside the building for Liz and Adam and Frank and Daniel, and Priscilla came up and asked to see my picture. I was so proud of it, I mistakenly showed it off to her. And what does she do? She drops it in a mud puddle—on purpose, of course." Josie's arms were waving around, and her face was animated to match the various dynamics of her tale. "Oh, I was so upset. I started bawling and carrying on, and Priscilla acted all sorry and tried to wipe the mud off, but all she did was make it worse."

David hid a smile. If she was this lively in front of her classroom of small students, she'd have no trouble holding their attention. "That sounds like Priscilla, all right."

"Doesn't it, though?" Josie raised her eyebrows and gave a quick nod. "I stood outside, crying my eyes out, and here comes Stephen. He was already a big boy by then—twelve or thirteen. Since he was a friend of my brother Frank, he knew me, too. He came over and asked me what was wrong. I pointed at Priscilla and blubbered out what she'd done to my picture. Well, he took Priscilla's leaf picture away from her, dropped it in the same mud puddle, and stepped on it. Then he gave it back to her and asked her how it felt to have her picture ruined. Oh, you should have heard her screech! She ran home, howling all the way— you could hear her from three blocks' distance!"

David laughed. "I can imagine. She does have a set of lungs."

"I found out later that Stephen got a whipping from his father for spoiling Priscilla's picture." Josie straightened her leg and turned forward again in the seat. "After that, Stephen was my hero. I thought he was bravest, most handsome boy in town." Her voice had lost its animated tone and now sounded melancholy. She paused, her head cocked sideways, lost in thought.

David sneaked a glance at her. Had he ever, in his entire lifetime, impressed anyone the way Stephen had impressed that little seven-year-old Josie? They rode in silence for several minutes before she turned to him with a deep sadness in her brown eyes.

"You know, David, when Stephen started calling on me, I was—" She paused, searching for the right words. "I don't know. Astounded, I guess. I'd had a crush on him ever since that day he got back at Priscilla in my defense. I idolized him, but I figured he only saw me as a little kid. He and Frank called me 'little tagalong' when I trailed after them on the playground. 'Go along, little tagalong,' they'd say when I dogged their steps. But while Frank scowled, Stephen would grin when he said it. I never felt like he was slighting me."

David had held the impression that it was all over between Josie and Stephen, but maybe that was because he wanted that to be the case. During these weeks on the road between Mountain Lake and Winston, she hadn't mentioned the man except in passing. But now David was forced to realize her feelings for Stephen went back a long ways—and they hadn't changed. From the longing in her eyes and her pensive tone, he could see she still cared for him deeply. David's hands tightened on the reins.

She went on in that same hurt tone. "I think I loved him even before he started courting me. I could talk to him so easily, and he always listened."

"Listened, but didn't understand." The words slipped out before he could stop them.

"Don't judge Stephen by his recent behavior, David." Defensiveness had crept into Josie's voice. "You haven't known him as long as I have. I can't understand why he's been so bullheaded about my teaching, because it just isn't like him. The Stephen I fell in love with is kind and considerate and giving. . . ." As her voice trailed off, David's heart sank further, and he tried to swallow the lump in his throat.

He remembered his initial impression of Stephen. He had liked him—genuinely liked him—and had thought they could be friends. But when Stephen had hurt Josie, David had pulled away from him, turning his attentions toward Josie instead. Now he wondered . . . had he gotten to know Stephen better, would he have found him to be the type of person Josie had just described? He remembered, too, Hulda Klaassen's description of Stephen as a fine young man, worth ten of Priscilla. David realized he had been casting stones without the right to do so.

He reached over and touched Josie's arm. When she looked at him he said, "I'm sorry. You're right—I don't know Stephen, and I have no business putting him down."

She gave a sad smile. "I suppose it really doesn't matter, because I'm sure I've lost him." Her brown eyes flooded with sudden tears, and she turned away to dash the moisture away. "He hardly even looks at me anymore, and we certainly don't talk. After all those years of following him around, dreaming of him, loving him . . . it just hurts to have to let go." She pressed her lips together, then burst out with, "If only I could understand."

David's thoughts turned inward. *If Stephen could have seen Josie bound out of that school after her first week of teaching, he'd realize Josie was born to this. Maybe the man would then put his own wants aside long enough for her to do what she was meant to do. But I guess when you've waited for years for a little girl to grow into a woman . . .*

Realization struck. *Why, that had to be why Stephen had been so adamant about Josie staying in Mountain Lake, marrying him immediately. He had been watching Josie grow up, waiting for her to be old enough to become a wife. And then when she was old enough, she wasn't ready for the role. How frustrating that must have been. David could almost sympathize with the man.*

Josie sat in silence on the seat beside him, obviously also lost in thought. Should he interrupt her contemplations to tell her about his observations? It might help her understand Stephen, maybe even encourage her to try to reconcile with him.

But did he really want to help her reconcile with Stephen? It pained him to see her sorrow, but wouldn't she eventually give up her childhood fantasy? And then she would see David in a new, deeper light. Right now they were friends—close enough for her to share her greatest hurt. If he continued to be her friend and confidant, surely she would be able to put those old feelings for Stephen aside and lean on a new hero.

David had a fleeting thought that a true friend would do everything possible to ease a burden. . . . What should he do?

While he was still debating the issue, Josie spoke. "David, I'm so glad it's worked out for you to take me back and forth to Winston."

"I've enjoyed it, too, Josie."

She smiled at him, but it didn't quite reach her eyes—she still looked sad. "I appreciate the friendship we've developed. You'd think with all the brothers and sisters I have, I wouldn't need anyone else to talk to, but there are some things I just couldn't say to any of them." She sent a quick glance into the backseat, making sure Teddy still slept. She looked at David again. "They are too close to me. They'd immediately jump to my defense, and while I understand that only means they love me, it isn't always helpful. Sometimes you just need to get everything out and look at it logically instead of trying to fault find."

David considered her comments. While he wanted to be more than a sounding board, he was pleased that Josie felt comfortable enough to tell him things she wouldn't share with someone else. He began carefully, "You mean a lot to me, too.

I want you to be happy." But I *want to be the one to make you happy, not Stephen.*

She sat quietly, biting her lip. He got the impression she was trying to decide whether or not to tell him something. He knew when she had gotten her thoughts straightened out, because she took in a big breath and turned to him, looking at the same time apologetic and determined. He braced himself.

"David, because we are such good friends, I feel I can tell you this without you misinterpreting my true intentions."

David held his breath.

"You've been so helpful, taking me back and forth every week, and I don't want you to think I don't appreciate it. It's a lot of hours of your time that could be spent elsewhere, and I've enjoyed the talks and the opportunity for us to get to know one another. I just wonder if . . ." She broke off, her eyebrows pulling downward.

David, on pins and needles, prodded, "You wonder if . . . ?"

She drew in a deep breath, then blurted out, "It's possible that if Stephen drove me back and forth, he wouldn't feel left out of my life, and maybe . . . maybe we could work things out between us," she finished in a rush.

David's breath came out in a long "Ohhh . . ."

Her face drew together as if she would cry. "I'm sorry, David. I didn't mean to say . . . well, I didn't mean it to sound like I'd rather be with Stephen than you."

David managed a low chuckle, his eyes on the horse's rump. "Hmm. I think you just did."

She turned crimson. "But I didn't mean I didn't want you to—oh! I don't know how to say it. Forget I said anything." Scooting down in the seat, she crossed her arms and turned her face away, looking like a disgruntled first grader.

Despite himself, David had to laugh. "Hey, what would you do if one of your young students behaved this way?" But she obviously didn't see the humor. So he bumped her with his elbow. "All right, Josie my friend."

She didn't budge but grumbled, "What?"

"Are you pouting?"

"No."

"You look like you're pouting."

"Well!" She shot him a scowl. "You're mad at me."

"I'm not mad."

"Yes, you are."

"Would I be laughing if I was mad?"

"I don't know. Maybe."

"Well, I'm not mad. Disappointed, perhaps, but not mad."

She finally looked at him and straightened up in her seat. "Disappointed?"

He shrugged. "I've enjoyed these rides, too. It gets me outside instead of being cooped up in your uncle's store all the time. And I look forward to . . . our conversations." His heart skipped a beat as he dared to add, "I cherish your friendship, Josie. I don't want to lose it."

"Oh, David," she said, leaning toward him, "I wasn't trying to get rid of our friendship. But it has developed and gotten stronger because of these rides, and I thought maybe it might do the same for Stephen and me. I love him so much, and I really miss him. . . ."

David's chest went tight once more. Oh, how he wished she could say such things about him. A friend. She considered him just a friend. He sighed. "Well, Josie, if that's what you want to do, ask him. I just hope he won't disappoint you—again." He peeked at her sideways without moving his head.

She was biting on her lip again. "You're sure you wouldn't mind?"

Oh, he minded all right. But how could he say that without opening himself up to a whole new conflict? No, the best he could hope for was that Stephen's stubbornness would hold out, and he'd be there to pick up the broken pieces of Josie's heart.

He tried a half truth. "It sounds like that would be worth a try, Josie. But would it be okay if I still made the drive occasionally? I think I'd miss it." *And you.*

Josie smiled joyfully, her cheerful spirit restored. "No, I wouldn't mind. Besides, I have to keep my best friend up to date on everything, don't I? When else would we get a chance to talk?"

Best friend . . . Those words caught him right below the breastbone and held with almost a physical pressure. No one had ever called him a best friend. Although it wasn't what he had anticipated when he began making these trips, it felt good. It warmed him.

By now they were both familiar with the road and knew the landmarks, and Winston was waiting just over the next hill. Josie perked up, looking ahead, going into her "teacher mode" as David called it. It tickled him the way her concentration turned inward when they reached this spot in the road. She most thoroughly enjoyed her position.

As he helped her down from the buggy in front of the boardinghouse, she woke Teddy to tell him good-bye, then gave David her usual sisterly hug. After turning toward the door, she suddenly slapped a palm to her forehead and exclaimed, "Oh! Dummy me! I nearly forgot." She came back and said, "Next weekend I won't be coming home. The other teachers and I have meetings with the school board on Saturday, and they'll be doing an evaluation on me, so I have to be here."

David protested, "But next Saturday evening is the party at the schoolhouse to celebrate the end of harvest. You won't be home for that?"

Josie's face scrunched together in disappointment. "I want to be there, but I can't. I have to go to those meetings. Please tell Ma and Pa for me, will you? And I'll see you in two weeks."

David heaved a sigh. "All right. I'll do that." He carried her satchel up the walkway and into the parlor. She took it with a thank-you and held on to it with two hands against her skirt. The landlady, Mrs. Porter, sat on her starched sofa with some knitting, observing them through her round-lensed spectacles.

"Thank you again for the ride," Josie told David primly.

Aware of Mrs. Porter's sharp ears, David responded formally. "Certainly, Josie, I enjoyed it. I'll pass the word along about next weekend, and then I'll see you the following Friday." He leaned forward and gave her a friendly kiss on the cheek that set Mrs. Porter's needles clacking.

"Bye, David, take care." Her customary parting.

He returned to the buggy, swinging himself into the seat and tugging the lap robe tight around his legs. He took a moment to pull on gloves; it would be dark and much cooler by the time they reached Mountain Lake. He looked up at the lace-shrouded window he knew belonged to Josie, and waited for the light to appear. He shook his head sadly. Two weeks. Maybe longer, if Josie asked Stephen to make the trip next time and he agreed.

In David's opinion, the man would be a fool to refuse her. One didn't cast aside a girl as special as Josie. If she and Stephen managed to work out their differences, he wondered how he'd survive it, and then felt guilty for his selfish thoughts. *Get your mind elsewhere*, O'Brien!

"Giddy up now," he said, flicking the reins slightly. He turned the buggy expertly and headed away from the lighted window and from the girl who had won his heart without even trying.

He sighed, his breath hovering in a little cloud around his face. The ride always seemed longer without Josie at his side.

Chapter Seventeen

*T*he post-harvest celebration was as well attended as a wedding or funeral, with every farm family plus most of the townspeople showing up to enjoy a full afternoon and evening of food and fellowship. Reverend Goertzen began the activities with a prayer of thankfulness for a bountiful harvest, then everyone dug into the mountains of dishes provided by the womenfolk.

Someone wisely organized games for the children which took them out into the school yard. The schoolhouse doors remained wide open, and the happy laughter and shouts of fun by the crowd of children echoed throughout the building. After weeks of hard field work with little time for relaxation, everyone enjoyed this time of socializing.

David was there too. As Samantha had pointed out, he was the brother of a farmer's wife, and that certainly made him welcome. Everyone knew him from the mercantile, so he didn't lack for conversation. But he sorely felt the absence of one farmer's daughter. As far as he was concerned, the entire community of Mountain Lake couldn't make up for Josie not being there.

He wandered to the food table and selected a ham sandwich. As he lifted it to his mouth, he watched the Koehn family enter the school building. The sight of Stephen brought a tight feeling to his chest. Had Josie written and asked him to drive to Winston to pick her up for her next trip home? Curiosity tangled his stomach into knots, but he certainly wouldn't ask Stephen. Deep down, he was afraid to know.

He turned his attention back to Samantha, who was engrossed in an animated conversation with several other women. They reminded him of a gaggle of geese, heads together, tongues wagging.

Anna and Frank had recently announced they were going to be parents somewhere around Easter the next year, and that seemed to be the topic of discussion. He listened in as advice was handed out to Anna.

"Now don't eat too much cabbage or beans right now. It's bad for your digestion, dear, and it will make the baby colicky" was just one tidbit of helpful information. David struggled to hold his mirth inside, but Sammy was taking it all in, an expression of longing in her eyes. He knew how much she wanted a baby too, and he hoped soon she would be the center of a circle of well-intentioned women, receiving their blessings and experienced advice.

A tap on his shoulder, and there was Stephen Koehn at his side.

"Hello, David. How are you this evening? Enjoying the party?"

"Oh, sure." David held up his half-eaten sandwich. "Plenty to eat. That's about all a bachelor can hope for."

Stephen gave the expected chuckle. He hitched his fingers in his back pockets, rocked on his heels, and he seemed to be carefully avoiding facing David. "So . . . I hear you've been carting Josie back and forth from Winston."

David took the time to swallow a bite before answering, "Yup." He, too, kept his eyes forward rather than on his conversation partner.

"She's not . . . here tonight? She didn't come home?" Questions rather than a statement. So he hadn't heard from her. He sounded wistful.

"No. She hated to miss the harvest party, but she had meetings today—an evaluation or something. She stayed in Winston for the weekend." Still they didn't look at each other.

A pause, then, "How is she?"

David could have said a lot of things, including "missing you," but he intentionally made his voice casual and matter of fact as he responded, "Oh, she's doing great. She really enjoys her time with the children. She's a wonderful, natural teacher. The kids love her as much as she loves them."

Stephen nodded slowly. "Yes, I can believe that. Josie has a kind heart; she'd be good with kids."

Was Stephen thinking along the lines of Josie being good with her own children? David wasn't sure how to respond to Stephen's last statement, so he stood quietly, observing the milling groups and finishing his sandwich.

Finally Stephen sighed. "Well, I reckon I'll get myself something to eat. It looks good."

David experienced a flash of unexpected irritation. Stephen had proposed to Josie, made her feel terrible for going off to teach, and the man couldn't even ask David to deliver a message to her? At the very least, he could have asked David to tell her hello. But David kept the impatience out of his voice, "Yes, go ahead. Enjoy the party."

David shook his head, watching as Stephen took a plate and ambled his way down the row of serving tables. What a stubborn cuss. Josie deserved better than a man who was as self-absorbed as Stephen seemed to be. David was still looking at Stephen when Priscilla crossed his line of vision, hanging on the arm of her current favorite flirtation, Lucas Stoesz.

Self-absorption must run in the Koehn family. Priscilla acted as if she were the only person in the room, fluttering her eyelashes at Lucas and simpering in a way intended to keep his attention. Lucas didn't seem averse to giving it to her, either.

David turned his gaze away from the pair, searching out Sammy once more. He smiled to himself. He had certainly lucked out in the sister department. Samantha was a jewel. And even more so when compared to Stephen's sister. He wiped his palms on his handkerchief and walked over to drop an arm around Samantha's shoulders. She smiled up at him briefly before turning her attention back to Anna and their friends. He let his gaze rove over her head and found himself being watched by a pair of bright blue eyes.

Priscilla clung to Lucas's arm, her head tipped toward him as he whispered something in her ear. But instead of looking at Lucas, her gaze was aimed right at David. He got the impression the smile on her face was intended for him, too. He maintained a deadpan expression. He was not inclined to give her the least bit of encouragement.

As he watched, Lucas removed her hand from his arm and held it around his waist, circling his own arm around her shoulders. Apprehension stirred through David's gut. What was Lucas suggesting? Whatever it was, Priscilla played along. She pretended to resist, pulling back slightly as he began to pull her toward the door. She threw back her head, making sure her eyes caught David's once more before allowing herself to be persuaded by Lucas.

The pair headed out the back door of the schoolhouse, and David shook his head, tightening his hand on Sammy's shoulder. *I'm a lucky man*, he told himself again with a shake of his head, and he put Priscilla from his mind.

"C'mon, Pris." Lucas tugged Priscilla none too gently across the school yard through the shouting throng of children. "It's too crowded around here. Let's go take a walk, get some air."

Priscilla gave him another dose of her eyelashes, puckering her lips into a practiced moue. When she'd noticed what she hoped was David O'Brien watching her with Lucas, her heart had leapt. A perfect opportunity to make David jealous! She couldn't explain why it was so important to win David's attention. After all, there were certainly other men—like Lucas—who were more than willing to shower her with it. But it was David's interest she wanted.

Lucas's wiry arm around her shoulders guided her down the walkway leading away from the school building. Priscilla laughed and pushed away his arm playfully. "You, sir, are incorrigible!" Without an audience, the game had lost its greater appeal, but it was still exciting to see how she could manipulate Lucas. If she couldn't have David's attention, she'd settle for Lucas. For now. He was certainly better than nothing.

Lucas grinned, allowing her to slip away from him. "I've been called worse," he quipped, and she laughed again. This was the kind of play Priscilla liked best—dangerous and forbidden, but always within her control.

They reached the main street of Mountain Lake, and Priscilla paused, looking back toward the school. Might David be watching for her return? "Where are we going, Lucas?"

Lucas shrugged. "Jost has a couple of new horses in. One's got a star on its nose—real pretty. Wanna go see it?"

Priscilla hesitated only a moment before turning her face to his and flashing her beguiling smile. "Are you sure you only want to look at horses in Jost's barn?"

Lucas laughed, his white teething shining in the moon- light. "What else?" His comment sounded innocent enough, but his eyes indicated he had something else in mind.

Priscilla punched at his chest with her fist. "I'll go with you, Lucas, but you better behave! Or I'll tell my daddy on you!"

Lucas feigned great fear, staggering around with one hand holding his chest and the other flung outward. "Her daddy! Oh, no! I would never want to tangle with her daddy! Oh, Pris, no, don't tell on me to your daddy!"

Laughing, she punched him again. "Lucas, don't make fun of me!"

He caught her hand and gave a tug that set her feet moving toward Jost's Livery and Blacksmith Shop. Priscilla shivered, hunching her shoulders. The late October air was crisp, and she had left her shawl at the schoolhouse. Lucas wrapped an arm around her, resting his hand on the curve of her waist. She peeked at him, considering voicing a protest, but the warmth was welcome, so instead she smiled acquiescence.

They reached the blacksmith's barn in a matter of minutes and stepped into the livery part of the large structure. The gentle snoring and snorting of contented horses greeted them. There was little light, but the air was warmer here and rich with the odors of hay, wood ashes, and horseflesh. Lucas led Priscilla directly to the stall of the new horse with the white star on his nose.

Priscilla reached between the bars of the stall door and cooed, "C'mere, girl, let me pet you."

Lucas laughed. "Silly goose. He's not going to come to you if you call him a girl."

Priscilla pretended to be insulted. "Well, how am I sup- posed to know what it is?"

Lucas gave her a calculating look. "Do you want me to tell you?" And his hand slipped around her waist.

She stepped sideways, twisting her body slightly to elude his touch. She arched her brows and assumed a tart tone. "No, I do not think that will be necessary."

Lucas laughed at her again. There was a gleam in his eye that Priscilla found slightly disturbing, and she was beginning to question the wisdom of coming here alone with him.

"I could tell you lots of things, Pris." Lucas moved stealthily across the hay-covered ground toward her. "And I guarantee you'd like every one of them."

Priscilla backed up just as quickly as he advanced, but with less grace considering her full skirts, the lack of light, and the uneven ground. "I don't think so, Lucas. And I know my daddy wouldn't like it."

Lucas grinned. "Ah, we're back to your daddy again, are we? Well, let me remind you . . . your daddy ain't here." His tone lost its teasing quality, causing Priscilla's heart to ram against her ribs in fright. "All right, Pris, it's time to stop teasing. A man can take only so much of that before he caves in. You've been asking for this for months, turning those brilliant blue eyes on me and batting your lashes, sending me come-hither smiles. The time has come. So stop teasing and come here."

She backed herself against a stall and could go no farther. She made to dart past him, but Lucas grabbed her by the upper arms, pushing her against the stall door again. Her lips parted in fright as he neared, and he lowered his head and placed his eager mouth over hers. She pushed at his chest, twisting her head and making sharp little sounds of panicky protest. At last she pulled her head free.

"Lucas, stop it!" Her demand exploded breathlessly against his cheek.

But Lucas didn't let go. He slid his hands down her arms until he gripped her wrists tightly, pushing them against her chest and pressing painfully against her breasts. Sandwiched between his hard hands and the unyielding stall door, she had no choice but to stay put, but she moved her head back and forth in frenzied motions.

His breath came heavily against her hair as he murmured, "Stop fighting me, Prissy. You've wanted this as much as me. I've seen it in your eyes. Kiss me back."

"No-o-o," she gasped out, struggling to free herself. But Lucas ignored her protest, pursuing her relentlessly. Her back hurt where it pressed against the wood of the stall gate, and the horse in the stall whickered nervously. Her mind raced, frantically seeking a means of escape. She pulled her left foot back, then swung it forward as hard as she could. The pointed toe of her shoe cracked against his shin.

He gave a grunt of pain, and in the moment of distraction, she shoved outward with her arms, throwing him off balance. Scrambling awkwardly, she darted around him and made for the entrance of the barn as quickly as her skirts would allow.

But Lucas was infinitely more sure-footed. His clumping steps closed the ground behind her. She released one high-pitched squeal as he caught her by an arm and swung her in a small circle to land solidly against his chest. His arms locked around her, pinning her there, and his eyes bore into hers with a hard, angry expression that made her blood run cold.

"Oh, no, Pris." His eyes snapped with temper. "You're not goin' anywhere. It's high time you gave me a little of what your eyes have been promising." He gave her a little shake as she continued to moan and fight against him.

She began to cry as his lips crushed down on hers once more.

Chapter Eighteen

A party without Josie was really no party at all. David said his good-byes, receiving a hug and a promise from Samantha to get together soon, and then he slipped on his jacket and left. It was a pleasant night for a walk. The air was cool but not biting, with the fresh promise of snow in the air. The moon provided enough light to see where he was going. Stars twinkled brightly in the clear sky, and a hoot owl called its echoing question from a nearby tree. When the nocturnal bird asked deeply, "Whooo? Whooo?" David smilingly answered, "Just me." The flap of wings cut the air as the bird departed.

His long-legged stride carried him quickly across the boardwalk, his steps echoing hollowly in the quiet evening. He whistled softly to himself, his breath whirling around him in a cloud as he moved briskly toward the boardinghouse and his own private room. His mind ran idly through the various tasks that would require his attention at the store tomorrow. He almost missed the low sound of a moan that came through the gaping door of Jost's Livery and Blacksmith Shop.

He paused a good ten feet from the opening, cocking an ear. Could that have been a horse? It sure hadn't sounded like one. Then it came again—a low, frightened sound that couldn't have been made by an animal. The muffled sounds of a scuffle followed. What on earth?

David crossed quickly to the door and looked in. In the dim light provided by the moonlight slanting through several high windows, he spotted two people. It was obvious even in the shadows what was taking place, and he considered moving on, but then he heard a woman's gasp in a fear-filled voice, "No, Lucas! Let me go!"

Lucas Stoesz—with Priscilla. And she was not a willing participant. Without further consideration he stormed into the stable.

Lucas had his back to the door, so the hand that clamped down on his shoulder caught him by surprise. David pulled him away from Priscilla with one hand and landed a felling blow against his jaw with the other, all before Lucas had a chance to react.

"Hey!" Lucas yelped as his seat hit the floor and he slid backward at least three feet.

Priscilla caught hold of David's arm, but he shook her off. "Get back, girl!" She skittered away.

Lucas bounded up, coming at David with both fists raised. For a moment David questioned taking on the stocky farm boy. Lucas was accustomed to wrestling bales of hay and obstinate calves. Could a skinny storekeeper come out the victor? But what David lacked in girth he made up for in indignation. He deflected Lucas's swings, delivering a punishing blow to the younger man's left eye and then sinking a fist into his midsection. Lucas clutched his stomach and sank to his knees, fighting for breath. Priscilla stood off to the side, shaking hands covering her mouth, tears raining down her pale cheeks.

David, winded, propped his hands on his knees and glowered at Lucas. "You ought to be ashamed of yourself, forcing yourself on a woman. Get yourself up and out of here before I give in to the temptation to beat you senseless."

Lucas pressed the back of a hand to his lip. It came away with blood on it, which he wiped on his pants with a growl.

"I wasn't forcing nothin'. I know you've seen how she prances around. . . . She's been askin' for it."

"Yeah, I've seen," David said, ignoring Priscilla's indignant gasp, "but when a lady says no, that means no."

Lucas snorted. "She's hardly a lady, O'Brien."

David glanced briefly at Priscilla, taking in her shame-faced expression, before retorting sharply in retaliation. "Well, then, what does that make you?"

Lucas's gaze narrowed angrily, but he didn't respond.

David straightened, his chest still heaving as he caught his breath. "Next time you make a pass and the . . . the young woman says no, you'd be wise to listen to it. A gentleman would listen. Now, pick yourself up and get out of here." Lucas sat on his knees, staring at David belligerently. David made as if to come at him again. "Out. Now."

Lucas stood up, dusted the hay from his knees in a deliberately slow gesture, then stalked out, his head high. The minute he cleared the door, Priscilla raced across the barn floor and threw herself, sobbing, against David's chest. He allowed her exactly ten seconds of self-pity before he took her by the upper arms and shook her hard. "You stop that right now, Miss Koehn."

Priscilla ceased her sobbing immediately. She stared at David through tear-filled eyes. "B-but, David, I thought—"

"You thought wrong." His fingers tightened on her upper arms. "I might've blamed Lucas for this, but you are just as much at fault. What were you doing here with him, anyway?"

"Trying to make you—" She bit down on her lip and wrenched free of his grasp. "I came to look at a horse!"

"Yeah, sure." David gave a sarcastic snort. "Girl, you don't have the sense God gave a goose. You knew good and well what Lucas was after, and you came anyway. I saw you leave with him, and you weren't resisting. What did you expect to happen in here?"

Priscilla started to cry again. "Nothing! I didn't expect anything to happen!"

"Then you are dumber than I thought." David's low voice rumbled with barely controlled anger. He shook a finger under her nose. "Let me tell you something you should have figured out long ago, Miss Koehn. When you ask for something, you're likely to get it. And when someone rises to your bait, you've got no right to cry and complain and act put-upon. You and your flirting ways nearly got you into serious trouble tonight. I hope this all serves as a good lesson for you."

She blinked away tears and lifted her chin in defiance. "What gives you the right to—?"

"The fact that I came barreling in here in your defense gives me the right, you spoiled little brat." He balled his hands into fists on his hips. "I'm thinking now I should've just left Lucas to have his way with you. Maybe that would've brought you down a peg or two."

Priscilla covered her face and dissolved into frightened sobbing which only angered David further. Why couldn't the girl see she'd brought this on herself? No, Lucas didn't have the right to force himself on her, but her actions had contributed to the situation. And further, why did it bother David so much that she didn't seem to understand her accountability?

David barked, "Stop crying before I do what your own father should have done years ago and give you a good reason for all those tears." She sobbed harder, and he shook her again, but gentler this time, and said in a softer tone, "Come on, Priscilla, it's over, and he's gone. Now it's time to dry up."

At the kind tone—and the use of her Christian name—Priscilla raised her chin and looked into David's eyes. Her face crumpled once more, and she choked out, "I'm sorry, David." She fell against his chest once more, sobbing brokenheartedly.

David let her cry for a few seconds, then firmly pushed her upright. "Priscilla, listen to me." He waited until she had released one more shuddering sob and wiped her face with her hands. When she finally lifted her face and was looking at him, he said, "You cannot carry on with young men—even me—like you have been doing. Do you understand me?"

She nodded and started to cry once more.

"I'm not sure you really do, Priscilla. I want you to look at me."

She stared into his face, and this time she seemed to realize the gravity of the situation from which she had just been rescued. Her voice breaking over the words, she said, "Oh, David, I'm very sorry. I didn't mean for him to . . . I really didn't know . . . ."

He just shook his head.

She admitted in a whisper, "I was so scared!"

David finally reached out to pat her shoulder. "I know, Priscilla. And I'm glad I came along when I did." He paused a moment. "I'm sure you've learned an important lesson tonight."

"Oh, I have. I'll behave from now on." The gaze she turned on David bordered on adoring. Even in her rather disheveled appearance, with puffy eyes and tear-stained features, her striking natural beauty was fully in evidence. David felt more ill at ease with this subdued, obedient Priscilla than he had the willful, obstinate one. At least he'd known how to handle the untamed Priscilla.

He turned stern. "I certainly hope so, because if I ever have to pull you out of a predicament like that again, I guarantee I'll haul you straight to the woodshed." He pulled his eyebrows down in a scowl.

To his surprise, instead of bristling at his threat, Priscilla gave a meek nod. She wore an expression of contrition and gratitude that made him wonder if she had indeed had a change of heart.

David said gruffly, "You'd better get home and clean yourself up, then head back to the party. Your folks will be wondering where you are."

She nodded, her eyes still on him, but she made no move to leave.

"Go on now, Pris."

She started to move away, then turned back. "Would you mind . . . well, will you walk with me, please?"

It was the first time in his memory he could recall hearing Priscilla Koehn use the word *please*. He hesitated.

"I'm afraid to be by myself in the dark."

He stepped forward and nodded, looking down at her. "All right, Priscilla, I'll take you to your house."

"Then back to the schoolhouse?"

He knew he should deny her request. After all, she was getting her way. Again. But her eyes beseeched him, and for once they held not a hint of coquettishness. Her sincere entreaty tugged at his heart in a way he found disturbing. At last he sighed and caved in. "All right."

"Thank you, David." She tucked her arm into his.

David didn't trust himself to answer. He merely nodded once more, and they made their way out of the barn, arm in arm.

Chapter Nineteen

*P*riscilla lay in her bed, staring at the ceiling. The lace curtain rose and fell in the breeze drifting through the open window, sending shadows across the rose-printed paper. She hadn't extinguished her bedside lamp. Never afraid of the dark before, her heart now pounded with fear and anxiety. Her eyes burned with the effort of keeping them open. Each time she allowed her lids to close, she saw again Lucas's leering grin as he forced her against the stall gate.

She rolled to her side, pressing her fist to her mouth and battling the urge to call out for Mama and Daddy. Why hadn't she told her parents what Lucas had done when David returned her to the party? Daddy would have pummeled the fellow into the ground. Her father wouldn't simply have landed a few blows and sent Lucas on the way, as David had. Wouldn't she find some satisfaction in seeing her attacker punished for the dreadful assault?

But deep down, she recognized the situation wasn't entirely Lucas's fault. Shame rose from her middle as she acknowledged David had been right. Her deliberate flirting had given Lucas reason to believe she wanted him to kiss her—and more.

Tears trickled down her cheeks and into a damp place on her pillowcase. She'd so wanted David to notice her and give her attention. Well, she'd gotten what she'd been after. Oh, how he'd paid attention! But instead of feeling victorious, she only felt ashamed. And sad. He'd risen to her defense like a knight in shining armor. Afterward, he'd certainly been angry, but he was also kind. She wasn't sure how she should act around him now. Priscilla Koehn, unable to discern how to behave around a man!

For as long as she could remember, she'd enjoyed using her wiles to garner attention from boys. Boys clustered around her like bees around a honeysuckle vine. She'd welcomed them, encouraged them, teasing and beguiling and enjoying every minute of control. Until the moment she lost control. *Or maybe I lost control long before then.* . . .

Lucas's disparaging comment—"she's hardly a lady, O'Brien"—echoed through her mind. How many others in town held his sentiment? Such an ugly reputation she'd established for herself. Maybe the face she saw in her mirror each morning was not beautiful. She swallowed, rubbing her fist beneath her nose, groaning out her distress at such a thought. Who was she, then, if not "the lovely lady, Miss Priscilla Koehn"?

But David had extracted a promise that she give up her flirtatious ways, and she fully intended to keep the promise. And maybe—just maybe—David would look at her as more than a fickle flirt. Maybe he'd see the lady she truly wanted to become.

*　　　　　∽◯*

"Here you go, David." The postman handed David a fistful of mail through the little barred window of the post office front. "All of Hiram's and Si's, plus one in there for you, too."

David gawked in surprise. "For me?" He began thumbing through the envelopes in his hand. Sure enough, he found one with his name on it. The address—Mr. David O'Brien, Mountain Lake, Minnesota—was spelled out in a neat, slanting script. He recognized the envelope from the stationery set he had given Josie for her graduation. His heart leaped just looking it.

He mumbled, "Thanks," before heading back to the mercantile. He held the envelope, unopened, in front of him, staring at his name as if merely looking at the handwriting would give a clue to the contents. What would she say? *Come for me—don't come for me—come for me—don't come for me.* . . . The words reverberated through his head, alternating with each step. Then realizing he was playing a childish game of chance, he pushed the letter into the middle of the stack and held them stiffly against his side as he walked.

Hiram looked up when the cowbell clanged above the mercantile's door. "Mail all in?"

"Yes." David pulled out the envelope of shell pink, pocketed it, then laid the stack on the tall counter. He kept his voice light as he inquired, "Mr. Klaassen, would it be all right if I took my lunch break now?"

Hiram pulled out his timepiece, snapped the cover, checked the time, and nodded. "Ja, David, go ahead. It's been slow today. Freight will not be in until two. Why don't you just plan to come back then?"

"Thank you, sir." He'd have plenty of time to stop at the café for some lunch, read his letter, and maybe even pen a reply. If one was required. He wasn't sure what was proper; he'd never received a personal letter before.

Minutes later he slid into one of the high-backed benches at Vogt's Café. The café's plump waitress, Maudie, came over to take his order. Unable to even think about what he might want, he requested the daily special.

"Ham and beans with cornbread today, David." Maudie's round face and dark eyes peered at him from beneath heavy eyebrows.

David fingered the envelope in his pocket. "That sounds fine."

"Want some coffee or pie to go with that?"

David didn't answer.

"David?"

"Um—sorry?"

Maudie's lips took on a teasing grin. "Wrong time of year for spring fever, but I'd say by your starry-eyed look your mind's not on food."

David ducked his head and gave a brief laugh.

Maudie repeated, "Want some coffee, or some pie?"

"Coffee would be fine, but no dessert today. Thanks anyway."

"Young folks . . ." Maudie shook her head and chuckled to herself as she headed back to the kitchen.

David folded his fingers around the square of paper in his pocket, wondering if he should read it here. It was still early, so few people were in the café, and, situated within the confines of his high-backed booth, he had some privacy. He removed the envelope from his pocket and laid it on the checked tablecloth. He spent a few moments admiring the neat handwriting, imagining how Josie's hand might have looked as she dipped the pen and set it on paper, forming the letters of his name.

Suddenly an image of Priscilla Koehn's hands placing a pair of suspenders on the counter at the mercantile flashed through his mind. *Where did that come from?* Determinedly, he turned his attention back to the envelope in front of him. He lifted it, and, after checking around to make sure he wasn't observed, he brought it to his nose and sniffed. There was no scent save the faint odor of glue. A little disappointed, he turned it face down on the table and at last slid a thumbnail beneath the flap to open it.

Inside he found two sheets of matching pink paper, folded in half. He began to read:

Sunday, October 21, 1918

My dear David,

He read her chosen greeting several times, his heart beating more rapidly each time.

After spending a fretful hour in thought and prayer, I felt I really must write to you and try to settle my aching conscience.

I feel terrible about the clumsy way I approached the subject of Stephen today. I should realize that you, as my friend, are committed to be as protective of me as my family has been, and would wonder at the sensibility of my asking anything of Stephen again. He has hurt me with his withdrawal, and although I don't wish to be injured again, I am having a hard time letting go. As I told you earlier today, I do love him. I actually can't remember a time when I did not.

Often, as you and I have laughed and talked, I have thought of Stephen. The hours of solitude, of one-on-one communicating, have helped you and me develop a wonderful, caring friendship. That is why I couldn't help but wonder if Stephen and I had time alone together, if we might be able to come to some sort of accommodation between his desires and mine.

That's why I suggested what I did. I know now how ungrateful and selfish it sounded, and I apologize. I certainly didn't want to offend you, or make you feel unappreciated. I really am sorry, David.

Something else has occurred to me during our rides, and I think you might be too much of a gentleman to speak of it. That is, you are spending so much of your free time carting me back and forth, not much is left over for you to pursue other relationships. I am sure that you could think of other people (or another young lady?) with whom you would like to spend time. I wonder if I'm being unfair to you, taking advantage of our friendship and your kind nature by counting on you more than I should, and perhaps these rides are hindering you.

I want you to know that if that is the case, you certainly can tell me. You won't offend me.

David lifted his head from the page as Maudie appeared, holding a crockery bowl of steaming soup and a plate piled high with wedges of cornbread. David tucked the letter under the edge of the table. Maudie set his food down with a curious glance at him but only said simply, "Enjoy your meal," before disappearing back into the kitchen.

David pushed the bowl aside and picked up the letter once more, sliding the first page behind the second. He continued to read:

> You deserve some free time, too, David, so even if Stephen refuses to come pick me up after this coming weekend (as I trust you are still planning to come for me this time!), I intend to speak to Father about making other arrangements. Now that harvest is over, he or one of my brothers should be able to make the trip without any problems. (When the snowfall hinders travel, there will no doubt be times when I will just stay here on weekends.) I wouldn't mind a bit if you still made the trip once in a while, but I don't want to be a burden on you and leave you the full responsibility for getting me back and forth. You have certainly performed your duty already!
>
> I just want you to understand, and I hope you will forgive my clumsy way of bringing up the subject earlier today. I do just fine when talking to a roomful of little children, but expressing myself clearly to a grown man is quite another thing. I hope you meant it when you said you weren't angry with me, because I cherish your friendship, David, and I don't want to do anything that would jeopardize it. You mean a great deal to me, and I imagine you always will.
>
> Affectionately yours,
>
> Josie

By the time he finished, he was pinching the bridge of his nose with one hand and creasing the pages of the letter with the other. She'd pretty much told him the same thing on that last ride together, but the words were somehow more real, more poignant, when written on paper and staring back at him, black against the pale pink. Slowly he set the last page down and lifted the first page to reread a section:

Often as you and I have laughed and talked, I have thought of Stephen.

How disconcerting to realize that all the time he thought they were becoming closer, another man was on her mind— that she was thinking about possible ways to restore a relationship with the man she really loved.

David honestly hadn't been angry before, but he battled the emotion now. Josie was making a mighty big assumption that he had other things he wanted to do with his time. Maybe he had waited too long. Maybe he should have come right out and told her what he'd hoped would be the outcome of these rides together.

But reality came crashing through his what-ifs. No, that simply would have ended their rides earlier. If she had known his feelings for her went deeper than friendship, she would never have agreed to these times with her. Not while she still loved Stephen. And, he thought further, not while I am an "unbeliever." Josie was honest and straightforward. She would have come right out and said it wasn't a good idea for them to have these long buggy trips together.

His eyes glanced down the page of even, slanted script.

I am sure that you could think of other people (or another young lady?) with whom you would like to spend time. . . .

Why did Priscilla Koehn's face seem to float above "another young lady"? He'd not viewed her as anything other than a spoiled, shallow, self-centered annoyance. And in light of the latest encounter, naïve to a fault. Oh, she was certainly beautiful, but she lacked all of Josie's sweetness and honesty. Yet with Josie's simple words, Priscilla's faced pressed into his mind and refused to depart.

He leaned his chin on his hand and sat staring out the window. He pictured Priscilla as she had looked after he had chased Lucas from Jost's barn. He remembered clearly her wide, tear-stained eyes and penitent expression as she'd begged him to walk her home. He remembered, too, the feel of her hand tucked into his arm; the gentle swishing sounds her skirts made as they walked together along the planked boardwalk; the sight of her tumbling, glossy curls cascading down her narrow back and shining blue-black in the moonlight. . . .

He sat up abruptly, slapping his hand on the tabletop. Good heavens, what was he doing, sitting here fantasizing about Priscilla Koehn? This letter from Josie must have had a more disheartening effect on him than he realized. He folded the pages and slid them into the envelope, then pushed it deep into his pocket.

According to the letter, Josie expected him to pick her up this Friday, presumably for the last time. Well, he'd set her straight on that one. He had four days to think of the proper way to word what needed saying. In the meantime, his soup was getting cold. He picked up his spoon.

⁓

A pink envelope was in the Koehn family's mail, too. Stephen recognized Josie's handwriting the instant his father placed it in his hand, and he ducked around a corner in the mill and tore the entire top off the envelope. He held the two pages side by side and scanned them briefly before laying them back together for more serious reading. He leaned against the wall as he began, taking time over each word and sentence.

The beginning paragraphs were chatty, newsy things— telling about the boardinghouse and the others who lived there. There was an anecdote about a little girl named Essie who, after a lesson on balance, cut off one of her braids to see if it might make her tip sideways. She mentioned an art project involving paper, paint, and leaves. And his mind carried him backward, remembering the adorable little pigtailed girl he had known many years ago. . . .

And then he got to the real purpose of the letter.

I have missed you, Stephen. We've been friends for such a very long time and were closer than friends for a while. I think of you often, wondering how your work is going, if you have time to play checkers with the old-timers at the mercantile on Saturdays, and if you ever think of me.

When we talked last, I asked you to leave me alone unless you could tell me you loved me. You've honored that request well, and I've regretted my hasty words. You said something, too, that has plagued me. You said when I was ready to stop "playing teacher," I shouldn't expect you to be sitting and waiting for me. I wonder if you have some regrets, too, about those words. A part of me certainly hopes you do.

I would like to spend some time with you when I come home this next weekend. I realize I'm not being very ladylike, just saying it out like that, but right now I think being honest is more important than being lady-like. I have missed my dearest friend, and I would like to "catch up," so to speak.

If you would like to see me, too, I will be at home Saturday. I can make us a lunch, and we can have a picnic in the barn loft. It would be warm in there, as well as quiet, so we could talk without interruption. I would like to try to regain our old easy friendship, Stephen. I hope you would like that, too. If you don't come, please know that I will not blame you. I'd rather you be honest than courteous. But I will then know you are no longer interested in pursuing a relationship with me, and I won't bother you again.

Well, I must sign the letter now and get it in the mail before I grade some papers. The third graders wrote their first essays yesterday, and I am eager to read them. I hope to see you on Saturday next. I will be praying that we make the right decisions concerning the future.

Take care, Stephen.

Affectionately yours,

Josie

Slowly Stephen folded the letter in half, second page on the top. She missed him. She thought of him. She wanted to spend some time with him, to talk. . . . He hadn't had a moment with Josie since that day in July in the bean patch, months ago. His heart hammered in his chest, thinking of some time with her again. Yes, he wanted to go on a "loft picnic" with her, wanted to talk easily and openly as they once had before her desire to teach got in the way. But could they? So many words had been spoken in anger, so much time had passed. Could things really be fixed now?

And did he really want to fix things? Josie wouldn't change her stance on needing to hear "I love you" from him—not just the words, but the meaning of those words—before she would marry him. And she obviously enjoyed teaching. Would she give that up for him? The things that had created the problems in the first place were still firmly planted. Was there any point in getting together again, talking, and risking another argument?

He held the letter tightly in his fist, unconsciously crumpling the pink sheets in his agitation. He remembered the advice his brothers had given him. They were quite certain he would never find contentment with Josie unless he "laid down the law" and let her know who was in charge.

Sadie, Mary, and Lillian obviously respected their husbands' positions as head of the household. His brothers were of the opinion that their marriages were the way it was supposed to be—with the man fully "in charge." The idea certainly represented his parents' marriage too. But what did it really mean?

Stephen couldn't help but wonder if being the head of the house actually meant being dominating and bossy. Because that's what his father and brothers were. In addition, the males in his family treated their wives as if they didn't have one brain between them. He could well imagine bright and assertive Josie's reaction to that kind of treatment.

As angry—and as hurt—as he had been by her refusal to accept his proposal, he had mixed feelings concerning what was the proper way according to his brothers and what was actually right. What if he went to one of his brothers right now and showed him the letter with Josie's invitation, what advice would he give? Stephen snorted. No doubt the response would be along the lines of "that woman is trying to dictate to you again" and "don't give in to her."

No, he wouldn't show the letter to his brothers. And his father was out of the question. John Koehn's dictatorial attitude extended beyond Millie to include his male offspring. Stephen didn't want to set himself up for a lengthy lecture. So who to talk to about this?

What about Ma?

Stephen chewed on his lip. A female viewpoint could be helpful. And if he was able to talk to Ma alone, without Pa around, maybe she could help him understand Josie's determination to hold out for what she wanted.

But there was no point in standing here stewing about it right now. Saturday was still five days away. He had time to think about it, talk to Ma, and—as Josie had said—pray about it as well. If it turned out that he showed up at the Klaassen farm Saturday, he knew he would be sending a strong message without uttering a word. He'd have to be very sure of what he wanted—what God wanted for Josie and for him—because if he accepted her invitation, there likely would be no turning back.

osie stood inside the schoolhouse, holding the door open a mere inch to look out like a child peering through a knothole. Cold air blew in the opening, carrying biting snowflakes that stung her eye. But still she remained, silent and waiting. What kind of a greeting would David give her? Would he feel awkward and uncomfortable after the letter she'd sent? She certainly felt awkward!

Josie hated conflict. Oh, she wasn't averse to it if the situation merited it; she would stand her ground as required. But she greatly disliked dissension, and that's precisely what she had created when she brought up the subject of Stephen with David. David was as close as family, and of course he would take her side, come to her defense.

She heard the sound of wheels on the road, and then David in the driver's seat came into view. She held her breath and watched as he brought the vehicle to a halt, set the brake, then looked toward the school. She opened the door more fully, and they looked at each other across the expanse. Embarrassment swept over her. What must he think of her, standing there in the cold watching for him?

But then his face broke into a broad smile. "Hi, Josie! Are you ready to go?"

As amiable as ever. Josie's heart lifted, and she beamed a smile back at him. "I sure am!" She pulled her shawl snug around her ears, stooped over to scoop up her books, and ran down the steps.

At the boardinghouse, even though Teddy clambered out to accompany her, David declined her offer to come inside. "I'll wait here for you. If I go in where it's warm, I'll just have to get used to the cold again."

Josie promised to be quick. In only a matter of minutes, she hurried a dawdling Teddy down the wooden steps and followed him into the buggy. Teddy crouched in the narrow floor space between the seats with a book, pulling a wool blanket clear over his head like a makeshift tent.

David handed her the lap robe. "Bundle up tight. It's really nippy today."

Snowflakes danced in the wind, clouds blew past the sun, and bare trees stood out starkly against the pale blue sky. Josie shivered as the buggy pulled out of town. She'd worn her warmest wool dress, a wool coat, heavy shawl, woven scarf, and gloves. Even with the lap robe pulled close, she still shivered.

From beneath the scarf, her voice sounded muffled. "It won't be long, I imagine, before I'll have to just stay in Winston for the weekends. It will be too cold to make this trip."

David glanced at her. "I suppose that would be preferable to getting frostbite—especially your nose." He lifted her scarf between thumb and finger a little higher, covering all of her face except her eyes. He smiled—a sad smile, it seemed.

"Josie, I want to talk to you about . . ."

Another tremor—a different kind of cold—struck Josie, and she shivered again.

David frowned. "You really are cold, aren't you?"

Hugging herself, she nodded. "Y-yes."

His breath hung heavy in the crisp air. "Well, I suppose it is too cold for conversation." He sighed. "You just hunker into that robe, and I'll get you home as quickly as possible. All right?"

"Th-thank you, David." She scooted down on the seat, pulling the lap robe up around her ears. They rode along in companionable silence, the buggy jolting over ruts in the road and the horse's steamy breath creating little clouds of condensation. Although she felt bad for having discouraged conversation—they'd enjoyed such pleasant chats in the past—she appreciated David's willingness to let her keep her attention on staying warm.

～⌒つ

Stephen drew in a breath for fortification, knocked and turned the handle on the door, and entered his father's office. "Pa?"

Pa looked up from the ledger, his bushy eyebrows low. "Yes? What is it?"

"Can I head home a little early today?" He tapped one finger against his jaw. "Tooth." The evening before, he'd suffered a toothache. Although the twinge was mostly gone, he couldn't think of another excuse his father would not question for letting him go before quitting time. And he needed to speak to Ma alone.

Pa waved him off. "You've put in extra hours since harvest ended. Go ahead—have your ma doctor that thing. Clove usually works." His father returned to his bookkeeping.

Relieved at having escaped further discussion, Stephen hustled home and accepted the clove bud Ma offered. He held the strong-tasting spice between his back teeth. Ma made hot tea for them both and brought it to the dining room. Stephen followed, choosing a chair across from her.

Ma clucked in sympathy. "You are quite uncomfortable, Stephen?"

Stephen lowered his head. Yes, he was uncomfortable, but not physically. He reached into his pocket and withdrew the pink sheets with Josie's neat handwriting and slid them across the table. Millie looked at him, puzzlement in her eyes.

He kept his jaw clenched to hold the clove in place. "Would you please read the second page, Ma?"

Ma placed a hesitant hand against her chest, her brows raised high in query. "Me?"

Stephen understood her confusion and guilt smote him. He'd never come to Ma with a problem before. He'd treated her with the same distant affection that Pa employed. He gentled his voice. "I need your advice, Ma. Would you read it, please?"

A smile of wonderment tipped her lips and lit her eyes. She set aside her cup, reached for the letter, and began to read. Stephen fidgeted, eager to hear what she'd say.

Her gaze lifted from the page, her expression hopeful. "Josie appears to want a reconciliation between you two. Is that what you want, Stephen?"

He shrugged. "I'm not sure, Ma. That's what I wanted to talk to you about." He paused, struggling with the choice of words. How could he ask his mother if she thought Josie was too independent to make a good wife? In the end, he talked around what he really wanted to know. "Ma, what do you think is the most important element in a good relationship between a man and woman?"

To his surprise, Ma didn't hesitate. "The most important element in any relationship is respect. If you respect each other, then your treatment of one another will always be what it should be." She seemed to lose herself in thought for a moment.

Stephen couldn't help but think of his father's attitude toward Ma. Did Pa respect Ma? He sure didn't act like it. Instead of questioning Pa's feelings toward Ma, Stephen decided to pursue his mother's feelings. "Do you respect Pa?"

"Of course I do." Ma picked up her cup and took a drink. "If I didn't, I couldn't be a good wife."

Without thinking, Stephen blurted, "Pa isn't a good husband, though, is he?" In an instant he wished he could take the words back.

His mother turned scarlet and set the cup down with a trembling hand. "Your father is a Christian man. He is faithful to me and a good provider. He has brought you children up to honor your parents and be good, God-fearing people. Of course he is a good husband."

Stephen moved to the chair next to his mother. He put a hand on her arm as he asked gently, apologetically, "But does he respect you, Mama?"

She hung her head.

Stephen went on quietly. "You just told me that respect is the most important part of a good relationship. I have to say, it doesn't seem to me that Pa respects you or your feelings much." A lump filled his throat as he recognized the truth of his words.

Millie's hands clasped together tightly on the tabletop, trembling beneath Stephen's touch. "Son . . ." Her voice broke. She lifted her face, and tears shimmered in her eyes. "I don't wish to speak ill of your father. He's my husband. I love him and respect him. But . . ." She swallowed, blinking rapidly, and raised her chin. Determination seemed to spread across her face. "If I speak truth and answer you honestly, I might be able to keep you from making the same mistake we—your parents—have. So listen to me carefully, son."

She looked Stephen full in the face and smiled weakly. "You are right, Stephen. Your father does not respect me or my feelings." Her tone gained strength as she continued. "But that isn't his fault. It was his father's way, and it is what he knows. In his mind, he is treating me the way a man should treat his wife. A man is to lead his wife. How he does it is his interpretation of a biblical concept. Your father believes he is right."

Stephen was amazed at the way she explained the difficult subject. "But is he?" he asked.

Ma gave another sad smile. "For me, it is enough that he thinks so, Stephen."

Stephen removed the clove from his mouth and asked softly, "Is it really, Ma?"

Ma's shoulders slumped. "In our early years, I told myself that if I was a good, obedient wife, then John would love and respect me. We've been together now for thirty-six years, and I've come to understand and accept that, in his way, he loves me. We've brought five children into the world, we've supported each other through good times and bad times and all the monotonous, unemotional times in between. Your father has always seen to my physical needs and has provided me with many extras my friends don't have. That counts for something. So yes." She gave a firm nod, her eyes glittering. "For me it has to be enough."

But then she leaned forward, taking Stephen's hand and squeezing it hard between her soft, warm palms. "But, Stephen, it doesn't have to be enough for you. I see a tenderness in you that your brothers lack. I see a . . . a fairness in you. I think you understand that what your father and I have isn't necessarily the only—or best—way. To lead lovingly, you need only to ask, not command."

Stephen thought back to the countless times he had thought Pa was unreasonably hard and domineering with Ma. At those times distress and sympathy for his mother had welled up. "You're right, Ma. Sometimes I have felt Pa doesn't treat you right."

"Well, then, son, listen to your heart. I know when children are small, they think their parents can do no wrong. But parents aren't perfect. You're a grown man, Stephen, and it is time for you to decide the kind of man you want to be. The kind of home you want to have—yes, to lead. You have a choice to make. You can be like your father—and I'm not saying that everything he does is wrong. He has good qualities, too, that I would be proud for you to follow. But if there are things you feel should be different, your other choice is to find another path to follow."

Ma paused. Her hands had been pressed around Stephen's, but now she released them and picked up the folded pink papers bearing Josie's words. Her gaze remained on the letter as she said, "You seem to wonder whether or not you really do love Josie. Do you want to know how to be sure?"

Stephen waited silently, heart pounding. This probably was the most important question he faced.

"When you want her happiness more than you want your own, then I would say you love her."

Stephen saw the wistfulness in his mother's expression, and his throat constricted with the effort to control his emotions.

Ma waited a moment, staring into her cup. "Loving another means respecting that person enough to let them be the kind of person they need to be." She looked up and searched his face. "If you can't do that for Josie, then you shouldn't meet her tomorrow, Stephen. You would be misleading her, and it would not be right or fair. And I think, Stephen, you want to be right and fair."

Stephen nodded. "Yes, Ma, I do." He meant it.

Ma passed Josie's letter across the table into Stephen's hands. "Then, son, I will encourage you to spend some time in prayer and consider what is in your heart. And I'll be praying, too, that you and Josie will both know what's best." She lifted her cup and Stephen's and turned toward the kitchen.

Stephen rose quickly and reached for the teacups. "I've got them, Ma. I'll put them in the kitchen for you." At her startled expression, he smiled. After everything she did for all of them, he could do a small act of kindness for her. "You sit here for a while. I'll join you again in a minute."

When he returned, he paused behind his mother's chair to clamp a hand on her shoulder and squeeze. Millie looked up to meet his gaze, and in that moment Stephen recognized the sorrow in his mother's eyes. No, he didn't want that for Josie. Not Josie. "Thank you, Ma, for what you have said to me today." He slid back into his chair. "Your wisdom and counsel have already helped me, and you've given me much to think about, pray about."

Her tremulous smile spoke volumes.

Swallowing a lump of regret for the mindless way he'd treated his mother in the past, he rose. "I'm going to search out Scripture about marriage." A grin twitched at his lips. "And about being a husband."

"Don't miss First Corinthians 13, Stephen," she said with a solemn nod. "It tells you just about everything you need to know."

As he passed through the hall, his thoughts turned inward, he almost missed seeing his sister standing in the shadows of their parents' bedroom doorway. Tears clung to her thick eyelashes, and instantly Stephen knew Priscilla had heard every one of their mother's heartfelt words.

osie took extra care with her appearance on Saturday. Normally she would have worn a work dress, but not this time. Not when she might be seeing Stephen. Her heart fluttered in anticipation, but she quelled the eager rush. He might not come.

Her royal blue wool dress wasn't showy by any means, but the crisp lace collar and lace-edged cuffs and sweeping skirt were attractive. She pulled the sides of her long hair upward, catching it in tortoise-shell combs and leaving it cascading down her back in a girlish style that suited her.

She took one last look in the mirror. With some surprise, she found her same familiar, freckled reflection peering back. She felt so much more mature since going away to teach. Why didn't it show?

In the kitchen, she shooed her sisters out from underfoot before frying a chicken and making a batch of baking soda biscuits. Holding her skirts, she went into the cellar to fetch a jar each of dill pickles and pickled beets. The food was simple by necessity; she couldn't prepare a fancy dinner and serve it in a barn. To compensate for the homely meal, she carefully packed two china plates, linen napkins, and two place settings of Ma's finest silverware. A jug of cool water and two mugs completed the essentials.

Hands on hips, she surveyed her preparations. With a sigh, she closed her eyes. *Dear Lord, You know my heart and how I care for Stephen. If we're meant to be together, open the door to reconciliation. Whatever happens today, let it be Your will for us.*

Another glance at the unpretentious offerings brought a smile to her face. The picnic items were not as important as what might be settled between Stephen and her.

At a quarter to twelve, Josie tapped on the boys' door upstairs. Teddy stuck his nose out. "Yeah, what'cha want?"

Josie clasped her hands in front of her. "I hoped I could talk you into helping me with something."

"What?"

"Carrying some food and stuff out to the barn."

Teddy's eyes popped wide. "The barn? What for?"

"Never mind what for," she retorted, her smile softening the words. "Will you help me or not?"

"But it's cold out," Teddy protested, "and I was putting a puzzle together."

Josie stifled a sigh. "Teddy, your puzzle will keep, but I need to have everything in the barn before noon. Will you please help me?"

Teddy narrowed his eyes and lifted his chin. "What'cha up to, anyway?"

"If I tell you, will you help me?"

He shrugged, grinning impishly.

"I'm setting up a picnic out there for Stephen and me."

"In the barn?"

Josie's patience waned. *Brothers!* "Yes, in the barn. Where else can we go to get some privacy around here? Teddy, please—"

Teddy threw up his hands. "Oh, all right. Let's go. But I think you're nutty, eating a lunch out in the barn when there's a perfectly good table and chairs right downstairs in the kitchen."

Josie muttered, "With six other people around it." No, the barn might be crude, but it would be quiet. It would have to be the barn.

By ten after twelve, Josie had swept a spot clean in the loft, spread a checked cloth on the planked floor, and carefully laid out her picnic. A fierce wind whistled and rattled the barn shutters, but the warmth of the animals within the solid log construction of the huge building kept it a comfortable temperature. She found she didn't need her gloves, but she left her shawl around her shoulders. All was prepared. Now it was a matter of waiting. And hoping.

She paced back and forth. Would he come? What would he say? In spite of best intentions, would it turn into a fight again, with each spewing angry words back and forth? Oh, she hoped not. She wanted so badly to find the kind, sweet Stephen she'd looked up to since she was a little girl. She prayed he was still somewhere inside of the demanding, stubborn man she'd seen lately.

The creak of iron hinges alerted her, and she dashed to the edge of the loft, peering down through the hole in the floor where the ladder descended. A man was pushing the door closed against the driving wind. He shut it with a muffled thump, then placed a length of wood through two clamps to keep it shut. His back still to her, he pulled the hat from his head and ran a gloved hand through the thick, dark hair. He hadn't turned around yet, but Josie would have known that figure and the wondrous head of hair anywhere.

He'd come! Her heart hammered in her chest so hard she was sure he'd be able to hear it over the whining wind and snoring cows.

He turned then and lifted his face toward hers in the opening of the loft floor. He stood stock still with the hat against his chest. His cheeks were ruddy from the cold, his hair uncombed. To Josie, he looked wonderful. His eyes met hers, and time stood still as the two admired, thrilled, worried—and wondered who would break the silence first.

Stephen did. "Hello."

One simple word, and her heart went winging. Her breath came in nervous little huffs, and she wasn't sure she could talk. So she let her beaming smile offer a welcome.

Stephen moved across the dirt floor, holding his hat by the crown, his uncertain blue eyes still locked on her hopeful brown ones. His pants must have been new and stiff; they made a swishing sound as he walked, along with the slight thud of his heels against the hard ground.

He reached the ladder and tossed the hat aside, then paused, his hands wrapped around the rails, one boot propped on the lowest rung. He looked upward at Josie. Was he holding his breath, too? A smile dimpled his cheek. "If you want me to come up, you'd better shift aside."

She scrambled a few feet away from the opening and watched until his head emerged, then his shoulders, and then he was sitting on the edge and with his legs dangling below. Josie found her voice and said with no small amount of wonder, "You came."

"Uh-huh." He rubbed one hand up and down tan fabric covering his right leg. A nervous gesture.

Josie sought to put him at ease. "Are you hungry?" She moved to the array of food laid out on the cloth. "I fixed chicken and biscuits, and got out some of Ma's pickled beets and sour pickles you like so well." She looked over her shoulder. He remained seated in the loft opening with the same tentative look on his face. "Stephen?"

In slow motion he pulled his legs up and swung them around, rolled onto one hip, then pushed himself to his feet. He crossed the wide planks and knelt beside her, looking over the china plates, the silverware, the baskets of food, and finally turned his gaze to meet hers. "This is all really nice, Josie. You went to a lot of trouble."

She shrugged. "Not so much." She tried a smile. "I wish it was more, but . . ." Her voice drifted off, and she dropped her gaze to the crusty biscuits.

"I don't deserve having a fuss made over me."

She sent him a startled look, taken aback by his penitence.

"After the way I've treated you, I don't know why you did this for me."

She reached out timidly, touching his sleeve with shaking fingers. Softly, honestly, simply, she said, "Because I love you, Stephen."

The words hung as heavily as if proclaimed on a banner. She hadn't planned to say it. She'd meant to keep things light and casual between them. But he'd been there less than five minutes, and she'd said it.

It would have been easy for Stephen to respond, "I love you, too, Josie." She held her breath, waiting and hoping, but although he didn't drop his gaze, those words were not spoken.

Disappointment washed over her. To hide it, she reached for the basket of biscuits. "Let's eat now. I'm sure you need to get back to work soon."

This time Stephen's hand closed over Josie's. With his other hand he reached out and lifted her chin, turning her face toward his. "I don't have to be back soon. I have lots of time, and I'm really not all that hungry. The eating can wait. Please—can we talk?"

"A-about what?"

He turned to face her, drawing up his knees and wrapping his arms around them. Once he was settled, he said, "Tell me about Winston—and the kids in your class, how the teaching is going."

Her eyebrows rose. "Really?" It seemed unlikely that he was really interested, given his past responses. "You'd rather listen to me talk than eat?"

"For now."

The teasing grin on his square face reminded Josie of sweet times from long ago. Her heart thumped hopefully beneath her wool bodice. She answered in a light tone. "Well, all right, but I have to warn you: once I get started, you might not be able to shut me up. I'm awfully fond of the children in my class, and I'm likely to brag for hours."

His dimple showed. "I can take it. Brag away. I want to hear everything."

She twisted around until she sat with her legs folded to one side, her skirt in a circle around her. She flipped her hair back behind her shoulders and dropped her hands, palms up, in her lap. "All right, Stephen. Let me tell you about . . ."

Chapter Twenty-Two

*S*tephen listened carefully as Josie told him about the first few days of loneliness when she only wanted to be home again, then of forming attachments to the smallest children in her care who were as homesick from their daily separation from their mamas as she was from her much longer one. She told him about planning lessons to keep three different grades busy and learning, and how challenging she found the task. She shared funny stories and touching moments, and while she talked, he found himself absorbed by the sincere, almost passionate expression in her face and voice.

He watched her countenance change from smiling and amused to thoughtful and introspective. He listened, and through her descriptions he was able to see and feel what it was like to be in front of a classroom of wiggly but responsive children. And he found himself thinking, *What a wonderful experience she's having. I wouldn't deny her the memories she's forming for anything in the world.*

And with that thought, something else struck him. For once he was thinking of Josie's happiness rather than his own. What had his mother told him? If he wanted someone else's happiness more than his own, then . . . His heart almost stopped, and he was so stunned by the realization that he didn't hear Josie's question.

"Stephen?"

He shook his head, still in shock from the revelation. "What?"

She gave a brief laugh. "I don't think you've heard a word. Did I put you to sleep?"

He stared, his mouth opened slightly in wonder. He loved her! It had taken her leaving him before he could find the truth, but now he knew. He loved her. He made himself answer calmly. "No, I'm not asleep. I just—" He grinned sheepishly. "What were you saying?"

Josie pretended to bluster. "Honestly! You men. Tell a girl to talk, then drift off somewhere into unknown places and don't even listen. I asked if you were ready to eat yet. The biscuits are getting hard."

Stephen couldn't wipe the grin off his face. He stared at her, awestruck. She looked so different to him now. He'd always thought her pretty, but now she seemed to glow with something even better than beauty. Was it the happiness she'd found in her new position or his love for her creating that glow? He couldn't be sure.

"Stephen?" She shook her head in mock impatience. "What on earth is wrong with you?"

He dropped his arms from his knees and turned slightly. He felt as though he'd awakened from a long nap—drowsy and warm and content. He shook his head. "No, I'm not ready to eat."

She stared at him, her brow furrowed, then gave a quick nod. "Oh." She flipped her palms outward. "Well, then—"

"It's my turn to talk, Josie." He waited until her eyes were focused on his. "There are some things I need to say, but first I have to ask. . . . Have I muffed up things between us for good?"

A soft smile crept across her face. "Would I have asked you here today if I thought that?"

He scooted forward until his knees touched hers. He took one of her hands, sandwiching it loosely between his own. Josie sat in silence with her lower lip caught between her teeth, as if half afraid. Her reaction stung, but what else could Stephen expect after the emotional battering he'd delivered? He must settle things once and for all.

"Josie, I owe you an apology." He leaned forward, bringing his face so close to hers he could count the pale freckles dotting her nose. "I've been bullheaded and obnoxious about your wanting to teach. I should have respected your feelings, but instead I only thought of myself." With as much sincerity as he could muster, he added softly, "I'm sorry. Would you forgive me?"

She stared at him, so silent and unmoving it seemed she'd turned to stone. He leaned back slightly, still holding her hand, and sighed. "I suppose it's pointless to explain why I acted the way I did."

Josie came to life. She tipped her head, strands of soft brown hair spilling forward over her shoulder. "Why, no, I don't think it's pointless, Stephen. I'd like to understand why you got so angry."

Stephen bolted to his feet and stalked four paces away before turning and facing her again. "I know this will be hard for you to understand, because I spoke to you as if I was angry. But I wasn't angry, I was . . . I don't know how to put it." He rammed a hand through his hair. "This is so hard."

Josie rose and crossed to him. "What is it, Stephen? What were you feeling?"

He rested his hand gently against her cheek. The feel of her soft skin beneath his rugged palm soothed him. He took in a great breath and admitted, his tone ragged, "I felt abandoned."

Josie didn't flinch. "Abandoned? By me?"

He caressed her cheek briefly and then lowered his hand. "Yes. Teaching was so important to you, you were willing to say no to my marriage proposal and just take off. I felt like I didn't matter that much to you. It hurt, so I reacted in a spiteful way. It was wrong—"

With a slight frown, she said, "Stephen, it wasn't just my desire to teach that made me decline your marriage proposal. There was another, more important reason."

He nodded. "I know, and I'm not blaming you. I should've waited until I was sure of my feelings before I brought up the idea. But I'm twenty-three years old, and my father still treats me like a child. I wanted to get out from under his roof, and I . . . well, I suppose I jumped the gun."

Josie stepped back a pace. "So you saw me as a means of escape?" She ducked her head.

Stephen moved to her side in an instant and took her hand. "No! No, Josie, I didn't propose to you just to get away from my father. That isn't true. Please, Josie, look at me."

He waited until she tipped her head to meet his gaze. "Josie, you are everything I want as a life's mate. You are intelligent. You have a sweet, caring spirit. You're a strong Christian with sound moral values. And to top it off, you were the cutest little tagalong I'd ever seen." A soft rose graced her cheeks, and he reached out to tap the end of her nose. "I want to see your delightful, adorable face across the breakfast table from me for the rest of my life." With a deep sigh, he dropped his teasing then. "When I got your letter, I was so uncertain. I knew that if I came out here, I'd be walking through a door that only went one way."

Josie drew in a breath and held it, her eyes wide.

"I wasn't sure I should come, because I still wasn't sure how I felt about you, in here." He placed a wide, work-roughened palm against his chest. "I wasn't sure, Josie, because I didn't know what it means to love a woman."

Josie's breath whooshed out, her expression dubious. "How can you not—?"

Stephen silenced her with two fingers gently against her lips. "Just listen to me, please? Withhold your questions till I've said my piece." He resorted to pacing—five steps away, five steps back—then took her hands again.

"Josie, in my house, my father is in charge. When he says jump, you don't question the order, you simply obey. That's the way it's been my whole life, and that rule applied to me, my brothers, and to my mother as well. I've not really known a give-and-take relationship between a man and his wife."

He laughed ruefully. "Well, maybe I have: Ma does the 'give' and Pa gets the 'take.'" Sadness washed over him as he admitted, "I'm not sure my father loves my mother, Josie. I know he has the capacity to love—he certainly showers Priscilla with his affection—but I haven't seen him treat my mother in a loving way."

Josie gave his hand an encouraging squeeze. He drew courage from the sweet pressure of her fingers, and he rubbed his thumbs against her knuckles.

"All three of my brothers are already married, and not a one of them is any less demanding with his wife than Pa is with Ma. Matt, Mitch, Stan . . . Every one of them is the boss—the deliverer of orders that better be obeyed. And their wives respond just like Ma. They do what it takes to please their men." He paused, cringing inside at the picture he was painting of his family. "I suppose it sounds as if I'm making excuses, and I don't want it to sound that way, but the reason I couldn't say for sure that I loved you is because I wasn't sure how a man who loves a woman acts."

Very slowly, Josie nodded. "Of course I've observed the favoritism your father has always shown Priscilla, but I hadn't realized the effect it had on the rest of the family. Do you feel as if you've been abandoned, emotionally, by your father?"

Although Stephen had never given the idea much thought, he realized that deep down he had never felt as though he measured up to Pa's expectations. A new awareness made his scalp tingle. He nodded slowly. "Yes, I think that's a good way to put it. Priscilla's always come before everyone else. Ma, my brothers, me . . ." He gulped. "I suppose when you seemed to make teaching such a priority, I thought I was . . . again . . . less important. When you insisted we wait to get married, it said to me you didn't care about my needs." Spoken out loud, it all seemed so petty. Heat filled his face.

But Josie didn't turn away. She smiled and gave his hands a reassuring squeeze. "Stephen, thank you for telling me about this. I know it wasn't easy for you. And I'm sorry, too—for making you feel you didn't matter to me. You do matter, so much so that it nearly tore me apart, making plans to leave with such hostility between us."

Stephen bowed his head. "I didn't like it either, but I didn't know how to set things right." He looked up. "So I talked to Ma. And she helped me understand some things about her relationship with Pa, and—well, some other things, too." He blew out a noisy breath. "I don't want us to be like my parents, Josie. I want you to be more than someone to make me happy. I want to make you happy, too."

Tears swam in her eyes. "You've made me happy by coming and telling me these things, Stephen. And I'm not upset with you anymore."

"Good." Stephen heaved out a sigh. He felt as though a great weight had been lifted. "Now that I've gotten that off my chest, maybe we can eat." He escorted her to the picnic on the floor, but before sitting, he caught hold of Josie's arms. "Josie? I need to know something."

"What?"

"You'll be finishing the year of teaching at Winston, right?"

Josie nodded. "I've made a commitment, so . . . yes, I will."

He stared at the floor for a moment, nodding. "I figured you would." Then he met her gaze, offering a smile. "I'll take you there myself Sunday, but before you go, there's one more thing you need to hear." Cupping her face in his hands, he lowered his head until he could see his own reflection in her irises. Then he said, clearly and fervently, "Josie, I love you."

She gasped and clapped both hands over her heart. Her lips parted in an expression of surprised exultation. "Ohhh . . ." The word was carried on a wavering breath of wonder. "Y-you do? You're sure?"

He nodded.

Grasping his wrists, she peered into his eyes through a veil of tears. "How do you know?"

"I figured it out when you were talking about teaching." Tears stung behind his nose, and he sniffed. "I could see the joy in your eyes and hear it in your voice. Teaching makes you happy, and suddenly I was glad you'd gone and found that happiness. Your happiness was more important than me getting my way. And that's love, isn't it, Josie?"

The tears spilled over and left silvery trails on her cheeks. "Yes, Stephen, that is love."

Stephen ran his hands through her tumbling curls, coiling the strands around his fingers. "My stubborn pride has been getting in the way of your happiness—and mine!—but from now on, things will be different. If I have to wait fifty years to marry you, I'll wait, because there's no other woman on this earth who could take your place in my heart. And if you'll accept me, I'll do my best to always treat you with the respect you deserve and to do everything in my power to make you the happiest woman who ever lived."

"Oh, Stephen." She swished the moisture from her cheeks with shaking hands. "Those words are all I need to make me the happiest woman who ever lived! Oh, I love you, too!"

Stephen opened his arms wide, and Josie stepped into his embrace, wrapping her arms around his torso beneath his jacket and clinging hard.

She wept against his shirt front. "How can I leave you now?"

Stephen shook his head, chuckling. "You mean now that I've told you I'm glad you want to teach, you don't want to go?"

"It doesn't make any sense at all, but . . . yes!"

Stephen laughed. "If you aren't a bundle of contradictions." He set her away and offered her a handkerchief. She used it to good advantage before smiling at him sheepishly. Stephen brushed her cheek with his knuckles. "Josie, you and I both know you have to go to Winston and finish the year. You've made a commitment, you love what you're doing, and you won't be happy with yourself if you quit midstream. You've had this dream for too long to give up on it now. I don't want to stand in your way any longer, so I'll get you back there myself, you hear?"

"Are you sure that's what you want, Stephen?"

He nodded with certainty. "Yes, I'm sure. I've had a long, lonely time of stewing to think about it. It's for the best. But"—he shook a finger at her, offering a mock scowl—"I will bring you home each weekend from now on. No more of these drives with David O'Brien. And you'll spend your free time with me."

She locked her hands behind her back and smiled. "That's fine with me."

"And when this term is done, we'll sit down and talk about whether or not you should continue for another year. It will be our decision—made as a team. Agreed?"

"Agreed."

"And the next time I ask you to marry me—and I will, soon—I will say 'I love you' first and 'marry me' second, so your answer will not be no. Right?"

"Absolutely."

Silence fell while Josie's brown eyes searched Stephen's face, as if seeking peace and contentment. She must have found what she was looking for, because she burst into a smile rivaling the bright ribbon of sunlight coursing through the loft's square window. She tipped her head. "Stephen, if you're done laying down all these new laws for us, will you kiss me, please?"

Stephen did so, gladly. When done, he said, "Now, woman, stop making demands and let me eat."

Chuckling, they seated themselves on the blanket. And it mattered to neither that the biscuits were as hard as sun-baked bricks.

Chapter Twenty-Three

W hat?" David stared at his sister. His hands clamped around the broom's handle so tightly his knuckles turned white. "When?"

Samantha held the tails of her shawl beneath her chin and blinked up at him. "Earlier today."

In a town the size of Mountain Lake, news traveled fast. In fact, he'd once heard Hulda Klaassen brag that she often knew someone's business before the persons concerned knew it themselves. He supposed he shouldn't be surprised to receive word of Stephen and Josie's reconciliation the very day it occurred. But did Samantha have to be so joyful about it? David snorted. "Isn't that just fine and dandy."

Samantha apparently missed his sarcastic tone because she nodded enthusiastically. "As a matter of fact, it is. Josie has said all along she loves Stephen. This change in his attitude is what she's prayed for. Aren't you happy for her?"

David regained control of himself and managed to reply in an even tone. "Well, of course, I want her to be happy. I just— well, I'm just taken by surprise, I suppose." *I wanted a chance to talk to her. I wanted her to know how I felt!*

Samantha smiled. "So am I. I certainly wouldn't have imagined Stephen giving her his blessing to continue teaching after the way he's acted. But his willingness to accept it has put the spring back in Josie's step."

David gave the broom a harder swipe than necessary against the mercantile's porch floor. Samantha jumped back as a cloud of dried leaves danced toward her feet. She stared at him, her eyes wide. "David!" Then she tipped her head, her brows pinched together. "Are you jealous?"

Despite the cold wind against his face, heat flooded his cheeks. "I—I'm . . ."

She touched his arm. "David, she was spoken for long before you came to town."

David bowed his head, not even considering an attempt to deny what Samantha intimated.

"I'm sorry if you thought otherwise." Tenderness glowed in his sister's eyes.

David sighed. "It's okay, Sammy. It was a fool notion anyway. What in the world would a woman like Josie see in a man like me?"

Samantha raised her chin, sparks flying in her eyes. "Now listen here! Nobody is going to insult my brother—not even you." She jerked his sleeve. "There's plenty to see in you, Davey. You're hardworking and kindhearted and one of the best-looking men around."

David made a face, and she glared at him fiercely.

"I won't let you think just because Josie doesn't see you as more than a friend there's something wrong with you. It just means Josie isn't the right one for you." She softened her tone as she added, "Besides Josie's longtime love for Stephen, there's something else you need to realize, David. Although Josie is friendly to everyone, she would not allow herself to consider a non-Christian in a more serious light than friendship."

"I know that," David snapped. "Why do you think I—?" He clamped his jaw shut on any admissions about his reason for church attendance.

Samantha gave him a seeking look which he did his best to ignore. Finally she spoke again. "Davey, I'm sorry if you're hurt, but sometimes when you really care about someone, you have to let them go. This may be one of those cases."

David nodded.

She threw her arms around him in a tight hug. "I need to run my errands and then get home. I'll see you in church tomorrow, won't I?"

He gave her a few halfhearted pats on the shoulder around the broom. "Sure." And at church, maybe he'd take Josie aside for a private chat. Before she committed herself to Stephen, she should at least know how David felt about her.

But when Josie entered the sanctuary of the Mennonite church Sunday morning, David found himself tongue-tied. Her joy was palpable. Her eyes sparkled with an inner joy, and she seemed to float rather than walk across the floor. An inner happiness kept a permanent smile on her lips.

He took his regular spot, and Josie took hers, at the end of the bench on his right. She turned her radiant smile on him. "Good morning, David! Isn't it a beautiful day?"

David had thought it windy, gray, and too cold for comfort, but he refrained from raining on her happiness. He cleared his throat. "You're in high spirits this morning."

Josie giggled—a sound that resembled creek water tripping over stones. "Yes, as a matter of fact, I am. And, David, I owe it to you."

David's eyebrows rose. "Me?"

"Well, yes." She lowered her voice and leaned into the space between them. "Remember that day I was so upset, and you told me everything would work out? You kept my hope alive, and you were right. I kept praying that if Stephen and I were to be together, it would somehow iron itself out. And everything has come together wonderfully. Stephen has professed his love to me and given me his blessing to go on teaching in Winston.

From now on, we're going to discuss together any decisions that affect both of us and work out a compromise. He's made me so happy!"

He couldn't respond because people were pouring in, filling up the aisle, and Josie sat up straight on her bench. In spite of everything Josie had said, David fully intended to catch her after the service for a private chat. But Stephen came up the aisle as soon as the service was over and took her arm. David watched her walk away, smiling up at Stephen with that brilliant glow. She seemed to forget David even existed. He stared after the pair, dejected and forgotten.

Adam and Samantha approached. Samantha tucked herself under David's arm and beamed up at him. "Come with us to Adam's folks'. Mother Klaassen invited us all over for dinner."

"We're having a celebration for Josie and Stephen," Adam added.

David's chest tightened. "I have some leftover chicken and corn muffins in my room that need to be eaten before they spoil."

Adam sent David a speculative look. "Are you sure? Josie will be disappointed."

Josie won't even notice I'm gone if Stephen is there. David held the errant thought inside. "I'm sure. Please give Josie my best, and tell her I'll try to see her soon." Although no one had said so, he knew he wouldn't be driving her to Winston this afternoon.

Adam shrugged. "All right then. I guess we'll talk to you later."

Samantha reached up to hug her brother, whispering in his ear, "Things will work out for you, too, David. Don't be sad."

David returned Samantha's hug a little too firmly. "I'm fine, Sam." He added with forced cheerfulness, "Go enjoy your meal. And eat enough for me, too. Laura's a wonderful cook."

Adam laughed and told David as the three made their way outside, "I'll tell her you said so, and maybe she'll save you a piece of pie."

"Sounds good to me." David jammed his hands into his trouser pockets and headed for the boardinghouse. In his room, he sat on the edge of the bed and nibbled on a dry corn muffin. He glanced around the quiet, unadorned space, absorbed in gloomy thoughts.

This room is no different than my room in Minneapolis—or the ones back in Wisconsin. I'm still alone. I sit alone, I eat alone, I sleep alone. . . . Sammy is here in Mountain Lake, but she has her own family and circle of friends, and I'm always the odd man out. I'm just as lonely as ever.

He put aside the muffin and crossed to the window overlooking the street. The wind waved leafless tree branches and swirled the powdery snow in snakelike patterns along the hard surface of the street. David unbuttoned his shirt and drew it off, tossing it across a chair in the corner. In long johns and pants, he looked outward. Not much to see—no one around. Sunday afternoons were family times. And he didn't fit anywhere.

He pulled the wooden chair next to the window and sat, his stocking feet propped up on the windowsill. He aimed his gaze out the window, unseeing, as self-pitying thoughts continued to roll backward, considering all the ways he'd been dealt a raw deal by life. Fathered by a man who loved liquor more than his children. Mothered by a good woman but who died far too young. Partly raised by a grandmother who went to heaven too soon.

How different his and Samantha's lives would have been if Mama hadn't died in childbirth. If she'd lived, he wouldn't have left home so early, losing his sister in the process. He wouldn't have ended up in Minneapolis, pretending to be someone he wasn't. All those years of loneliness would have been filled if he could have stayed in his childhood home with his parents and sister.

His self-pity changed quickly to recriminations as a stab of guilt pierced through his heart. The choice he'd made his last night at home—the long-ago night when he had sneaked into Sammy's room—overwhelmed him. If he closed his eyes, he could still see the look of complete trust on his sister's face as he promised he'd come back for her. But he'd failed her, believing Pa's lie that she'd run off too. His stupidity and helplessness to forge ahead anyway and find her had cost her years of suffering.

Sammy had forgiven him. But he couldn't forgive himself.

He sat up abruptly, his feet hitting the floor with a resounding thud. His head sank low, his hands clutched his head, his back curled forward as if carrying a burden too heavy to bear. What kind of a person leaves a little girl in a home like that? He knew the answer: a person unworthy of love. Someone like himself. A person who had harbored feelings of hate and resentment for years, who had lied about his own identity for his own selfish ends. A man who was even now misleading the people he supposedly cared about into thinking he was interested in their God by sitting in their church services with them. Yes, he was unworthy of love.

It must be true. Surely if he was worthy of love, he would have it by now. Surely if he was worthy of being loved, Josie would have returned his feelings. He pictured her again as she had looked in church that morning, smiling and happy and glowing. Glowing with love—for someone else.

He hadn't known a heart could actually ache, but his pained him with an intensity he found frightening. He rose slowly, painfully, and stumbled to the bed with its rumpled sheets and leftover muffin crumbs. He dropped across it, burying his head in the pillow. No, he wasn't worthy of Josie's love—he firmly believed that—but he still longed for her presence, her goodness, her gentleness. In his mind, she was the epitome of perfection.

"And too good for you, you fool," he berated himself.

Josie was better off with Stephen, the man she prayed would come to her. It was for the best. She could never be happy with the likes of David O'Brien. David was a grown man, not a child, but he finally gave in to his aching heart and wept.

Chapter Twenty-Four

*D*avid awoke with a dull ache at the back of his head. He groaned and sat up, rubbing itchy eyes. Unfolding his stiff muscles, he stood and padded to the window. The shadows were long now—late afternoon. He must have slept for several hours.

He crossed to the wash basin that sat next to the bed and splashed some water from the pitcher into the washbowl. After scrubbing his face, he lifted his head and encountered his own reflection in the small, square mirror hanging from a nail above the washstand. His face was pale, the freckles standing out like poppies in a field of daisies. He looked just the way he felt— washed out.

Glancing at the small wind-up clock on the bachelor's chest across from the bed, he realized it was nearly time for the evening service at church. Although the idea of listening to a sermon had no appeal, the thought of staying alone in this room the rest of the evening appealed even less. After his soul-wrenching time of loneliness, he needed to be with people. He had time for an all-over wash and a change of clothes, and then he would attend the service.

Evening services were much less formal than morning worship times, David had discovered the few times he'd gone to the second one. There was more singing, less structure, and instead of standing behind the wooden pedestal and delivering a sermon, Reverend Goertzen came down to sit on the organ stool and presented a simple lesson. During the winter months, he had spent Sunday evenings expanding on the character traits of various Bible-era men.

Tonight the minister opened his Bible to the book of Psalms and began to read. "'Why are you in despair, O my soul? And why have you become disturbed within me? . . . O my God, my soul is in despair within me . . . I will say to God my rock, "Why hast Thou forgotten me?"'" He paused, glancing over the congregation. "Do these sound like the words of a happy man?"

David stifled a snort. The words sounded like him.

Reverend Goertzen continued, "These are the words of a man named David."

David? He sat up, intrigued.

"I know we've all heard stories about David," the pastor was saying. "David the shepherd boy, protecting his sheep by killing a lion and a bear with only his hands. David as a boy on the battlefield, winning the battle against the giant Goliath, using only a sling and stones as his weapon."

David listened closely. A child had done such things?

"Even as a youngster, David had a mighty faith in God. And he grew up to do great things for his God." Reverend Goertzen held up a finger, and one eyebrow raised high. "But—he was also human, and he made many mistakes. Those mistakes, and the guilt he experienced as a result of those mistakes, led him to write the words of anguish I just read for you."

David found himself captivated by this namesake in the Bible. Perhaps it was the common name that had caught his attention, perhaps it was the despairing words the man had written, perhaps it was that this man from the Bible was human and made mistakes. Whatever the reason, he leaned forward to hear what would be said next about this other David.

Reverend Goertzen set his Bible on the organ and placed both hands on his knees. "I can't help but acknowledge David as a great man of faith. He firmly believed that God was the power that undergirded his own strength. He knew God's protecting hand kept him from harm. He looked to God before battles, asking for God's wisdom. And the Lord was there." He looked once again out over his audience. David, from his seat in the back of the room, wondered if the preacher was looking for him.

"But David, despite his great faith, also made terrible mistakes. He once murdered a man, so he could take that man's wife. And he engaged in adultery. Many times, he went off on his own selfish excursions, ignoring God's leading. Because, you see, David was human."

David found it interesting that the minister could refer to a man who had performed such atrocities—adultery, murder—as a man of great faith. How could this well-known Bible figure have faith and still do such horrendous things?

"And God, in His great wisdom," Reverend Goertzen said, "recognized David's humanness and therefore could forgive him his transgressions. David was always sorry for his wrongdoings. Oh, he made attempts to hide them from God. Once he even cried out"—he picked up his Bible again—"'Turn Thy gaze away from me, that I might smile again. . . .' I believe David knew he had been wrong and was ashamed to have God seeing his weaknesses. But we can't really hide anything from God, can we? He sees our hearts just as clearly as he saw David's, and He is willing to forgive us just as He was willing to forgive David."

David's brows came together in puzzlement. Could this really be true? God could look on a man's evil heart and still be forgiving?

"You see, it's a matter of faith," the minister went on, almost as if he was answering David's questions. "This man of such contradictions, when all was said and done, had faith. He knew deep down that God was bigger, wiser, and more powerful than King David could ever be. God knew what was best, and David knew that, too. It didn't keep him from going his own way, doing some abhorrent things—that was the human part of him coming through. But because David had faith, his heart ultimately was open to God's guidance, and he was still able to receive God's blessings."

Reverend Goertzen smiled at the people gathered in the small church. "Those same blessings can be ours, even with our imperfections and unworthiness. All it takes is faith—the same faith David had—in a wise and loving God. Our fears and feelings of worthlessness can be set aside, knowing that God cares for us and wants to guide us along the pathways He knows are the best."

David glanced up the aisle at Josie, who sat near her mother. Maybe Josie was being guided down the right pathways with Stephen at her side. Should David stand in the way of what was best for her?

The minister said, "Once we believe, as David did, that God is sovereign—the One who is all powerful, all knowing—then we give Him the reins of our life, the control, and we are then ready to receive the precious gifts He wishes to bestow on us. All it takes is the laying down of our selfish notions, and by faith receiving Him into our lives."

He paused, thumbing through his Bible again. He looked up. "Let me read to you some more of David's words: 'For the Lord God is a sun and shield; the Lord gives grace and glory; no good thing does He withhold from those who walk uprightly. . . . How blessed is the man who trusts in Thee!'"

He closed the Book, laid it in his lap, and smiled once more. "Those are not words of despair. Those are words from a man who had done wrong, but who has not lost his faith. May we learn from David's life."

David could hardly wait for the closing hymn to end. Unmindful of the others in the congregation, David shot up the aisle's pine boards to the minister. He clasped Reverend Goertzen's hand and blurted, "I want to learn more about this David."

The reverend drew back momentarily, as if startled, but he quickly recovered his smile. "Why, certainly. Come with me." He led David to a small bookshelf at the back of the church and removed a leather-bound Bible from the top shelf. He placed it in David's hands. "You can read about David in First and Second Samuel. That will give his background and tell the events of his life. In Psalms, you will find words that David himself wrote, including those I quoted tonight."

Reverend Goertzen put his hand on David's shoulder. "I believe you will learn from David's humanness and his desire to do what was right. And of course if you have questions or if I can be of help to you in any way, please call on me anytime."

David looked down at the Book in his hands, eager to get back to his room and begin reading. "Thank you. I'll do that." Intent on beginning his journey into David's life, he said a quick good-bye to Samantha and Adam and left the church. He lengthened his usually long strides to get him home quickly. He hoped to find how this man David could still be worthy of God's blessings when the man had failed in so many ways.

Without the deliveries to Winston filling the weekends, David had extra time on his hands. He spent Friday evenings with Samantha and Adam and Sunday afternoons reading the Bible Reverend Goertzen had provided. After reading about David, he went on to read about other biblical characters, and he found he could relate to many of them. But after he discovered the Gospels, he found he liked reading about Jesus most.

He engaged Adam in many in-depth discussions that seemed to thrill Samantha as much as they intrigued David. He began to understand that sometimes the all-knowing God allowed difficult things to happen in life that could potentially result in good. With that understanding came a blessed acceptance that, although his thoughts and actions were often far from perfect, he could still find forgiveness and happiness.

The hardest thing, though, was coming to accept that Josie was meant to be only his friend. He truly missed those times spent with her and wondered if someone else would ever be able to fill the empty void left by those treks back and forth to Winston with Josie.

The freezing temperatures of November were keeping her holed up in Winston instead of coming home on weekends. He missed her, even merely seeing her in church, and he was sure Stephen must miss her too. Sometimes he even could sympathize with the man instead of envying him.

Fortunately, the store kept him busy. Hiram and Hulda had established a relationship with him that he found touching, ". . . almost like the son we never had," Hulda told him once. He was fond of them, too, and was glad to be included as part of their family. It made him work all the harder, wanting to please these two who put so much trust in him.

The Tuesday before Thanksgiving celebrations, Priscilla Koehn and her mother came into the mercantile to make some dinner purchases for the coming Thursday. While Millie picked through a basket of yams, Priscilla wandered the dress goods section, idly smoothing her hand across bolts of cloth. Hulda was helping Millie, so David wandered over to offer Priscilla assistance.

He hadn't spoken to the girl in weeks, although their paths had crossed many times. Each time, Priscilla had averted her gaze, and David had not tried to get her attention. It seemed odd, not having her look for occasions to spar with him.

He experienced a prickle of unease as he stopped on the other side of the fabric table. "Miss Koehn, can I help you with anything?"

She turned, her wide-eyed expression containing none her coy and flirting manner he had come to expect. Her lips tipped into a small smile before she shook her head. "Oh, no, I really don't need another dress. I was just looking. I enjoy seeing the new fabrics."

She was cordial—very pleasant, with no undertones—and she had said she didn't need a new dress. *This is* Priscilla? "Well, then . . ." he turned to leave her on her own. "I guess I'll just—"

"David, wait a moment, please." Priscilla scuttled around the table and reached out a hand that didn't quite touch him.

He paused, looking into those blue eyes. "Yes?"

She twisted her fingers through the fringe of her shawl. "I—I never really thanked you. You know, for . . ." She turned her face away.

David nodded his understanding. "It's all right, Miss Koehn. I trust he—I hope you have not been bothered anymore?"

Priscilla shook her head, her wide blue eyes still locked on David's. "No, and I haven't given him any reason to."

Despite himself, David had to smile. She looked like a little kid giving a report on her school grades. He felt almost fatherly as he replied, "Well, I'm glad to hear that."

She dropped her gaze then, still fussing with the fringe on her shawl. After a few minutes of awkward silence, she looked up and asked, "So, do you have plans for Thanksgiving?"

"Thanksgiving?" The abrupt conversational turn caught David off guard. He gathered his thoughts. "Why, yes, thank you. I do. The Klaassens have invited me to join them."

Priscilla nodded and smiled. "Oh, that's nice. I would hate for you to be all alone on Thanksgiving. I think Stephen will be having dinner with our family, then go out to spend the afternoon with Josie. He's looking forward to it. He hasn't seen her in three weeks."

"Yes, well . . ."

"Priscilla? I'm finished," Millie called. "Are you ready to go?"

"Yes, Mother." She gave David a last sweetly shy smile. "Have a happy Thanksgiving, David."

"Yes. You too, Priscilla." He watched her go. *She's a beautiful girl, and today was even enjoyable. So what do you think about that, David O'Brien?*

Chapter Twenty-Five

*P*riscilla's thoughts remained in the store with David during the walk home through the brisk air. Actually, her thoughts had been on him for weeks, ever since he'd rescued her in Jost's barn. The way he'd fought Lucas and then turned around and scolded her still confused her. There were many times her father had jumped to her defense even when her behavior had been questionable, but he had never then accused her of bringing it on herself. She couldn't understand David at all.

He intrigued her. He had never succumbed to her teasing and flirting. She supposed she should find that insulting, but for some reason it gave him a strength of character she found attractive. She discovered that, deep down, she didn't really want to be able to lead him around by the nose; if she could, it would demean him. For once she'd found a man who wouldn't put up with her nonsense. But why did she find that appealing?

She helped Mama put the groceries away before shutting herself in her bedroom. Stretching out on her stomach across the bed, she propped her chin on her hands and let her thoughts drift. Closing her eyes, she could picture David clearly—his tall, slender frame, his unruly hair of autumn shades, his pale blue eyes that watched her warily.

His eyes were always wary, except that time in the barn, after Lucas had left, and she was crying. He had looked at her differently then. She remembered his expression—that odd, unreadable look—before he'd begun to scold. He'd first been comforting her, and he had become stern again. Her heart lifted with hope. Could it be possible that he found her just a little bit attractive?

She swung herself off the bed and crossed to the large mirror in the corner. She gazed at her reflection, trying to see herself as David might see her. She'd been blessed with the best of both parents' features—Mother's high cheekbones, heart-shaped face, and perfectly formed nose, and Papa's full lips and eyes of deep, dark blue. Her almost black hair required little attention, thanks to the natural waves passed on by Papa. Her figure was trim—not skinny, but she was without any unnecessary padding. All in all, she was a pleasing package. And she'd always figured out ways to show it off to good advantage.

How many hours had she spent in front of this mirror, practicing pouty looks and secretive smiles and fluttering, flirtatious gazes meant to capture the attention of any available male? Those hours seemed wasteful now, when what really mattered was what David saw.

And she knew what he saw: a spoiled, selfish brat! He'd made that clear enough when he'd said those very words.

It stung once more, reliving the humiliating way he'd berated her. She threw herself back across her bed with enough force to make the springs twang. It was frustrating and mortifying, but who could blame him? She knew he was right, that she was spoiled and manipulative, and she usually acted without conscience. She'd been that way since she was a very little girl; her earliest memories were of being pampered and petted and told how pretty she was. It hadn't taken much practice to learn to manipulate everyone around her, and she'd always enjoyed it.

Until now. Now, impressing David was much more important than getting her own way. She wanted him to see her differently, but first she had to be different.

She certainly felt different. Ever since the frightening experience with Lucas, she'd been less sure of herself. Just as she'd promised David, she had given up flirting and teasing. When balanced against the possible consequences, it had lost its appeal.

She'd tried very hard to be demure and polite in the mercantile today, and she thought David had noticed. She hoped David had noticed. . . .

Rolling onto her back, she threw her arms above her head and stared at the rose-papered ceiling through the veil of the lace canopy. Somehow, she wanted to win David's heart. But how?

A tap on her door interrupted her thoughts, and she sat up. "Come in."

Stephen stuck his head in. "Sorry to disturb you, Prissy, but Ma needs your help with supper."

She set her thoughts aside and stood up. "I'm coming." Stephen was turning to leave when an idea struck. She ran to the door. "Stephen, just a minute, please."

He stopped. Was her use of "please" the reason he stared at her so thoughtfully?

"What is it, Pris?"

"You're going out to the Klaassens' Thanksgiving afternoon, aren't you?"

"Yes . . . why?"

"May I come along? I haven't seen Josie lately either, and I'd love to find out how she's doing with teaching and everything. Do you think it would be all right?" All right, she was gilding the lily as was her habit, but maybe just this once more . . . ?

Confusion clouded her brother's face. "You've never been overly friendly with Josie before. Why now?"

Priscilla sputtered, "I—I'd like to catch up. If she's going to be my sister-in-law, shouldn't we try to be friends?" She could tell Stephen didn't believe her and was ready to say no. Old habits rose to the fore. "I suppose I should ask Papa instead of you."

Stephen rolled his eyes. "I suppose there's no point in arguing with you. All right, Pris. You can go out with me."

Priscilla smiled. "Thank you, Stephen. And I'll stay out of your way, I promise." A trickle of guilt followed her to the kitchen. She shouldn't have fabricated a reason, and she shouldn't have used her father as leverage against Stephen. But this was the last time, she told herself. It was necessary, this time. Once she'd won David over, she'd never do it again.

~⁓~

David sat in the midst of the sixteen people crowding around the kitchen table. Two high chairs side by side at the foot of the table held Liz's twins, who added more than their share to the lively conversations.

"Mama?" Sarah's voice carried over the din.

Laura leaned forward to locate Sarah sitting at the other end of the table. "Yes, sweetheart?"

"When we're all done, can we go skating on the pond?" Sarah's bright face looked hopeful. David had helped celebrate her ninth birthday a week ago, and his present was her first pair of ice skates. Hiram had given David a nice discount from the mercantile stock. Sarah's eagerness to try them out sent a little shiver of pleasure through him.

The girl continued, "Frank says it's frozen solid. Can we go?"

Laura turned to Frank. "You've been out to the pond, Frank, and it's frozen?"

Frank swallowed his last bite of mince pie and nodded. "Anna and I have been out there twice already."

Arn joked, "You've had Anna on ice skates? How does she keep her balance with her belly sticking out in front?"

Laura laughed with the rest but made an attempt at admonishing her brash son, while Anna threw her napkin at the teenager. "Now you hush! I can still see my feet."

More chuckles, then Laura looked to Si for his approval before turning back to Sarah. "All right, if your older brothers go with you, you may go ice skating. But—" with a gesture she stopped Sarah from jumping up and running off immediately—"first we need to get this mess cleaned up. You can help with that."

Sarah made a face, but at her father's warning look stood up and began clearing dishes. Becky, Josie, Samantha, Liz, and Anna joined in while the men rose and headed off in various directions—some to the barn, others to the parlor. David chose to stay at the table and sip another cup of coffee, content to be in the warm kitchen listening to the women's cheerful chatter along with rumbling snores from well-fed males in the parlor.

In short order, the table was cleared, the few leftovers were stored in the icebox, and the dishes were washed and put away. The minute the last plate was on the shelf, Sarah ran over to her mother. "Now can we go? Please?"

Laura laughingly hugged her daughter. "Yes, little monkey, you may go now. Wait for Frank and Adam. . . ."

Sarah clattered up the stairs with Becky close on her heels before Laura could finish her sentence. Laura looked at David. "Would you wake Frank and tell him Sarah is ready?"

In the end, half the Klaassens plus David went out to the pond. David and Samantha were the only ones without their own skates, but Josie had decided to stay at the house and watch for Stephen, so she lent hers to Samantha. Frank offered David the use of his skates, but David shook his head.

"I've never ice skated, Frank, and I reckon I'd just end up freezing my backside."

Frank smirked and looked David up and down. "Well, maybe you're wise. They say the bigger they are, the harder they fall. You'd probably crack the ice." They all chuckled, including David, and trudged onward through the snow. Sarah prodded them forward with impatient calls.

"The ice will keep, Sarah!" Adam told her, his arm around Samantha to help her through the drifts. He looked down at his wife. "Are you excited? This will be your first time on the ice too."

Samantha sent a dubious look his way. "I don't know, Adam. If I fall, I won't crack the ice, will I?"

Adam and Frank both laughed hard. "You?" Frank smirked. "A little pipsqueak like you wouldn't even make a dent! But now, Anna here . . ." He let his words drop away as he patted Anna's rounded coat front.

Anna rose to the bait, scooping up a handful of snow and trying to push it down in Frank's collar. They tussled briefly, both of them laughing, before Frank came up with a mock apology and gave his wife a kiss.

At the edge of the pond, they found places in the snow to sit and attach the metal skate runners to the bottoms of their boots. When they all were ready, Frank warned everyone, "Now stay along the edges. I'm pretty sure the middle is not solid enough yet to hold us up."

Adam helped a shaky Samantha to her feet, and she bit down on her lower lip as her ankles turned wobbly on her. Adam assured her, "We've all skated out here every winter for years, honey. Just do like Frank says and stay along the edge. We'll be fine." He kept a firm grip on Samantha's hand as they ventured onto the ice.

David, the only one without skates, cleared snow from a spot on the bank and sat down to watch. He chuckled to himself, observing Sarah's unsteady shuffling in between frequent falls. Teddy and Arn weren't all that graceful, but they managed to stay upright. Tomboy Becky proved surprisingly agile, and Frank and Anna glided along together with practiced ease despite Anna's additional bulk. Samantha didn't do badly, either, holding on to Adam's elbow with two hands and sliding her feet one at a time. David smiled at her as she sailed by his perch, and she tried a little wave and almost lost her balance.

Sarah landed hard on her backside for the umpteenth time. "Ouch!" She slammed a small mitten-covered fist on the ice. "Oh, this makes me so mad!"

Arn skated over and offered a hand. "Come on, Sarah, I'll help you."

Sarah pushed him away. "No! I want to skate by myself!"

Arn backed away, palms raised. "All right then, Miss I-Can-Do-It-Myself."

He skated off as Sarah struggled to her feet, her mouth set in a determined line. She kept her eyes on the tips of her toes as she started out again, elbows high and rear poking out behind her. David propped his elbows on his knees and observed her fledgling efforts with amusement.

But suddenly concern gripped him—she was almost to the center of the pond! He leaped up and waved his arms. "Sarah! Come back this way!"

Sarah paused and looked toward David, fear blooming across her face. She stood stock still, looking around, clearly uncertain what to do.

David considered hollering for Adam or Frank, but they'd skated to the other side of the pond, unaware of Sarah's predicament. He'd waste time waiting for them to return. So he headed onto the ice, moving gingerly. "Hang on, Sarah. I'm coming. Just hold still."

Teddy and Arn skated up and halted near David. Arn said, "David, you're heavier'n me. Let me go."

David held up his hand. "No, you go for help. I'll get her, don't worry."

Arn shot away, calling over his shoulder, "I'm going after Frank and Adam. Teddy, you stay here." And he zinged off.

Teddy hunkered down on his heels to watch as David slid one foot and then the other across the ice. Sarah had obediently remained still but reached her arms for David as he approached. It seemed to take years to reach her, his feet slipping precariously. But at last he took hold of Sarah's hand and gave her a reassuring grin.

"There." He pulled her toward him. "Nothing to it."

The pair turned, Sarah's hand clasped tightly within David's, when a strange noise—a roll like thunder—seemed to come from beneath their feet.

"David!" Sarah's scream combined with the frightening sound of cracking ice.

David reacted instinctively, putting his hands around Sarah's waist and giving her a mighty push. Her arms waving wildly, she went sailing across the ice a good twenty feet before losing her balance and landing face first, spread-eagle. She skidded another four feet before twisting to a stop. Teddy skated to her, grabbed her hand, and pulled her, still on her belly and crying, to safety.

Chapter Twenty-Six

*P*riscilla was laughing and chatting with Stephen and Josie as they walked to the pond to see how the skaters were doing. After trailing Stephen into the house, she'd seen the look of surprise on Josie's face, but within a few minutes Josie was her happy, relaxed self and acting as if Priscilla had visited dozens of times. Priscilla discovered she enjoyed visiting with Josie and berated herself for her prior ill-treatment of Stephen's girl. She hoped they'd be able to become real friends.

When the little group topped the hill, Stephen pointed. "What's David doing out there? That's not safe."

Priscilla's mittened hands went to her mouth, and fear shot through her whole body.

"Come on, hurry," Stephen ordered. He grabbed both women's arms, and the trio took off, awkwardly running and slipping down the hill. They were almost there when they saw the ice beneath David's feet open up.

Priscilla's shrill scream echoed over the ice as she watched David scramble for some kind of handhold along the edge of the hole, his face filled with terror. The ice gave another loud crack! . . . and he disappeared.

Priscilla stood, frozen, a few yards from the edge of the pond while activity exploded on the bank. The ones in skates were at the spot where Sarah and Teddy were huddled together, crying. They all tore off their skates while Stephen snatched up a dead tree branch from beside the pond and rushed onto the ice, skidding toward the spot where David had disappeared. Samantha, terror etched on her face, started to follow, but Adam held her back. "Sam! No! Stay here—we'll get him. I promise."

Anna caught hold of Samantha, holding her back with both arms, and Adam and Frank inched their way over the ice. Stephen stretched out on his belly and thrust the branch into the hole. He called over his shoulder, "Careful! Down! Too much weight on the ice!"

Adam and Frank dropped to crawl the last few feet.

Stephen swept the branch back and forth, his face crunched in concentration.

Adam yelled, "Can you find him?"

Stephen's excited shout echoed across the pond. "Yes, I think so! I've grabbed something, and I think it's his coat. But I can't pull him up—help me!"

Priscilla's heart leaped with hope. She found the ability to move, and she bustled to Samantha, pulling her snug in a helpless effort to shield her from the awful sight. Josie and Anna stood in a huddle with Arn, Becky, Teddy, and Sarah.

Sarah cried, "It's my fault! I'm so sorry—it's my fault!" Priscilla wished someone could comfort the distraught child. To her great relief, Josie knelt and put her arms around her little sister.

Frank slid on his belly to one side of the hole with Stephen on the other. They both reached into the water, their bodies shuddering in response to the frigid water and fear. Priscilla trembled from head to toe as she held tight to Samantha, who sobbed within the circle of Priscilla's restraining arms. Priscilla resisted watching the drama out on the pond, but she seemed unable to tear her frantic gaze away.

Then Stephen gave a triumphant yell. "Got 'im! Help me pull, Frank!"

The men pulled together at the fragile edges of the hole, and first David's arms and head, then his shoulders, emerged. He lay face down on the ice, with most of him still dangling through the hole. Drenched and limp, he might have been a large, discarded doll. Priscilla bit down on her lip, withholding a cry of alarm as his body seemed to slide back toward the opening.

"I'm going to lose my grip on him." Desperation tinged Frank's tone. "Adam, help us!"

Samantha pulled away from Priscilla's grasp, her fist pressed to her mouth. She moaned, "Oh, please, please don't let him drown . . . or any of them out there." Priscilla wrapped her arms around the frightened woman once more, finding a small measure of comfort in her attempt to soothe Samantha.

Adam inched forward on his stomach. Minutes dragged like hours until Adam took a grip on the back of David's coat. With three of them tugging, they finally managed to drag David from the water and onto the ice.

Once David was clear of the jagged hole, Samantha squirmed to get away, but Priscilla held tight. "No! We can't have any more weight on the ice. You've got to stay here!"

"But I—"

"The danger isn't over yet," Anna barked, her tone severe. "Don't get in the way, Samantha. Do you hear me? They could all go in!"

Samantha collapsed in Priscilla's arms, wailing, "Oh, God, please let them be safe! Don't let them drown. And please, please, help David—"

Priscilla held tight to David's sister, willing Samantha's words to find their way to heaven and be honored.

Still on their stomachs, Adam, Frank, and Stephen snaked backward, pulling David's unresponsive body with them. Snaps and crackles accompanied the men, giving every moment an increasing sense of urgency.

Finally the rescuers reached the edge, and they struggled to their feet and pulled David to safety while everyone else gathered around. Adam immediately began stripping the water-soaked coat from David's inert frame. Samantha hung over his shoulder. "What are you doing? Why are you taking his clothes off?"

"We've got to try to warm him up, Sammy," Adam said through clenched teeth.

Frank had already yanked off his own coat. He and Stephen wrapped it snugly around David while Adam used his own coat to dry David's face and hair.

Samantha leaned forward to touch her brother's chalky face. "Davey?" The tall man gave no response—not even a flicker of his eyelids. "Davey, please be all right." Her broken plea caught at Priscilla's heart, and she hugged herself as a deep fear chilled her from the inside out.

"We've got to get him back to the house." Adam turned to Arn. "Run on ahead and have Pa go for Dr. Newton. Tell Ma to get a bed ready and some hot water going. Hurry!"

Arn scuttled off through the snow.

"Do you think you can carry him?" Anna asked.

"We have to." Stephen took a firm hold on David's legs, and Adam and Frank each grabbed an arm, with Adam sliding a hand beneath David's neck to support his head. "Ready?" Stephen asked. The others nodded, and he said, "All right—lift!" They struggled to their feet.

"Girls, you're going to have to lead," Adam panted. "Break us a wider path. We can't carry him and get through the snow too."

Josie directed, "Anna, not you in your condition. You follow behind with Sarah and Teddy. The rest of us can do it. Come on, four abreast—and quickly!"

Priscilla hurried to Josie's side, joined by Samantha and Becky. They linked arms and began stamping a wide path in the snow for the men to follow. Priscilla risked a glance over her shoulder and caught sight of David's white face bobbing up and down with each uneven, staggering step. A sob rose in her throat as she looked at his blue lips and motionless form. Surely they were too late. It didn't appear as if there was any life left in him.

Chapter Twenty-Seven

A solemn group waited in the parlor for the doctor to come down and give them news. Priscilla sat in the corner, away from the others, chewing her thumbnail in nervous anticipation. With no downstairs bedrooms, David had been placed into Si and Laura Klaassen's bed after an arduous trek up the stairs. Laura and Samantha stripped him of his wet clothing, rubbed him down with towels, and dressed him in some of Si's warm, woolen long johns and a nightshirt. They'd then bundled him under several layers of sheets and quilts.

Samantha tearfully told the rest of the family that all the time they worked with him, David never opened his eyes or made a sound. "But he was breathing, even though it was awfully shallow," Samantha finished.

Adam took his wife's hand. "Then we have hope." And Samantha nodded before slipping into his embrace.

Arn stood staring out the window. He released a sudden huff. "This is all my fault. I knew he was too heavy to go out there, but I didn't stop him."

Sarah, cuddled on her father's lap, argued in a tear-choked voice, "But if I had let you help me skate, I never would've ended up in the middle, and nobody would've had to come after me. It's my fault, Arn, not yours."

Frank added, "I feel to blame. I was off laughing and having fun. I should have stuck close to keep an eye on Sarah. If anyone is to blame, it's me."

Samantha lifted her head from Adam's shoulder and frowned at everyone. "It's nobody's fault. It just happened, and blaming yourselves isn't going to help anything. David wouldn't want us down here faultfinding and feeling sorry for ourselves."

Priscilla blinked in amazement as various family members tried to take responsibility for David's accident. After years of pointing her finger of blame at others, she found their selflessness admirable, and she experienced a prick of conscience at her past self-serving behavior.

Adam hugged Samantha close again, resting his cheek against her tousled hair. "Sammy's right. It's a waste of energy to try to decide who's to blame here. I think we'd be better off using our time to pray for David."

Priscilla jolted, a wave of recognition washing over her. Her heart had risen into her throat the moment she'd seen David fall below the surface of the ice, and it was still lodged there, pumping hard enough to hinder her breathing. But in all the time of worry and fear, not once had she thought about praying. For the first time in her life, she wanted to pray, but she didn't know how. The realization frightened her.

Hiram charged into the parlor and announced, "Dr. Newton is coming down."

Samantha and Adam rushed to the stairway, followed closely by everyone else. Priscilla joined the throng near the center, held in place with the crush of expectant bodies. The small, wiry doctor came down, with Hulda making her plodding progress right behind him. His feet had barely reached the bottom step before Samantha addressed him.

"Dr. Newton, is my brother going to be all right?"

The doctor placed a hand on Samantha's shoulder. His eyes behind the spectacles glowed with compassion. "Samantha, come here. Let's sit down." He held his hand toward the table, but Samantha shook her head.

"I can't sit there right now." She turned her glittering gaze on Adam. "We gathered there just a few hours ago—a lifetime ago—laughing and talking and enjoying Thanksgiving dinner together. . . ." Her voice broke. "I—I can't sit there."

Adam nodded, his arm pulling her tight to his side. "It's all right. Doc, just tell us, please."

Priscilla held her breath, begging for good news. Samantha had lost so much; it hardly seemed fair she might lose her only brother, too.

The doctor sank down in the nearest chair and removed his spectacles. Then he gave Samantha a serious look. "I'm not going to lie to you. David is in a very serious state."

A collective gasp traveled through the little group.

"He was in the water, without oxygen, for quite a while from what I've been able to piece together from everyone here. There's no doubt he took water into his lungs as well. His body temperature is below normal, and he's having a hard time breathing. The lack of oxygen could result in brain damage."

"B-brain damage?" Samantha clutched at Adam, and his hand patted her back. She asked the question quivering on Priscilla's lips: "When will we know?"

"Not until he wakes up." The doctor took in a big breath. "Right now we need to keep him warm, make sure we give him lots of liquids, and as a safeguard I'm going to set up a mist tent and keep steam going for him to inhale. It will help clear his lungs and aid his breathing. I wish there was more, but . . ." He broke off to rub the bridge of his nose. He returned his glasses to his face, looked at Samantha again, and said kindly, "We'll just have to wait and see. If we can see him safely through the next forty-eight hours, then I think there's a good chance for full recovery."

Samantha nodded woodenly. She turned to Adam. "I'll stay here and help care for him."

"Of course, sweetheart. I wouldn't ask you to leave as long as your brother needs you."

Samantha spoke to the doctor. "May I go up to him now?"

"Can we all go?" Josie added. Priscilla strained forward, eager to see David for herself.

Dr. Newton nodded but held out a restraining hand. "Only if you promise not to cause a commotion. You can all take a peek at him—assure yourselves that he's safe now—but then you've got to clear out. And another thing . . ." He placed his hand on Samantha's arm, delaying her passage. "He might seem to be asleep right now, but I'm convinced he can still hear you. No crying or saying anything negative up there!" His gaze swept over everyone assembled in the room. "There may be no scientific basis to it, but I still believe positive thoughts and comments bring about positive change. So remember that when you go into his room."

Samantha promised, "I'll be positive. I have to be. I can't bear the thought that I might lose him."

She hurried upstairs with Adam close behind her. Priscilla moved along with the throng, and when she got a look at David lying still and white beneath the pile of covers—his breath coming in rattling gasps—she forgot Dr. Newton's command to be positive. Tears sprang into her eyes, and a low moan crept from between her lips. She pressed her fist to her mouth to hold back any other sound as Samantha turned and flung herself against Adam's chest, clinging and crying soundlessly.

Adam rubbed his hands up and down across her shaking back. "Shh, now, Sammy. Remember what Doc said?"

"I kn-know, Adam, but he—he looks—"

Don't say it! Priscilla's thoughts commanded.

Adam whispered firmly, "None of that, Sammy. He's alive, and we're going to do everything in our power to keep him that way."

Samantha gained control, taking in a deep shuddering breath that halted her tears. Priscilla determined to be just as brave. She sniffed hard, blinking rapidly to clear her vision, and watched Samantha make her way to the bed. She sat gingerly on the edge of the mattress and stroked David's wild hair. "David, I'm here. And I'm going to stay here until you're all better."

Priscilla thought her heart might break as she listened to Samantha speak to her brother.

"You were so brave, going after Sarah. I'm so proud of you. You were thinking of her then, and she's fine because of it. Now it's time to think of yourself. We're all fighting for you, Davey, so you fight, too. Try really hard to get well. B-because if you d-don't, I—I—" Her shoulder convulsed.

Adam gripped her upper arms and lifted her from the bed. "Come on, Sammy. Let Ma see to David for now, and you rest. You can come in later and spell her, okay?" He bobbed his head at the others, and as a group they shuffled out the door. Priscilla held to the doorknob, waiting until everyone passed.

Adam led Samantha out the door, and Laura Klaassen approached Priscilla. She offered a tender look. "Go on with the others, Priscilla. I'll take good care of David." With a gentle nudge, she urged Priscilla out the door.

Priscilla tipped sideways as the door slipped closed, receiving one final peek of David's colorless face. She feared the image would be imbedded in her memory forever.

*It's cold—so cold! And dark . . . God—oh, God, I can't breathe...
Sarah? Is she...? Where is she?*

"Sarah! Sarah!" His own voice rasped in his ears, and a
rustling penetrated David's fuzzy brain. Someone caught his
hand and pressed a kiss to its back. "It's all right, David." The
soothing voice—his sister's voice—seemed to come from far
away. "Sarah's fine. You saved her. Rest now." He could hear the
words, but they didn't make sense.

David flailed beneath the covers, yanking his hand free to
clutch fitfully at the edge of the quilt. The voice continued to
murmur, a hand touched his hair, his cheek, while he thrashed,
frantically trying to fight his way through the darkness.

Exhaustion claimed him, and he ended his fight. With a
rough expulsion of breath, he collapsed against the bed and
submitted to the welcoming blackness once more.

◦◦◦

Samantha allowed Hulda and Laura to talk her away from
David's bedside occasionally, with the caution that she wouldn't
be able to care for him at all if she totally exhausted herself. The
three took turns sponging him down with cool water to combat
the fever—his body temperature had risen during the first night
and then refused to go back down—spooning clear broth and
water into his slack mouth, applying soothing glycerin to his
chapped lips, filling the kettle to keep a steady stream of steam
clouding the room. . . . It was an enormous effort for all three
of them, but especially for Samantha for whom the mental and
emotional stress was far more draining than the physical.

The critical forty-eight hours had passed three days ago,
and David was still with them. Except for the one time he had
called out in his sleep, though, he hadn't spoken or opened his

eyes at all. His lack of response was especially disheartening to Samantha, who sat beside his bed and whispered encouragement for him to open his eyes until her throat was hoarse.

Dr. Newton checked in twice a day, monitoring David's temperature and listening to his chest. David had contracted pneumonia, Doc determined the second afternoon, and he added application of mustard poultices to the list of necessary duties.

After the sixth day, the doctor took Samantha downstairs and sat her in a rocking chair. He pulled a kitchen stool close and told her she needed to get a day or two of rest at home.

"But I can't leave him!" Samantha exclaimed tearfully.

"Yes, my dear, you can, and you must. Your brother is in very good hands here, and you will not be able to participate in his care if you are sick yourself." He patted her on the shoulder, picked up his hat and coat, and turned to her before stepping out the door. "Doctor's orders," he said with a little smile. But the finger he shook at her delivered a strong message.

Laura stepped into the kitchen and sat on the kitchen stool. She cupped Samantha's cheek with her hand. "*Liebchen*, I heard what Dr. Newton told you. And I agree. I promise you Hulda and I won't leave David for even a minute."

Samantha put her face into her hands as fresh tears welled. How could a body manufacture so many tears? "B-but what if—what if he slips away," she finally gasped out, "and—and I'm not here to say good-bye?"

Laura embraced Samantha and scolded gently, "What kind of thoughts are those? You can't sit by his side waiting for him to die."

Samantha pulled back, sniffing hard. "I can't help it. He looks so—so deathly white. And he's so still."

"He's gaining strength." Laura spoke with certainty. "This is the body's way of healing after the kind of trauma David has faced. And now you must rest too. Please, Samantha. Go home for a little while. Get some sleep in your own bed, see Adam, and then you can come back. Take a little time for yourself. We'll take good care of David. I promise."

Samantha looked into her mother-in-law's face. At last weariness won out, and she dropped her head. "All right, I'll go. But if anything—anything—changes, send Arn or Papa Klaassen for me right away, please?"

"Of course," Laura promised.

"I'm going upstairs once more just—just to tell him where I'm going, that I'll be back. . . ."

"Yes, that's fine, Samantha. I'll have Si take you home."

When Samantha returned to the kitchen, ready to go home after nearly a week away, she was surprised to find Millie and Priscilla Koehn sitting at the table.

Chapter Twenty-Eight

*P*riscilla sat primly at Mama's right with her hands crossed on the tabletop and her shoulders set in a determined angle. She'd see David today if she had to fight for the opportunity.

Laura Klaassen placed mugs of steaming coffee on the table as Samantha stepped into the room. Samantha sent a puzzled look at Priscilla and her mother. "What brings you two out in this cold weather?"

Mama sighed, sniffling. "Priscilla brings me out. She said she simply had to see how David was doing and wouldn't take no for an answer. So here we are."

Laura smiled, as relaxed as if Priscilla and Mama visited every day. "It's sweet of you to be concerned. David is still sleeping. He roused once the second night, apparently having a dream, but he drifted back off again. We continue to give him liquids, keep a mustard poultice on his chest, and the steam kettle going. . . . Other than waiting, there's not much more we can do. Isn't that right, Samantha?"

Samantha sat sideways on the kitchen bench, resting an elbow on the table to prop up her chin. Priscilla reached across to pat Samantha's arm. "How are you holding up?" Samantha's brows furrowed, and Priscilla sat still and unwavering beneath the other woman's perusal. Finally Samantha sighed. "As well as can be expected, I suppose. The waiting is just so hard. . . ."

Honest sympathy welled in Priscilla's chest. "You look as if you need a rest."

"Yes, she does," Laura put in, "and Samantha has just agreed to take one. Hulda and I will be watching David so Samantha can go home and get some sleep."

Priscilla sat up straight. "Mrs. Klaassen, may I help, too?" The women stared at her, open-mouthed. Heat flooded Priscilla's face at their obvious shock. She ducked her head, shamed. She deserved such a reaction. "I know what you're all thinking, and I don't blame you. But I—I care for David too, and I want to help. Really, I do."

Her mother leaned close. "It isn't easy, nursing. Are you sure you know what you're asking, Priscilla?"

"Probably not, Mama." Priscilla's straightforward answer earned another round of wide eyes. "But I want to try, anyway." She turned to Samantha. "Please, I can understand why you might not even want me to help; I've been awful to you and to David. But—" Her eyes welled with tears. "But I feel if I don't do something to help him, I might die. I hurt in here." She placed a shaky hand against the bodice of her dress. "I need to help."

Samantha looked at Laura, who looked at Mama, who gawked at Priscilla as if seeing her for the first time. Priscilla waited silently for Samantha to make up her mind.

At last Samantha sighed. "It's all right with me if Mother Klaassen doesn't mind showing you what to do. I must be on my way home before I change my mind."

Mama rose. "I brought our sleigh, so I'll take you home myself, Samantha. Prissy, I'll send Stephen or your father out for you later."

"Thank you, Mama." Priscilla stretched both hands toward Samantha. "Rest well." Samantha nodded, bundled herself in her coat, and followed Mama out the door.

Upstairs, Priscilla listened attentively as Laura explained how to keep the steam billowing, how often to change the poultices, and the best way to prop David's head to keep him from choking when spooning liquids into his uncooperative mouth.

The woman touched Priscilla's arm. "Are you sure you want to do this?"

Although her stomach rolled with apprehension, Priscilla nodded. "I am very sure, Mrs. Klaassen."

"All right, then. I'll be downstairs fixing supper if you need anything."

"Thank you, ma'am." Priscilla removed a cloth from the pan of water next to David's bed and wrung it out, then gently draped the cool cloth across David's forehead. She listened until Mrs. Klaassen's footsteps faded down the stairs then she scurried to the door. Peeking right and left, she ascertained no one was near enough to overhear. On tiptoe, she returned to the bed and sat on its edge, placing her hand lightly on David's chest.

"David?" She watched his face for any reaction. "David, it's me, Priscilla. I know you didn't expect me, but I'm here just the same. I had to come. There are things you have to know. So I want you to listen to me, please."

Leaning forward, she spoke directly into his ear. "I've been a rotten, loathsome person my whole life. You called me spoiled and selfish, and you were right. I've always treated everyone around me badly, and I never cared if I hurt someone. All I cared about was getting my own way. When you came along, and you wouldn't pay any attention to me, it made me mad, and at first all I wanted was to get even with you. But then that changed.

"I went off with Lucas that night just to get your attention. Did you know that? You probably did; you're the only person who ever truly saw through my games. You defended me, then got irritated with me, and I wasn't sure if I should be mad or thankful that you'd come."

Her breath stirred the curls near his ear. She smoothed the hair with her fingers as she continued. "But I've had time to think about it, and, David, I'm thankful for it. I needed someone to wake me up and make me see that the way I was behaving was all wrong."

She sat up straight, tossing her head. "Oh, you've infuriated me with your smugness. But at the same time, I've admired the way you've never given in to me. And maybe you've not given up on me either."

She wasn't sure now if she was talking to David or to herself, but she went on. "I know it sounds funny, but I needed someone to make me be good. And you're the only one who's been able to do that. I hope it's because you cared about me, that you scolded me and told me that I needed to grow up. Because I care about you, David."

Tears clouded her vision, and her throat felt so tight it was hard to speak, but she leaned down again. "David, can you hear me?" Her lips encountered his soft curls. "I'm telling you I love you. I love you! For the first time in my life, I'm thinking about someone other than myself, and it's because of you." She pressed both palms against his chest, feeling the thready beat-beat of his heart. "David, you have to wake up and hear me. You have to know that I love you. I can't go on if you don't know. Even if you don't love me back, I still have to let you know how I feel. David? David!"

She stared at him, waiting for some sort of reaction—a flicker of an eyelid, a twitch of a finger, anything.

Nothing.

Priscilla lifted her face to the ceiling and spoke in a tear-filled voice. "God, are You listening? Do You hear me? I'm praying to You now. I know I've never talked to You before, and I probably shouldn't expect You to listen to me now, but I'm not asking for anything for myself." A choked chuckle escaped. "That sounds very strange coming from me, doesn't it? But it's true." Closing her eyes, she pleaded, "God, heal David. He's such a good person, and his sister loves him so much. What would Samantha do without him? What would I do without him . . . ?"

She paused, lowering her gaze to take in David's relaxed face, white as the pillowcase beneath his head. Her head drooped low as she continued to pray. "God, I know we're not supposed to bargain with You. I have been hearing those sermons all my life. And I hope You won't hold this against me, but I have to offer You something. If You let David live—if You answer this prayer—I'll be Yours from now on. I know I'm not much right now, but I can be good. I really can! And I will be, for You, if You'll please just heal David. It doesn't matter if he never loves me back. I don't want him well for me, I just want him well. Please, God, please . . ."

In time Priscilla opened her eyes. David slept on. She checked the poultice. It was cool. She lifted it and moved quietly across the room to a basket which she then scooped up to take downstairs. She paused by the door, peering back at him, her heart aching with the desire to see him sit up and smile or scold or even tell her to get out of there.

"I'll be right back, David." In a whisper, she added, "I love you."

Fog everywhere. Thick, white, choking clouds. *Where am I? I can't see. . . . A voice out there somewhere . . . What? What did you say? Oh, you love me. . . . You love me? Who loves me? Who's there? Come where I can see you.*

The man strained beneath the weight of bedclothes. He tried to lift his head. It was so frustrating, the pressing weight.

If he could get out from beneath this heaviness, maybe he could escape the cloying fog.

The voice came again: "Can you hear me?"

Yes, I hear you. . . . But who are you? You are saying you love me. . . . Who? Who?

Suddenly an image of a little girl broke through the clouds, rushing at him. Her hands were held in a gesture of entreaty, her face wore an expression of pain, and he could tell she'd been crying.

Sammy, Sammy, baby, it's all right. I'm here, Sammy. Don't cry. The image faded, sliding backward. . . . *Sammy, where are you going? Wait, Sammy. Wait, come back!*

But she was gone, lost in the swirling mists. Someone else was there now—a man with a leering grin and foul breath. His face loomed, pulled back, then loomed again. He raised a fist and shook it, threatening. . . .

Pa? Is that you? What are you doing here? The man reached out a stubby hand and laughed raucously. "Comin' with me, boy?" *No, Pa, leave me alone! Where did Sammy go? I want to be with Sammy. . . .*

The clouds swallowed the man then changed from white to gray, spinning angrily like a wild, errant whirlwind. He had to get away. He jerked his hands, fighting the grayness that threatened to surround him.

Someone—anyone—help me, please! I don't want to be here all alone. I'm afraid. I know someone is there. Who is it? Sammy, is it you? Reach for me, Sammy. Please, help me out of here.

A voice came as if from a far distance, echoing and resounding, and he couldn't understand the words, only the tone. It was a sad voice, pleading—no, not pleading, it was praying. Praying for him. His heart beat in sudden hope.

Yes, pray for me. Call upon God. He can bring me out of here. God has the strength to push away these clouds and help me find the sun again. *Pray for me. . . . Yes, please, pray for me. . . .*

Slowly, painfully, the gray mists lightened. The swirling clouds slowed to the gentle swaying of wheat tips touched by a sweet spring breeze. Comforting motions, backlit by a yellow brightness. Light dawned—at first, from far away, but drawing closer, closer.. . . Warmth touched him. He felt strength filtering through him as the light beamed around him and the warmth spread from his head to his arms, his chest, his legs. . . .

He struggled, concentrating. It took more effort than anything he'd ever attempted before, but slowly, surely, with great difficulty, he opened his eyes.

Chapter Twenty-Nine

A shaft of sunlight from somewhere on David's left hit him square in the face, and he winced. He snapped his eyelids shut again. It was much easier to keep them closed. But where was he? This wasn't his room at the boardinghouse. He braced himself and fought to open his eyes once more. He wished he could raise his hand to shield his eyes from the bright sun, but his arms felt weighted. He didn't have enough strength to lift them.

He squinted, taking in his surroundings, struggling to raise his head slightly from the soft pillow. With effort he turned his head. Unfamiliar wall coverings greeted him—a yellow floral instead of the gray and white stripes of his own room. And furnishings he'd never seen before, part of a bedroom suite with matching etchings and the same maple finish. Where were his own mismatched pieces? His eyes settled on an overstuffed chair in the corner. A woman slumped in it, apparently sleeping. A tangled mass of auburn hair hid her face.

What in the world?

Too tired to make sense of it, he closed his eyes again and let his head slump back against the pillow. As his head fell, the bedsprings creaked gently, and someone yawned noisily. The yawn ended with a startled gasp. Hands curled around his shoulders, and his sister's voice blasted in his ear.

"David, are you awake?"

David forced his heavy eyelids open once more, focusing.

Samantha leaned over his face, her eyes swimming with tears. A smile of hosanna lit her face. "Oh, David, you are awake!" Her hand pressed to his forehead. "You're cool. The fever's gone!"

David, completely disoriented, asked croakily, "Where am I?" He winced. His throat felt parched and sore. He rasped, "What are we doing here?"

But Samantha raced to the open door and called, "Everybody, come quick! David's awake!"

The clattering of footsteps on the stairs multiplied David's confusion while the entire Klaassen family, in various stages of dress, congregated around the bed, smiling and laughing and crying and hugging each other. Samantha remained at the forefront of the joyful throng, leaning across David with a look of wonder on her face. "Oh, David, thank the good Lord, you've come back to us."

"Come back?" David battled to make sense of the commotion. "Where have I been?"

Samantha laughed—a joy-filled laugh that several others echoed. She shook her head. "It doesn't matter now. How do you feel?"

He grimaced. His head felt fuzzy, and his whole body felt weighted down with a pressing weariness. It took great effort to form an answer. "I . . . feel . . . lousy." He hadn't intended to be humorous, but his reply earned another round of laughter.

Laura stepped up, stroking his forehead then taking his hand. "Do you remember what happened, David?"

He shook his head. At least, he thought he shook his head; it was so hard to move. "I'm not sure."

Sarah pushed her way in front of Laura. "You saved my life, David, remember? You pushed me away from the crack in the ice—then you fell in. Remember?"

And then it all came back—the opening beneath his feet, the frantic scrambling to get himself above water, the engulfing darkness and bone-rattling cold of the freezing pond, the terrifying battle to breathe. . . . But beyond that, he couldn't recall a thing—how he got out, how he got to the Klaassens' . . . or why images of Priscilla floated around in the back of his mind.

There was something else, too. Somebody had been talking to him—and praying for him. Somebody who had said she loved him. The effort of putting it all together was too much. He opened his mouth to ask, but nothing came out. Instead, his eyes slid closed, his jaw fell slack, and he drifted off to sleep.

∽◑

When David woke next, instead of a disheveled Samantha hovering near, he found himself being thoroughly perused by Dr. Newton. When the doctor noticed David's open eyes, he smiled broadly. "Well, good day, Mr. O'Brien. I can't tell you what a relief it is to see what's underneath your eyelids."

David yawned. "How long have I been asleep?"

"Eight days." Dr. Newton used a cheery tone. "Are you hungry?"

He did feel empty. He nodded, the motion causing his head to spin.

"Well, we'll get you fixed up in just a minute, but first—" The doctor placed an odd silver cone with a tube attached to it on David's chest, plugging the other end of the tube in his own ear. He listened, scowling, for several seconds, then straightened, a grin splitting his face. "Much better. The poultices and steam seemed to have done their job." He shoved the instrument down into the belly of a black leather bag and shut it with a snap. He perched on the bed, his left leg crossed over the right, and folded his arms across his chest. "So . . . do you have any questions?"

Remembering not to nod, David answered slowly. "Yes, I do. Is Sarah all right?"

"Right as rain. Only a bad scare. Anything else?"

"How'd I get here?"

"Stephen, Frank, and Adam pulled you out. From what I understand, Stephen got hold of you under the ice, and the others helped fish you out. Then they carried you here."

David guessed he owed a few men some thank-yous.

"Any more questions?"

"Yes, one." David was so tired. Talking was torture, but he had to know. "There was somebody here . . . when I was sleeping. Somebody was talking to me, praying for me. . . . Do you know who it was?"

Dr. Newton uncrossed his arms and patted David's shoulder. "Yes, young man, I've got a good guess on that. But I think I'd better let her tell you her name. Now—" He stood up, clapping his hands together. "I'll see if I can't find something for you to eat. It will be a while before you regain your strength, so don't try to get up too soon. Let the ladies baby you a bit longer. I'll be back to see you tomorrow." He pointed an official finger at David's nose. "After your lunch, rest."

"Yes, doctor." He'd have no trouble obeying the order.

The doctor hadn't been gone five minutes before Samantha came in carrying a tray with a bowl of thick vegetable soup, two slices of bread, and a glass of milk. She smiled when she saw he was still awake.

"Hi, Davey. Dr. Newton says you're hungry. I'm sure glad to hear it." She set the tray on the table next to the bed and scolded, "I'm pretty tired of forcing liquids down your throat."

"Sorry to be a bother." His throat felt raw.

Samantha sat on the bed near his hip. "You're not a bother, my dearest brother. And I intend to feed you right now, so open up."

David grinned, his eyelids drooping. "You're bossy."

"Uh-huh, I am. Open up."

David ate some of the soup, half a slice of bread, and drank most of the milk before holding up a hand. "No, Sammy, no more."

She set the spoon aside. "Dr. Newton said your appetite would return slowly, so I won't force any more on you." She sat back, smiling at him.

David held his eyes at half-mast. With his stomach full, he felt stronger and ready to talk a bit. "What are you smiling at?"

"You." Samantha released a happy sigh. "It's just so wonderful to see you awake and to hear your voice. You really scared me."

"I'm sorry. I think I scared me, too."

"Please don't ever try to be a hero again." Samantha's eyes filled with tears. "If something had happened to you—" She covered her face with her hands.

David reached up to the back of her neck. His grasp was weak, but he pulled until Samantha rested her head on his chest. He let his arm lie across her back. "Don't cry now, Sammy. I'm fine. And Sarah's fine. I couldn't let another little girl down. . . ."

Samantha cried harder.

He gave her several weak pats. "All right, the time for tears is over."

"I know," came her muffled voice. "These are relief tears."

David chuckled briefly, which made him cough. Samantha sat up quickly and gave him another drink. When he had calmed, he said, "You women cry for the strangest reasons. . . ."

"Yes, well, you had lots of us crying," Samantha informed him, swishing away the tears with her fingertips. "Me, Josie, Sarah—even Priscilla."

His body jolted with surprise. "Priscilla?"

"Yes." Samantha shook her head, wonder in her gaze. "Priscilla was there when you fell in, and she stayed with me, comforting me. Then she helped take care of you so Mother Laura and Tante Hulda and I could get some rest. She was like a different person; she surprised all of us. I could get to like her, if she would stay this way."

"Priscilla Koehn?"

Samantha nodded. "I think she was as worried about losing you as the rest of us were. You came so very close to slipping away from us, Davey." Her voice wobbled as she battled another bout of tears. "I'm not sure what kept you with us, but I'm thankful for it."

David knew what had kept him from slipping away—the call from the person who claimed to love him. He was convinced of that. But he still wasn't sure who the person was. "Sammy, did you talk to me when I was sleeping?"

Samantha nodded. "Yes. Did you hear me?"

David frowned, trying to remember. Had it been Samantha's voice he'd heard—the one that had called him back? It had been a familiar voice, one he should know, but he didn't think it was Samantha's. "I heard someone, but—" He paused, pressing his memory. "Did anyone else talk to me?"

"Well, yes. Dr. Newton, and Adam and Frank and Josie. Mother Laura and Tante Hulda—all of us talked to you nearly constantly. Priscilla did too when she was here."

Priscilla . . . Could the voice he had heard—the one that prayed for him and told him "I love you"—have been hers? "Where's Priscilla now?"

"Arn took her home yesterday evening. Why?"

"I . . . I should thank her for helping." His mouth stretched in a yawn.

Samantha rose. "Thank-you can wait, big brother. Right now, you need to sleep some more. So I'm going to leave you to it." She kissed his cheek. "Rest well."

David gave a smile in answer and settled back against the pillows once more. Before he drifted off, he thought hazily, *It must have been Priscilla. . . . She loves me, and she prayed for me. . . .* The significance of the realization wouldn't strike him for some time. He slid back into blissful sleep.

Chapter Thirty

*F*or the first few days after David's "reawakening," he spent most of his time in peaceful slumber. He would wake to eat, visit a bit, then sleep again. By the third day, he was ready to sit up in bed with the doctor's blessing, and on the fourth day he even walked with Samantha's protective arm around his waist to the overstuffed chair across the room. They celebrated with cups of hot cocoa, David seated in the chair as proudly as a king on a throne, but with the room reeling around him. He didn't fuss about climbing back in bed.

But by the sixth day, he was restless and making noises about returning to his own room at the boardinghouse and his job at the mercantile. Hiram put that idea to rest in short order.

"Absolutely not!" the little man decreed, his volume belying his diminutive stature. "You will stay right here until you have completely regained your strength. Hulda and I are managing, and your job will keep." He softened, placing a hand on David's shoulder. "You have been through an ordeal, David. We appreciate your dedication to us and the mercantile, but it is more important to take care of yourself right now."

"That is right, David," Hulda added, stepping forward to pat David's hand. "You came dangerously near death, my dear boy, and we must take special care of you now."

Their concern warmed him. He wouldn't worry them by arguing. "All right, Mr. Klaassen and Mrs. Klaassen. I promise to be lazy and demanding for at least another month."

The older couple laughed, with Hiram joking that they couldn't hold his position that long, and bid David a fond good-bye. As they left the room, David pondered their acceptance of him. They viewed him as family, and he felt as close to them as if they were kin. With a jolt, he noted that he'd become an honorary member of the entire Klaassen family. He'd thought Josie was the key, giving him access to belonging, but belonging had been there all along. He simply needed to recognize it. The realization whispered peace around his heart.

Hiram and Hulda weren't the only ones who looked in on David regularly. Frank and Anna, Liz and Jake, Stephen, Reverend Goertzen, and all of the young Klaassen family members stuck their noses in his room to express their joy at his recovery. And of course Samantha visited so often he wondered if she spent any time at her own little home. Adam kidded that he had to visit David to see his own wife.

One person remained pointedly absent, though—Priscilla. He wondered about that during quiet moments when he'd been left alone to nap but didn't feel like napping. If she had helped care for him while he was unconscious—and if she had been the one to plead with the Almighty for his health and proclaim her love for him—then why didn't she come now that he was doing better?

Between visits and between naps, David had time to contemplate not only Priscilla's odd absence, but some other things as well that had pressed on him since he'd regained consciousness. From what he had been able to piece together from the various sources willing to tell their share of the story, it hadn't been an easy feat to get him out of the pond. He'd been in the water for a considerable length of time, eventually developed pneumonia which was often fatal, and had required round-the-clock attention to keep him from dehydrating when he was unable to even sit up for a sip of water on his own volition. By rights, he could have died three different ways. So why hadn't he?

He'd been saved. Certainly all the people caring for him had played a role in his recovery, but he couldn't help but believe there had been something more, some Divine Intervention, as he'd heard the reverend call it, as well. Could there be some purpose he had yet to fulfill—a destiny he was meant to serve? Although the thought seemed egotistical, he couldn't set it aside.

He recalled hearing the sweet voice raised in prayer on his behalf. He was sure that had been a significant one of many prayers that had saved his life. And in one quiet moment two weeks into his recovery, he walked unsteadily to the window, knelt before it and looked out at the beautiful snow-laden landscape. With the golden sun on his face, he spoke his first prayer.

"God, I can't say I understand everything about You yet. But for now, I reckon it's enough that I believe You sent Your Son into this world to be my Savior, just like Reverend Goertzen said. I believe You care. You had Your hand in bringing me back to life, so from now on, my life is Yours. I ask that You forgive my past unbelief, and I trust You to guide my pathways. I know whatever You have planned for me will be what's for the best. Use me in any way You see fit, for You've convinced me I'm a person worth Your love and attention. I surrender my heart to You, God."

A lump of emotion blocked his throat as he gazed outward at the beautiful day. Was it his imagination, or did the sun shine brighter than it had been before?

The morning after placing his life into the keeping of his heavenly Father, David decided it was high time he got some questions answered. When Laura brought in his breakfast, he started, "Mrs. Klaassen, I don't want to be a bother, but—"

Laura's eyebrows rose. "And who has said anything about you being a bother?"

He shrugged sheepishly. "Well, I've been sleeping in your bed, eating your food, taking up your time. . . ."

"And not a one of us have had a single complaint. Now, what do you need?" Laura's no-nonsense attitude put David at ease.

"I hoped someone could get word to Priscilla Koehn that I'd like to see her." He paused, fidgeting under Laura's unwavering gaze. "I've thanked everyone else for their part in caring for me, but Priscilla hasn't been around. I'd like to express my gratitude to her as well."

Laura smiled. "I think that's a lovely idea, David. I'll send a note into town with the school children this morning, and I imagine it won't take her long to arrive." She cocked her head and looked him over. "Before you have a female guest, though, may I make a suggestion?"

Hesitantly, he nodded.

"Now please don't be offended, but you are a mess. Your whiskers have been growing all this time, your hair has gone unwashed, and we've only given you sponge baths. Would a long soak in a tub and a shave feel good?"

David rubbed a hand across the scraggly growth on his chin and scratched his head. "You're right. A bath would be wonderful. But, Mrs. Klaassen . . . ?"

"Yes?"

"You've washed me for the last time. This one's up to me."

Laura laughed. "That, Mr. O'Brien, is exactly what I was thinking."

A knock at the door interrupted the Koehns' breakfast. Stephen rose. "I'll get it."

Teddy Klaassen stood shivering on the doorstep. "A note for Priscilla," he said, thrusting a folded piece of paper into Stephen's hands. The boy's breath came in puffs, and his cheeks glowed red from the cold.

"Come in and get warm," Stephen invited.

Teddy shook his head. "Nah—gotta get to school. See ya!" He took off at a trot.

Stephen handed the note to his sister and slid back into his chair. Fork forgotten in his hand, he watched her face as she read. When she lifted her head, her eyes held a mix of apprehension and elation. She looked from her father to her mother then back down at the note. She waved it slightly. "It's from Laura Klaassen. She—she says David has requested a visit . . . from me."

Pa scowled. "Well, young lady, I didn't complain when you spent most of the day out there nursing him. After all, he was at death's door and needed all the care he could get. But from what I hear, he's doing just fine now. And I'm not sure I can spare the time to take you—"

Intrigued by something in his sister's expression, Stephen put in, "I could run her out there at noon, Pa."

Pa plucked the note from Priscilla's hand and scowled at it. "What does he want?"

Mama sighed. "I'm sure everything will be fine, John."

Pa read the brief note then dropped it on the table. "Well, I don't know . . ."

Priscilla rested her clasped hands on the edge of the table. "I would like to see for myself that he's doing better."

Pa blustered, "But you don't even like the man. You've said so many times."

Priscilla's cheeks flooded with pink. She appeared flustered—unlike his normally self-assured sister. Slowly, she raised her head to meet her father's gaze. She spoke with forthrightness that held everyone at attention.

"Daddy, I know what I've said. I acted like a perfect ninny, and the only reason I said I didn't like David was because he wouldn't put up with my nonsense. But David made me see some things about myself that needed to be changed—and I'm trying to change them. I owe him a big thank-you, and I'd like to tell him so."

Stephen gawked in wonder. This was Priscilla speaking? Their Priscilla?

Several minutes of stunned silence passed before his mother finally cleared her throat. "Well, John, the visit would be supervised by Laura Klaassen. I . . . I think it would be all right, if Stephen is willing to give up his noon break to take her out there."

Pa opened and closed his mouth several times like a banked fish gulping air. At last he seemed to find his bearings. "It seems . . . settled then." His Adam's apple bobbed above his white collar as he swallowed. "But you be home well before dark, young lady, do you hear?"

"Yes, I hear." Priscilla sent a grateful smile around the table. "Thank you, Mama, Daddy. You, too, Stephen." She headed for her bedroom.

Pa hollered, "You haven't finished your breakfast!"

Ma said, "Oh, let her go, John. She's excited."

"About what?"

The look Ma sent her husband said everything. Stephen hid a smile. It was Pa's turn to turn red.

Chapter Thirty-One

When Priscilla climbed the staircase in the Klaassen farmhouse at half past twelve, she carried David's lunch tray. Samantha had planned to bring it up, but Priscilla begged for the honor. She was trying to figure out how to balance the tray against her hip and turn the doorknob when the door swung open.

There stood David in a pair of brown broadcloth pants, a pale blue chambray shirt, and leather house slippers. He was pale and looked thinner, but his cheeks were clean shaven, his hair was neatly combed, and he smelled of Ivory soap.

Her heart set up a wild kawumping. "David! You're up and around!"

He stepped aside to let her enter. "I've been on my feet for several days, off and on. You would have known that if you hadn't been making yourself so scarce around here."

Priscilla set the dinner tray on the small table beside the chair and began rearranging things that didn't need rearranging. "Yes, well, I thought perhaps I would be in the way."

David's feet scuffed across the floor as he moved toward her. He gently took her arm and turned her to face him. Her pulse galloped, having him so near. The smile in his eyes nearly melted her. "From what I understand, Priscilla, you were very helpful. Thank you."

She swallowed. She couldn't take her eyes from his. "You're welcome." Then she gestured to the plate of food. "Y-you'd better eat, before everything is cold. There's nothing worse than cold dumplings."

"Dumplings." David patted his flat belly and sank into the chair. "They'll have me fattened up in no time."

While David consumed his meal, Priscilla roamed the room and pretended to examine Mrs. Klaassen's few pieces of bric-a-brac. But her gaze flicked in his direction frequently. The very sight of him ignited a joy she found difficult to restrain. Every ounce of her being longed to throw herself into his arms and cry tears of delight at his recovery. But she'd promised to curtail her flirting ways, and he might misconstrue an embrace. So she ambled aimlessly about the small space, hands clasped behind her back, hoping to present a picture of decorum David might find pleasing.

～◯

David watched Priscilla as he ate. Was she acting bashful because she'd murmured words of love in his ear when he lay ill? Or did she prefer to be somewhere else? This shy demeanor was a far cry from the obnoxious girl he'd met several months ago.

When he'd finished, he set the tray aside and sighed. "That Laura is a very good cook. Have you ever made dumplings, Priscilla?"

She angled an uncertain look at him. "Are you making fun of me?"

He blinked. "I don't think so."

She sucked in her lips for a moment, her brows low, before answering. "No, I don't make dumplings. I've not spent much time in a kitchen, I'm afraid. I've never had to."

David nodded slowly.

"But I've been helping Mama lately. She seems to appreciate the company, and I've found it's not as tedious as I always

thought. I'm sure I'll learn to make dumplings. Eventually."
She drew in a deep breath and folded her arms. "But I'm sure
you didn't ask me here to find out about my skills—or lack of
skills—as a cook. Why did you send that note, David?"

David couldn't stop a short huff of laughter. "You're nothing if not direct, Priscilla."

Priscilla ducked her head and shrugged. "I suppose I am."
She lifted her face. "Does that bother you?"

"No, not particularly. I prefer honesty to mealy mouthed
platitudes. How about you?"

"Me?"

"Yes, you. Do you prefer directness or beating around the
bush?"

Priscilla examined him for several seconds, as if seeking
hidden motives. At last she brought an embroidered stool over
from beneath the vanity and seated herself on it, her hands in
her lap. "I prefer directness."

"Good." David leaned back in the overstuffed chair and
propped his elbows on the armrests. "I would like to ask you a
few direct questions, Priscilla."

Priscilla's blue eyes grew wider as she stared at him. The tip
of her tongue wet her lips, then disappeared again. "All right."

David looked at her unblinkingly. "Priscilla, when I was unconscious, did you pray for me?"

"Yes, I did."

David's eyebrows shot up at her unfaltering response. Ah!
Then she likely was the one. He found the next question a little
harder to ask. "Did you also tell me that . . . that you love me?"

Priscilla stiffened. Her fingers wove together as her dark blue
gaze fell to her lap and then up again. She looked him full in the
face. Her chin lifted proudly. "Yes, I did. And I meant it." When
David sat in stunned silence, Priscilla went on evenly, "I do love

you, David. I'm not sure why or how, but I do. When you were sick, I—I thought I might die, too, if I didn't get the chance to tell you how I felt. So I told you I loved you." She paused, her breath heaving in little puffs. "I didn't realize you could hear me."

"Yes, I could hear." David shook his head. "I just wasn't sure who it was. So it was you. . . ."

Priscilla jumped up and paced around the room, her skirts swishing. "I can't understand my feelings at all. You've called me spoiled and selfish and willful and impudent. . . ." She whirled to face him, her expression serious. "And I thank you for it. I needed someone to wake me up, to make me see how wrong I was. I'm glad I have the chance to tell you so. You've helped begin a big change in me."

David stared at her, flabbergasted. Would he have ever imagined her—prim and proper, with those bright eyes wide and truthful and her curling hair framing her perfect, beautiful face—thanking him for his bluntness? What could he say in response?

In time, he found himself. "I need to thank you, too, Priscilla."

She waved her slim hand in dismissal. "You've already thanked me, David, for helping with your care."

He shook his head. "No, not for that—although I am grateful. I owe you a thank you for praying for me. There were lots of people praying for me. But I believe it was your prayers that brought me back."

To his surprise, Priscilla's eyes brimmed and spilled over. She sank onto the stool and covered her face with her hands. One sob rent the silence of the room. David crossed to her, bending down to touch her shoulder. "Why, Priscilla, what did I say? How did I upset—?"

She shook her head, her spiraling curls bouncing over her shoulders. "Y-you didn't upset m-me."

"Then what is it?" Honestly, he'd never understand women and their tears.

She wouldn't uncover her face, so her voice was muffled. "You said—you said my prayers brought you back. Oh, David! That means so much to me. They were my first prayers ever, and if God heard them and answered them, then—." She lowered her hands until her fingertips rested on her lips. Her tear-filled eyes glowed with some inner wonder. "Then that means He really does care. For me . . . and for you too. Don't you see?"

David sank to one knee beside her and ran his hand down the length of her hair, his heart lifting with the joyous recognition of God's unfailing love. "Yes, Prissy, I do see."

Priscilla rushed on, "When I prayed, David, I wasn't asking for anything for me. I was asking for everything for you. It was the first unselfish thing I've ever done. I told God—" Suddenly she seemed shy, and David had to prod her a bit with a smile and a reassuring pat on her shoulder.

Her voice quavered as she continued. "I told Him if He let you live, I would spend the rest of my life doing what He wanted me to do, instead of what I wanted to do. I wasn't sure He'd answer, because I'd never done much for anybody, ever, and I wasn't sure I was even worthy of His attention. But He answered, and you're well, and that means—Oh, David! That means I'm worthy too!"

David was touched by her amazement. "Of course you're worthy, Priscilla. But not because of anything you did or can do. Just because . . . He loves." The truth of his words ignited a new fire of joy. How he wished he hadn't wasted so many years hiding from God's deep love. He leaned in slightly and shared, "I made a similar commitment myself."

"You did?"

"Yes, I did and don't look so surprised. It just occurred to me that perhaps God let me live for a reason. I don't know what the reason is, but He must, and I want to be open to His leading."

They sat staring at one another. David marveled that they had reached out to the heavenly Father at the same time. It gave him a common ground with Priscilla, a common bond. He found it sobering and exciting and frightening all at the same time. Where might this take them?

David's knee complained about being pressed on the hard floor. He rose awkwardly and moved the few steps needed to reach the chair and sit again. From his vantage point, he could look at Priscilla's face.

There was much to admire—not only her physical beauty, which had always been eye catching, but the beauty now shining from the inside as well. It stirred him in a way he wouldn't have thought possible. The expression on her face was serene, confident. . . . She was like a completely new person.

He chuckled. "Can you believe this?"

"What?"

"You—me. Us. Sitting here relaxed and talking, not sparring with each other."

She smiled. "It's nice, isn't it?"

"Yes, it is, Priscilla."

"Do you think it means anything?"

He frowned slightly, puzzled. "Like what?"

"Well, I told you how I feel about you, and I don't want you to feel obligated to me, but I was just wondering if—well, if maybe—you might come to feel the same way about me."

David gave a disbelieving laugh. He rolled his eyes and said, "When I called you direct. . . ."

She plunked her fists on her hips. "I think it's a fair question."

He laughed again. "You would!"

She crossed her arms and set her face in a teasing scowl that was still prettier than most women smiling their best smiles.

David stifled his mirth. "Come here, Priscilla. Please?"

After a moment she sighed, rose, and stood before him, head tilted to the side.

He smiled up at her. "Yes, Miss Priss, I think there's a very good chance of my returning those feelings you divulged while I was lost in sleep."

With a triumphant grin, Priscilla perched on the arm of the chair like a sparrow on a fencepost. "Well, it's about time you admitted it."

He shook his head indulgently. "You are about the sassiest thing I've ever known."

"Well, you needn't worry," she replied, "because I am going to be the most agreeable, most complacent, most unsassy wife in the whole world."

David leaned into the opposite corner of the chair, staring in open-mouthed amazement. "Priscilla Koehn, did you just propose to me?"

"Of course not." Her eyes sparkled with mischief. "That would be presumptuous, to say the least. And it's far too soon for us to consider matrimony. Daddy will insist on a lengthy courtship. But just so you know—when you propose to me, the answer will be yes."

He chuckled, taking her hand and weaving his fingers through hers. "You really are something, Priscilla." One thing about it, with Priscilla as his wife, life would never be dull. He turned his head to gaze out the open window, admiring the crystal blue sky streaked with wisps of white.

His thoughts turned inward. "Well, God, You sure have a way of working things out. I came to Mountain Lake just to be with my sister. But You had much more for me, didn't You? With surrendering of my heart to You, I found a place to call home and someone who loves me . . . someone I can love back. You brought me down some rocky roads to get me to this place, but I know now Your Word is right—all things do work together for good. Thank You."

LAURA KLAASSEN'S
VERENIKE (Cheese Pockets)

Dough:

1 cup water or milk

1 egg white

1 tsp. salt

2 1/2 cups flour

Cottage cheese filling:

1 egg yolk

salt and pepper to taste

2 tblsp. finely chopped onion, if desired

1 pound dry curd cottage cheese (or farmer's cheese)

Roll out the dough to about 1/8-inch thickness. Cut into 3- or 4-inch squares. Place a heaping teaspoon of the cottage cheese filling in the middle of the square. Bring the opposite corners together. Pinch the edges firmly. Drop the *verenike* into boiling water and cook slowly for about ten minutes. Drain.

Serve with fried ham or sausage. Make a gravy of the meat drippings to pour over the *verenike*.

LAURA KLAASSEN'S
CHERRY MOOS

1 quart sour cherries
2 quarts water
2/3 cup sugar
5 tblsp. flour
1 cup sweet cream

Add water to cherries and cook until soft. Add half of sugar to cherries.

Combine remaining sugar with flour and add cream to make a smooth paste. Add paste to cherries and cook until thickened, stirring constantly.

Serve warm or cold, as desired. (Makes 6 to 8 servings.)

Acknowledgments

Mom and Daddy, my first teachers, who taught me to trust in Jesus . . . Thanks to your showing me how to surrender myself to Him, I am never alone and always have a place to call Home.

My husband, Don, who often cooks his own supper and puts up with me sneaking away in the middle of the night to play with my imaginary friends . . . I'm grateful for your support and understanding.

My band of prayer warriors—Connie, Eileen, Margie, Darlene, Sabra, Miralee, Kathy . . . You're always there when I need you. I appreciate you more than you know.

My agent, Tamela, who goes "above and beyond the call of duty" on my behalf . . . Thank you for your consistent encouragement.

Finally, and most important, God . . . You bless me beyond imagining. May any praise or glory be reflected directly back to You.